THE HESS ASSAULT

By the same author

The Wotan series:
DEATH RIDE
SLAUGHTER AT SALERNO
MARCH OR DIE
THE OUTCASTS

The Submarine series:
THE WOLF PACK
OPERATION DEATH WATCH
CONVOY TO CATASTROPHE
FIRE IN THE WEST

The Stuka Squadron series:
THE BLACK KNIGHTS
THE HAWKS OF DEATH
THE TANKBUSTERS
BLOOD MISSION

The Rebel series:
CANNON FODDER
THE DIE-HARDS

THE
HESS ASSAULT

LEO KESSLER

CENTURY

LONDON MELBOURNE AUCKLAND JOHANNESBURG

First published in Great Britain in 1987 by
Century Hutchinson Ltd
Brookmount House, 62–65 Chandos Place
London WC2N 4NW

Century Hutchinson South Africa (Pty) Ltd
PO Box 337, Bergvlei, 2012 South Africa

Century Hutchinson Australia Pty Ltd
PO Box 496, 16–22 Church Street, Hawthorn
Victoria 3122, Australia

Century Hutchinson New Zealand Limited
PO Box 40–086, Glenfield, Auckland 10
New Zealand

ISBN 0 7126 1680 2

Photoset and printed in Great Britain by
WBC Print Ltd, Bristol

AUTHOR'S NOTE

It is common for authors of popular fiction to receive readers' letters. You know, the kids who want to 'do' you for their O-levels; those American autograph hounds who probably flog your signature anyway; those nitpickers who write indignantly to tell you that the German Mark III tank was *not* armed with the 1942 model machine-gun but with the 1934 model, etc.

However, it is rare for an author of my kind to get a letter from a solicitor (unless it's a warning or a summons). But some six years ago or so I did receive a letter from a solicitor in Stirling 'advising' me that his client 'knew' of my work and would like to offer me the opportunity of 'ghost-writing' his story.

It was about here in the letter that I prepared to throw it into my waste-paper basket. My previous experience of ghost-writing the story of a Czech spy had not enamoured me of the task. Fortunately, however, my eye caught the name of the man the solicitor's client wanted to write about. It was Rudolf Hess, the lone prisoner of Spandau Prison who had been – and still is – in captivity since 10 May 1941.

I bit, of course. The *real* reason why the deputy to the most powerful man in Europe had taken it upon himself to make that bold flight to Scotland back in 1941 has always fascinated me. I arranged to meet his 'client' on neutral ground in a northern town, not far from Stirling. The solicitor had insisted on the 'strictest discretion', for his client was still 'holding a sensitive post in Her Majesty's Service'.

His client, Mr George C., turned out to be pretty old to be still serving Her Majesty, I thought. I would say he was a good seventy, with one of those typical red, big-nosed Scottish faces, jolly yet canny, very canny indeed. He had cop written all over him.

It turned out that he wasn't a cop, but a professional prison officer, whose service went back right to the thirties. In 1941, while serving in Shanghai, he had been captured by the Japs and had served four years behind bars in his own jail. 'Ay,' he grinned over his 'dram', as he called it, 'I ken what it's like outside – and *inside!*' Now, in spite of the fact that he was well over the statutory retiring age for prison guards, he was still serving in that capacity. In Berlin, at Spandau Prison to be exact. His sole prisoner was Rudolf Hess, whom he had been guarding now since 1947. 'Ay, I know yon Hess better than his own mother. Sit with him on the sofa every night watching the telly with him. Ay, I'll have another wee dram, if yer buying one.'

My first question as to why he was still working, when he was obviously in his seventies, met with the same sort of reply he gave to most of my subsequent questions, 'Well, I'd like to tell ye, Mr Kessler, but ye ken the Official Secrets Act. Ma lips are sealed!' And all the while he would smile his broken-toothed smile in that canny way of his. Old he might be, but he was well versed in the ways of men, smart and stupid, high and low. After all, he had had nearly fifty years of dealing with criminals of one kind or another.

But what little he did say wetted my appetite for sensation. Yes, there had once been an attempt, never made public, to try to get Hess out of Spandau by helicopter. Since then there were anti-aircraft guns posted on the prison's towers. Both sides, East and West, had spies and informers in the staff of the kitchen that fed Hess, who apparently was very weight-conscious. ('Ay, he watches his waist does yon Hess. No like me,' and the Scot patted his own generous stomach.) Apparently both sides were frightened that one of them would attempt to snatch Hess out of the jail when it was their turn to do the month's spell of guard duty at Spandau.

Yet when it came to asking why he had contacted me in the first place – what exactly did he want me to ghost-write – the old Scot shut up like a clam, save to say, 'It's as much as my pension's worth to tell ye now. They'll take it away from me if

I did. But I'll talk the day I retire – *in Berlin!*' In truth he was a very canny Scot.

We arranged to meet again two weeks later in Berlin. He would retire on 1 April and then he would reveal the great secret about Hess that would make for a sensational book. 'Ay, nae doubt, there'll be a tidy wee bit o' money in it for us both, Mr Kessler.' And that was about it.

But, of course, that first meeting set my brain working overtime. Obviously the old Scot knew something about his prisoner that had caused the authorities, presumably British (they had enrolled Mr C. back in 1947), to keep employing him long after the mandatory age of retirement, which was sixty-five. Did the Scot know whom Hess had really flown to Scotland to see?

Officially he had flown to Scotland on 10 May 1941 to meet a relatively obscure Scottish nobleman, the Duke of Hamilton. The latter, according to the official story, was to arrange a meeting between Hess and unspecified top political leaders in order to conclude a peace between Britain and Nazi Germany. But what power did the Duke, who was serving in the RAF at the time, wield? Besides, Churchill would never have discussed peace terms with Hess – or anyone else for that matter. Any attempt to bring about a peace between Germany and Britain would have been conditional on removing Churchill from office, perhaps even imprisoning him.

But perhaps Hess had *not* come to see the Duke of Hamilton? Perhaps he had come to see what we would call today 'the wets' of the then Establishment? There were of course men who *were* prepared to do a deal with Hitler, some because they felt Britain couldn't beat Germany; others because they believed a peace was the only way to save the British Empire; a few because, cynically enough, they knew Germany would soon attack Russia. Let the Germans and the Russians beat each other into the ground, they opined, and we'll be the winners. Oh yes, that spring, when Britain's fortunes were at their lowest ebb, there were leading politicians, whose activities have been discreetly left out of the official accounts of World War Two, who were ready to talk peace with Nazi Germany. Could the name of the person whom Hess had really come to see be the secret that Mr C. possessed?

I saw him one more time in Berlin, just one week before he was due to retire. He had a little modern flat a mere hundred yards from the start of the Russian sector, surprisingly enough. In seven days he'd tell me everything and the 'Queen in London can keep her pension'. He downed a very large duty-free whisky and smiled cannily. 'It's no very much in the first place, ye ken. What d'ye think, Mr Kessler, how much are we gonna make on this one?'

It was no use trying to tell him that it all depended upon the 'story' he had to tell. Publishers would only be interested in him, an obscure prison guard, if he had something sensational on Hess. He simply wouldn't be drawn. 'I promise ye, it'll be sensational,' he declared towards the end of that long evening, his broad Scots face flushed with whisky. 'There's plenty of money in it for both of us, laddie.' The next day he was dead.

Later they said he had died of a massive heart attack. Who knows? He had appeared hale and hearty enough that last night, drinking his whisky and eating the *Wurst und Sauerkraut* prepared for him by a doting, middle-aged German lady, who, I half-suspected, was more than 'just a guid wee friend'. At all events it was perhaps a very convenient heart attack for a person or persons unknown. Just before he was 'going to spill the beans', as he was fond of declaring in that antiquated slang of his, he had passed away.

But what were 'the beans'? Was the old Scot going to tell me that Hess had really flown to Scotland to see R.B., who was still alive at that time, or perhaps even D.H., who is still alive, barely? What the devil had his secret been?

I didn't know it then, but I was barking up the wrong tree, *completely!* George C. had known something infinitely more sensational than that. It was a tremendous story, perhaps the last secret to come out of World War Two. It was the 'Schulze

Letter', as it became known in Hamburg press circles, that put me on the right track, though of course none of the cynics who staff the Hamburg *Bildzeitung* or the *Stern* believed in its authenticity. They had been badly bitten already with the forged Hitler letters to the tune of a couple of million marks. The 'Schulze Letter' – *'nein danke!'*

By the time it had done the rounds of the Hamburg press world (including Springer's *Die Welt*) and been returned to *Forsthaus Zwei*, the old folks' home in the nearby town of Bad Oldesloe, which an aged Schulze had managed to terrorize with his illicit drinking and trying to 'get into the knickers' of the old biddies resident there, ex-Sergeant Schulze was dead. An unfounded rumour has it that he died in action, 'dancing a mattress polka', as he would have put it, with an eighteen-year-old Italian cleaning maid.

Yet rogue that undoubtedly he had been, those fat, white-haired gentlemen who forty-odd years before had once been the scourge of Europe buried the ex-SS *Oberscharführer* with due ceremony. Certainly he had not been one of the SS's most obedient soldiers, but his combat record was second to none. After all, he had been one of the few surviving NCOs who had won every medal Nazi Germany had to bestow, including the Knight's Cross.

Discreetly, for the German Federal Republic is a country without a history (it does not like to be reminded of the SS), but solemnly the old reprobate was placed to rest in a lonely sector of the great Hamburg cemetery at Wandsbek. In due course the local Hamburg HIAG* group published a brief account of Sergeant Schulze's military career in the SS's national journal *Der Freiwillige*, detailing how he had won his medals.

It was in this account, published earlier this year that I stumbled on the first clue to what that canny old Scot had been really about to disclose about Hess before his unfortunate death. For, quoting briefly from the 'Schulze Letter',

* The national organization for ex-members of the SS.

which no one in the Hamburg press business was prepared to believe, the unknown chronicler states: ' "I got the Iron Cross First Class sent to me in a little box when we were right up to our hooters in the crap outside Smolensk. I could have used a flatman* better than the piece of tin. But it surprised me, because I didn't think they wanted to know any more about the crappy mess we made at Little Saxton." '

'*Oberscharführer* Schulze was well known throughout SS Assault Regiment Wotan for his somewhat forceful language,' the unknown chronicler of his military career added a little apologetically.

'*Little Saxton!*' The English place name had stabbed into me like a sharp knife. What had SS Sergeant Schulze been doing in England in 1941 (the SS had captured the Russian city of Smolensk in the autumn of that year, so I reasoned it had been 1941) to win the Iron Cross First Class? The record shows that no single member of the German Armed Forces, save naturally Hess himself, ever set foot on British soil throughout the whole of World War Two, except those who came as prisoners or fell out of the sky, *dead!*

But there was more to it. After Hess had made his dramatic parachute descent near Dungavel Hill in Scotland, and before he was sent to Mytchett Place, where he would remain until June 1942, he had been temporarily imprisoned in a former hotel in a lonely Suffolk village, which finally, after years of erosion, had disappeared beneath the North Sea during the great flood of 1952. That lost village had been called – Little Saxton.

So what had the Black Guards attempted to do all those years ago in Little Saxton? What had ended, as Sergeant Schulze had put it in his letter to the *Bildzeitung*, in a ' crappy mess'? The answer to these questions is, I believe, told in the *Hess Assault . . .*

Leo Kessler
Autumn 1986

* SS slang for a hip flask.

DAY ONE

Saturday, 10 May 1941

CHAPTER 1

He came in low over the hamlet of Eaglesham, perfectly on course. Now he began to follow the grey snake of the road that led to the village of Dungavel, sweeping along it in a loose curve. The engines were now red hot after such a long flight at full throttle, but still the untested prototype was bearing up well. His friend Willi Messerschmitt could be proud of his new fighter-plane.

Now he ripped back the stick and started to climb. Hastily he glanced at the green-glowing needle of the altimeter. It was already heading for two hundred metres, the minimum height from which he could jump. He knew the professional *Fallschirmjäger* of General Student's Parachute Corps jumped at one hundred and fifty metres. But they were trained young men, half his age. If anything went wrong during the jump, he needed altitude to rectify things and select his landing place.

Routinely he prepared for what was to come. He cut the engines. Abruptly everything was silent, save for the hiss of the wind. Carefully he feathered the two twin propellers so that they could not be started again by the wind. He was afraid that if they did, the propellers might get entangled with his shroud lines. That would be disastrous. Nothing must be allowed to interfere with the success of this mission, which had brought him all the way from Germany to this remote part of rural Scotland.

For a moment he hesitated, wondering when he would ever be allowed to fly again. For he had always dearly loved flying ever since that day back in the Old War when, as a thrice-wounded Bavarian infantryman, he had transferred to the Imperial Air Corps and had become a fighter pilot. After the war, as an impoverished student at Munich University, he had not had enough money to afford to fly. Later, however, when he had met the Führer – 'the greatest event of my whole

life', as he had often maintained to his few friends – he had
begun to fly once more. But then the Führer had insisted,
once the party had come to power, that the *Prominenz* should
not fly because of the danger of accidents. In essence, the ban
only applied to himself and 'Fat Hermann',* the only two
trained pilots in the whole of the party leadership. Anyway,
'Fat Hermann', the one-time ace and commander of the
Richthofen Squadron, had been too gross to clamber into a
cockpit.

Of course, he had obeyed the Führer as he had always
done. But after the fall of France last year he had begun to fly
secretly from Augsburg Air Port once more. With the help of
his friend Willi Messerschmitt he had accustomed himself to
the latter's new secret Me 110, though he had not told the
designer why. He had allowed Willi to think that he merely
wanted to fly for the pleasure and thrill of being airborne once
more.

The pilot grinned in the glowing darkness of the hot
cockpit. Poor Willi certainly *would* be in trouble when the
Führer discovered what had been going on all the time at
Augsburg behind his back. Still, he reflected, all would be
forgotten once his mission succeeded and the whole course of
the war changed. He was certain of that. He forgot Willi and
Augsburg and flashed a glance at the altimeter. It read two
hundred and fifty metres. It was time to go!

Now he worked swiftly for such a big man. Reaching up
with both hands he slid back the cabin roof. It moved easily.
He stood up. To his horror the fierce wind slammed him back
against the leather seat with such force that he gasped! For a
moment he simply slumped there, his mind racing, wondering how he was going to get out. At this stalling speed and so
low every second was vital. *What was he going to do?*

To his front in the silver gloom, Dungavel Hill raced up to
meet him. He tried again, gritting his teeth and exerting all
his strength. To no avail! He still couldn't heave his shoulders

* Air Marshal Hermann Goering, known thus because of his enormous
belly.

out of the cockpit. The Hill loomed ever larger. He had only
seconds now. Desperately he remembered an old trick from
his wartime flying days. He ripped back the stick. The ground
fell away and suddenly he was upside down. That was the
way they had always escaped when one of their Fokkers had
been hit in 1918 and was hurtling down to its doom.

The blood drained from his head. Silver stars exploded
before his eyes. His eardrums seemed about to burst. A red
mist enveloped him and momentarily he blacked out. Thus
one of the most powerful men in Europe flew on unconscious,
his plane flying upside down at almost zero feet, about to
disintegrate on impact at any moment.

Vaguely he became aware of his surroundings again. He
shook his head groggily. Everything swung into focus.
Centimetres from his face were the altimeter and air speed
indicator. *Both stood at 'zero'!*

The danger made him act. Adrenalin pumped new energy
into his bloodstream. His twenty-five years of flying told him
instinctively what to do. Somehow or other he bunched up his
legs in the tight confines of the cockpit. He grunted and
heaved. Suddenly he was out!

Cold air slapped him across the face. He gasped with the
shock, falling at a tremendous rate. He was going to die. He
grabbed the brass handle and pulled hard. A crack. A brutal
tug at his shoulders and above him the white silk canopy
flowered and blossomed. His mad progress ceased. The wind
died abruptly. Suddenly all was peace and silence and he was
falling gently, swinging slightly but not alarmingly from side
to side. He had done it. *Himmelherrgottnochmal*, he had done it!

He came lower and lower, falling into the mist over the
empty fields that diffused the silvery light of the full moon. He
craned his neck, trying to spot the landmarks he had studied
back in Germany for months. Away to his right there was a
row of cottages, which he recognized. But they were blacked-
out and there was no smoke coming from them. He might
well have been the last man alive in the whole world;
Scotland seemed so empty.

Now the plane went into its last dive. It shrieked towards a line of trees. He prayed that it would be burned out or disintegrate on impact. He didn't want the wreckage to reveal any of Professor Messerschmitt's secrets to the experts of the English Royal Air Force.

The Messerschmitt slammed into the ground, sending up a shower of angry red sparks. An instant later it was completely obscured by a huge cloud of dust and smoke. Then he forgot the plane and Willi's secrets. The rough ground below was looming up at an alarming rate. He tensed.

He hit the field hard and gasped, stumbled forward under the impact. Sprawled like a drunk, he lay trying to catch his breath, still holding on to the shroud lines, his whole big burly body lathered in a cold sweat. Now through the thick padded leather of his flying helmet he could hear faint shouts of alarm and cries, perhaps even curses. Soon they would find him. The white parachute billowing limply in the faint breeze would give him away. No matter. He *wanted* to be found.

Still struggling for breath, he released the parachute and pulled off his helmet to wipe the sweat that trickled down his high forehead and lodged in the thick bushy eyebrows above his strangely hypnotic, staring (some might have said mad) eyes and waited patiently for what had to happen. The cries were getting louder. They were coming...

CHAPTER 2

Slowly, deliberately, Major Geier, Commander of the SS Assault Regiment Wotan, lowered his binoculars, the wind from the Channel below whipping his uniform against his skinny frame. Silently, Captain von Dodenburg standing next to him on the cliff top, did the same. The Vulture, for so he was known, not just on account of his name,* but also because of the monstrous beak of a nose that dominated his skinny arrogant face, took his time. He screwed in the monocle he affected, though he had perfect eyesight, stamped first his right boot and then the left so that his breeches sat perfectly and then cleared his throat with a rasping noise.

Kuno von Dodenburg had heard it all before. With another person he might have laughed, but not with the CO. Wotan's commander tolerated no amusement at his own expense and he was a dangerous man to cross. His sole ambition in life was to become a general, just as his late father had been. He would let no one and nothing stand in the way of achieving that aim. So von Dodenburg, who towered above his commander, remained silent, his harshly handsome face emotionlessly watching the dull red glow over England, ears taking in the drunken singing coming from the officers' mess behind them and the steady throb-throb of the bombers coming back from tonight's raid on London. This evening, it was said, 'Fat Hermann' had sent nearly one thousand *Luftwaffe* planes to finish off the job of wiping the English capital off the map of Europe. By the look of the sky on the other side of the Channel, it seemed he might well have succeeded. The whole horizon burned. God, von Dodenburg cursed to himself, why did the stupid English keep on fighting? It only caused unnecessary suffering. They had not a

* *Geier* is the German word for 'vulture'.

hope in hell of ever again engaging the Greater German *Wehrmacht* in battle. They had been soundly thrashed at Dunkirk and had fled the Continent for good.

The Vulture lit a cigar and said, almost as if he could read his young subordinate's mind, 'The English are finished. Why they didn't surrender after Dunkirk God in heaven only knows? Now they waste Wotan's time, keeping us here while the men rot, indulging themselves in drink and those French whores. What piggery! What decadence! The regiment will go to pieces if your Führer doesn't act in the East soon.'

Von Dodenburg ignored 'your' Führer. It was a deliberate jibe, he knew. The Vulture felt nothing for Germany's sacred mission to bring new life to a corrupt, weary Europe. Indeed the CO was completely cynical about national socialism and the Führer, and did little to hide his views. Instead he said eagerly, 'Do you think we are going to march against the Russians, sir?'

The Vulture nodded and rolled his cigar from one side of his tight cruel mouth to the other. 'Of course. Why, daily troop trains are leaving France for the East, and – keep this under your hat – the "Bodyguard" has been alerted too.'*

Von Dodenburg whistled softly. It seemed an age now since they had charged triumphantly through France, driving all before them. Day after day, week after week, the eager young blond giants of the Wotan, their filthy grey uniforms reeking of sweat and explosive, racing through the smouldering countryside of *la belle France* under the blood-red ball of that summer sun, had mercilessly overcome all opposition, what little there had been of it. The yellow of the uncut corn and white of surrender had been the predominant colours that June. For everywhere had hung the symbol of France's decadence and defeat, white flags, bed-sheets, towels, underclothes, on cottages, farmhouses, churches, apartment houses – anything white to symbolize that the

---

* 'The Adolf Hitler Bodyguard Division' to which Wotan belonged.

French would or could not fight. Now it was all to begin
again, and at last after years of waiting, the Führer, in his
infinite wisdom, was soon to make his final reckoning with the
Reds, as he had always promised he would.

'Yes,' again the Vulture seemed to read the eager young
officer's mind, 'the invasion of England, for which we have
been preparing stupidly these last few months, is to be
abandoned. The *Luftwaffe* will bomb them into surrender, no
doubt' – he indicated the burning horizon – 'but by then we'll
be long gone, driving for Moscow, winning tin* by the
basketful, and naturally promotion, too. This time there'll be
plenty of casualties, I am certain.' He chuckled suddenly, as if
pleased at the thought. 'There'll be gaps higher up. Why,
mein Lieber, give us one year of combat in Russia and
undoubtedly I shall be a divisional general, don't you think?'

All that von Dodenburg could do was to stutter a little
stupidly, 'Yessir. I suppose so, sir.' What else could one do in
the face of such overweening, self-centred egotism?

The Vulture took one last puff at his cigar, and ground out
the butt with the heel of his riding boot on the turf, the spurs
he affected jingling slightly. 'Well, I for one am going to turn
in. Soon we'll all be getting precious little sleep, I should
imagine.' He shot a glance at the green-glowing dial of his
wrist-watch. 'About curfew time for the decadent frogs.
You're duty officer, von Dodenburg. Ensure that the men are
all in their barracks by twenty-four hundred hours. We don't
want any of the drunken sots coming out of their dirty
whorehouses causing trouble with the chain-dogs.' He meant
the military police. 'There is some kind of alert on the whole
length of the coast as it is. Red alert, in fact.'

Von Dodenburg showed surprise. 'Red alert, sir?' he
echoed.

The Vulture shrugged carelessly. 'Something to do with
the *Luftwaffe*. You know how those flyboys panic easily. Well,
gute Nacht, von Dodenburg. It's up to you now.' And with that

---

* SS slang for military decorations.

he stumped off into the glowing darkness, his spurs jingling slightly, heading for his quarters, where undoubtedly, as was his wont before turning in, he would drool over the pictures of naked boys he kept in a locked drawer.

Von Dodenburg stiffened to attention and then relaxed, staring out over the dark mass of the sea towards the fires that burned over London. How much longer could the Tommies stand it, he wondered. The *Luftwaffe* had been bombing the English capital and the surrounding areas for four solid months now, night in, night out. Surely the English had to weaken soon?

Then he dismissed the English at the thought of the great adventure to come, his harshly handsome face set in a thoughtful frown. Soon, out there to the East, the greatest battle the world had ever seen would be fought between the two ideologies that dominated the twentieth century – national socialism and that perverted Jewish creed communism. He had no doubts about the outcome, of course. National socialism would triumph, but the cost worried him.

Captain Kuno von Dodenburg was a typical SS officer of his time: tall, lean, blond, with one of those peaked, ruthless, slightly arrogant faces that seemed the fashion in the SS Officer Corps of the early forties before the great bloodletting of Russia commenced. But unlike most of his comrades he was not eager for an early death on the battlefield for the sake of 'Folk, Fatherland and Führer'. If he were to die, he wanted it to be for a realizable, valid objective. Not that he lacked courage. The close combat badge, the black wound medal, and the Iron Cross, first and second class, adorning his black tanker's tunic, showed he had displayed bravery enough on the battlefield and willingness to shed his blood for the Fatherland.

But he had seen the Vulture operate during the campaign in Poland back in 1939, flinging away the lives of his men recklessly for the sake of his personal prestige and advancement. Then he had sworn he would never allow the CO to do that again with the men in his charge and he had managed to realize that aim during the lightning campaign in France the previous summer. But could he do the same in the coming battle in Russia? He knew just how much the Vulture lusted for promotion, whatever the cost in human lives. He bit his bottom lip, worried, as yet another bomber limped home from the great attack on London, its engines spluttering and back-firing. What would the new campaign against Soviet Russia bring?

> '*Tante Hedwig, Tante Hedwig, deine Nahmaschine geht nicht....*
> *Ich hab' die ganze Nacht probiert und mein ganzes Ol versch-*
> *miert.... '*

The dirty song, followed by bursts of drunken laughter, cut into his thoughts. The young officer sighed and straightened up. The drunks were already coming home from the brothels and inns of nearby Calais. He'd better get back to the lines in case he had to help the orderly sergeant with them. A drunken SS trooper, especially if he were one of Wotan's 'old hares',* was too much for one man to handle. He grinned at the thought and then he was striding back to the camp energetically, ready for trouble.

* Name given to the veterans.

CHAPTER 3

The tin alarm clock on the night table next to the big bed shrilled urgently. Someone moaned. 'Great crap on the Christmas tree!' a deep masculine voice groaned. 'Is there no frigging peace for a poor old soldier man?' A brutally muscled, hairy arm reached out to turn it off in the same instant that two other arms, thinner and paler, and undoubtedly female, reached out to do the same. In the dim red light cast by the lamp, over which they had draped a pair of Gerda's red silk knickers, the trio found the clock and turned it off.

Sergeant Schulze, one of those few surviving 'old hares', licked his parched lips and told himself he had taken a lot of suds aboard this night. His mouth tasted like the bottom of a parrot's cage. Then with an effort of will he looked at the 'grey mouse'* next to him in bed. It was Gerda. 'Hey,' he said thickly, as the naked woman opened her eyes, 'you was on my right when I dropped off.'

On the other side of the huge sergeant, Erna, the other grey mouse, tittered and chirped, 'We're wanderers, *Schatz*, nocturnal wanderers.' She giggled and winked across his massive chest at her twin sister.

Schulze wasn't amused. He felt the first definite stirrings of his loins. 'Well, whichever you are, Erna or Gerda, wander over this. Grab a hold of it. It ain't no frigging hiker's pole, I can tell yer!' He guffawed coarsely and pointed down to where the sheet had suddenly become tent-like.

The two twins, who were both signals operators at the *Luftwaffe* radar station just outside Calais, shook their blonde

---

* Name given to the female auxiliaries of the German Service on account of their grey uniform and supposedly demure behaviour.

heads as one. 'Can't do, *Schulzi*. We've got to be back on the job at twenty-three hundred. There's a red alert on, you know.'

'Get back *on this job!*' Schulze said, and there was a note of pleading in his voice. 'Don't yer know yer cutting into my love life? I've only had it twice.'

'Yes,' Erna said firmly, slipping out of the big bed and reaching for her grey uniform knickers. '*Twice* – with *both* of us!'

Her sister also slipped out of bed and began to dress. Schulze groaned. 'Shit on the shingle, I don't know what to do for the best, have another litre of frog suds or go and have a wank! And will you get a load of that little shit next door. His piece ain't worried about no red alert!'

Next door the floor boards were creaking as his running mate Matz clattered up and down in his jackboots, singing and groaning at the same time, *'And this is the way the ladies ride, clip, clop, clip, clop!'* His grey mouse, the massive Brunhilde, groaned pleasurably.

'Well, at least he's up,' Gerda said, carefully settling each large breast into the cups of her bra.

Schulze licked his lips greedily at the sight and grumbled, 'Yer, I know what that perverted banana sucker's up to.' He clenched a fist like a small steam shovel and hammered on the wall. 'Stop that perverted piggery in there! I'm trying to say a loving good-bye to my fiancées, horseshit!'

'But I'm only having a little bit o' pleasure, Schulzi,' Matz panted. 'Surely you don't begrudge me a bit of the old two-backed beast. Be reasonable, old house.'

'Knock it off!' Schulze snorted angrily. The twins began to slip on their shoes and he knew that the orgy was over. 'If I don't fuck, nobody fucks, especially lowly corporals who are inferior in rank to me.'

'But if I'm quiet, Schulzi,' Matz began to plead, 'real quiet, you won't hear. Brunhilde, get off!'

But a downcast Schulze was no longer listening. The twins were dressed now in full uniform and he realized he couldn't tell the difference between them now he couldn't see the mole that adorned Erna's delightful right flank. 'Which is Gerda and which is Erna?' he asked. 'You've got me all confused again.'

They laughed in unison. 'Well, *Schatzi*, you'll just have to wait till we get our next day off, won't you?' they chirped together and kissed him on both cheeks, giggling like silly schoolgirls.

Morosely, Schulze, sitting up naked in the bed, knowing that the hardness of his loins would have to find its own solution now, accepted the kisses as his right and muttered, 'Pay the old cow downstairs for the room, will yer, girls. I can't speak frog like you. Besides,' he added, more to the point, 'I'm skint to next pay-day.'

Dutifully they said they would. Then they were gone, clattering down the ancient stairs in a hurry to get back to the 'graveyard shift', leaving Schulze to drag himself morosely out of the rumpled hired bed, not even caring now that next door Matz was still attempting to have his 'bit of the old two-backed beast' on the quiet. There was no mistaking the urgent squeaking of the bed springs.

Ten minutes later the two old comrades were back on the street, standing under the shadow of the ornate Hotel de Ville, staring in blank comprehension at Rodin's statue of the Burghers of Calais, waiting for the truck that would take them back to camp, the rest of the 'beer corpses' littering the pavement and the excited 'green-beaks', flushed and happy, boasting about their adventures with the local whores.

Schulze took the dewdrop hanging from the end of his big nose and flung it from him almost angrily, just missing a drunken *Sturmmann* snoring happily on the cobbles. 'Frigging Army!' he cursed. 'Allus frigging getting in the way of the simple pleasures of yer little man! Now I'm not gonna be able to dip my wick in the old honeypot till next pay-day.'

Matz looked up at his friend's massive bulk. 'Didn't yer get enough tonight to last yer, old house? Anyhow, you can allus have a bash with the old five-fingered widow,' he added brightly. He made an explicit and obscene gesture with his clenched fist.

Schulze glowered at him, 'None o' that. I'm not going to have that kind of filthy talk around here. What are them green-beaks gonna think of the NCO Corps when they hear the likes o' that? One more piece of dirty mouth from you, Corporal Matz, and I'm going to sew yer arse cheeks together so that you're gonna have to crap through yer ears! Do you get that?'

But before Sergeant Schulze could carry out that terrible threat, a harsh metallic voice, magnified a dozen times by a megaphone, cut into the conversation, as an armoured car swung round the corner of the big square, searchlight sweeping from left to right. *'Achtung, achtung, hier spricht die Feldgendarmerie?'*

'Chain-dogs!' one of the green-beaks breathed in alarm, as he became aware of the heavily armed military police, the silver half-moons of their hated profession around their necks, marching to both sides of the armed car.

Matz kicked the nearest beer corpse in the ribs and whispered, 'On your hind legs, you horned ox. It's the frigging chain-dogs!'

'This is an official order,' the harsh voice continued. 'A state of red alert has been proclaimed all along the coast. All soldiers, sailors and airmen will return to their units forthwith. Do you hear me, this is an official order, all men will return to their units – *at once!'*

Matz looked at Schulze curiously. 'What's the flap?' he asked. *'Was ist los?'*

Schulze caught a glimpse of the open-necked tunic and yellow air force eagles of the officer on the armoured car and spat contemptuously into the gutter, again narrowly missing the drunken *Sturmmann*. *'Luftwaffe* aren't there?' he snorted, as if that were sufficient explanation. 'Pissing their pants as usual.'

'But there's some kind o' flap going on, Schulzi,' Matz

objected. 'Brunhilde mentioned it, too. Their place has been on red alert most o' the day.'

The big NCO remained unconvinced. 'Shit in the wind, ape turd!' he growled. 'You and yer frigging flap. Anyhow, whatever it is, it's nothing to do with Wotan. And here comes the truck...' With that he started to barge his way through the crowd of soldiers, crying, 'Make way for a naval officer there. Come on, get out of the frigging way!'

But for once Sergeant Schulze, the one-time terror of the Hamburg waterfront, was wrong. What was now beginning to happen on this Saturday night on both sides of the English Channel would very *definitely* affect SS Assault Regiment Wotan.

CHAPTER 4

'Come on, *Hauptmann* Horn, this way!' The Home Guard officer, who wore a steel helmet, but whose feet were clad in battered carpet slippers, thrust a great, old-fashioned pistol into the captive pilot's back and pushed him out of the little Morris.

Obediently their captive obeyed, though his dark brooding face under the thick eyebrows exhibited some signs of impatience, as if he were not used to dealing with such inferior mortals as these, and wished he could be confronted with his equals, people who wielded power.

Horn, that was the name he had given them as soon as they had captured him in the field, allowed himself to be led down to the dark smelly corridor of the Home Guards HQ in what had once been a Boy Scouts Hall, blinking at the sudden light after the total blackout outside. Suddenly a voice called in that sort of English he found exceedingly difficult to understand, 'Who's there?'

His captors halted. 'The police and the Home Guard,' one of them rasped. 'Open up, we've got a Jerry prisoner. A pilot who bailed out of his fighter.'

Horn smiled sardonically. So that was what they supposed. Well, it would be as good a cover story as any until he was able to meet people in authority and tell them who he really was and what his mission was.

A lock was turned, a rusty bolt was drawn back. The door was opened hastily to reveal an old man without teeth, dressed in a corporal's blouse, with a striped collarless shirt beneath. He snapped to attention when he saw the officer with the revolver and said thickly, 'Sorry, I ain't got me teeth in, sir. Didn't have time. They're in the glass – '

The officer waved his revolver for silence and thrust his

prisoner forward into the room, which smelled of stale cigarette smoke and unwashed feet. It was occupied by thirty or so middle-aged and old Home Guardsmen in various stages of undress, as if they had been just about to go to bed. Others were squatting on their bunks under the litter of military equipment – gas masks, packs, rifles – hanging from nails, eating fish and chips out of newspaper.

The officer flushed at the sight. 'Turn out the guard!' he bellowed.

The men sprang into action, bumping into each other as they grabbed for their rifles and equipment, snatching their boots from beneath the bunks, cursing one another when someone took the wrong ones. The pilot allowed himself a half smile at the sight and next to him the middle-aged officer with the pistol snapped, 'Suppose this kind of thing wouldn't happen in Germany, eh?'

The pilot thought it wiser not to answer and he waited, his smile gone, until the civilian soldiers were lined up at the position of attention, while the officer eyed them sternly, pistol still drawn, as if ready to shoot any one of them who didn't react promptly enough.

With his men at the ready now, the officer gestured with his pistol to the door on the far side of the room on which was tacked the notice in pencil, *'Guard Room'*. 'In there!' he commanded.

The pilot drew himself up to his full height, towering above the officer and his soldiers. 'I am a German officer,' he announced proudly.

The officer thrust the muzzle of his pistol into his stomach. 'I'm giving orders here, *Herr Hauptmann*!' he barked. 'Now get in there, or it will be the worse for you!'

The pilot paled, but walked into the guard room, which was blacked out, lit by a single naked bulb and devoid of anything save the old Boy Scouts training charts still pinned to the peeling wall. He paused, shrugged and then lay full length on the floor, staring at the fly-specked bulb without moving.

Time passed. As the officer and his second-in command examined the contents of their prisoner's pockets on the table in the big room, Home Guardsmen tiptoed forward to peer in at the open door of the guard room at their charge. For all the world he might well have been dead, or so it seemed to them. He lay there with his hands under his dark curly head totally still, as if he had fainted or gone into a coma.

But the pilot was well aware of their presence. He had not fainted and nor was he in a coma. As a boy back in Alexandria, where his father had been a businessman, he had often watched nomadic Arabs prepare for long arduous journeys through the desert by lying down in the sand and relaxing every muscle. Within minutes, the hook-nosed, swarthy nomads would arise refreshed and prepared for the rigours of the weeks to come.

He had taken up this elementary form of yoga himself and had found it had worked. As a pilot before a mission, later as a student readying for a difficult examination, and then a party leader just prior to giving a long speech, he would stretch out full-length for five or ten minutes, deliberately making his mind blank, to arise full of energy and confidence, prepared to tackle anything. And on this particular night, he knew he would need all his physical strength and peace of mind for he was now about to attempt his greatest mission.

'Will ye no take a cup o' tea, sir?' A kindly voice broke into his reverie. 'Real ol' sergeant-major's tea, we used to call it in the trenches in the Old War.'

He turned his head. An old grey-haired Tommy with no teeth was proffering him a chipped white enamel mug from which the steam rose.

The pilot smiled. He forgot all his fads about food and accepted the cup, blowing away the steam and thus not noticing the old man's suddenly changed expression. 'Thank you,' he said. 'It is very kind of you.'

'Thank you, sir,' the Home Guardsman said like a head waiter pleased that his attentions and service were appreciated. Then he sped away, wrinkled old face puzzled, to where the officer was still going through their captive's possessions – a small hypodermic syringe, a flat tin that contained tablets, possibly drugs, a sealed letter on which was scrawled in a florid continental hand, *'His Grace, the Duke of Hamilton'*. At this the officer whistled. But he did not attempt to open it. Instead he announced to the room. 'None of you men are to touch this envelope. Leave that to the boys from Intelligence. It might be important.' He stopped short suddenly and frowned at the man who had taken the pilot a mug of tea.

Standing there in his ill-fitting uniform, he had his skinny hand raised like a schoolboy urgently requesting leave to go and have a pee. 'Well, Hamish, what is it? What do yer want, man?'

Hamish licked his lips, face a mixture of bewilderment and purpose. 'D'ye think, sir, I could have a wee word with ye in private, sir?'

The officer frowned and put down the Leica camera he had just picked up, wondering as he did so why a pilot would need a camera. What did he think he was, a ruddy tourist come north to snap pictures of the glens! 'Why in private, Hamish?' he demanded. 'Can't the rest hear what you have to say.'

Hamish pulled a face. 'Ye ken, sir,' he wheedled in that typical Scottish fashion. 'I dinna want to make a fool o' myself. If – '

'All right, don't make a bloody big song and dance of it, man!' the officer snapped. 'Come on out into the corridor.'

In silence they walked outside into the dark corridor with its walls of fading posters, encouraging the populace *'To Keep Mum'* and asking *'Is Your Journey Necessary?'* 'Well?' the officer barked. 'What is it, Hamish?'

'Yon Jerry officer, sir,' he croaked. 'I think I ken who he is. I've seen him in the pictures more than once.'

'In the pictures!' the officer exploded. 'Our prisoner. But what would a Jerry pilot be doing in the pictures?'

'In the newsreels, I mean, sir,' Hamish stuttered. 'Not in them Hollywood things.'

'Get on with it, before I have you up on a charge!' the officer snapped.

'Can I whisper, sir?' Hamish asked pleadingly.

The officer caught himself in time, his fat face underneath the steel helmet almost purple now. 'Yes, any damned thing you like, man, but will you bloody well get on with it?'

Hamish reached up on the tips of his toes and whispered the name into the officer's ear, who gasped and pushed Hamish from him. 'My God, man,' he cried, 'have you been drinking?'

'I've nae touched a drop the whole long day, sir. I swear that on the Holy Book.' Hamish looked offended.

The officer mopped his brow beneath the helmet with a khaki handkerchief. 'But you can't mean that the pilot is . . . ' His words ended in a gasp. Then he took control of himself. 'All right, get back to your post, I'll take care of it.'

Hamish went, looking downcast and muttering to himself, while the officer stood in the gloomy corridor, mulling over what the Home Guardsman had just whispered in his ear. Could it be possible? he asked himself. Surely it couldn't be *him*? What the devil would he be doing landing by parachute in this remote arsehole of the world?

The officer sucked at his bottom lip. But all the same what was a German, who was obviously in his forties, doing piloting a fighter? Besides, what military objective had he hoped to find up here in rural Scotland? And there was the business of the letter, too. What was the Jerry doing carrying a letter addressed to the Duke of Hamilton?

The Home Guard officer looked at his watch. It was already nearly midnight. Time had flown since he had picked up the German. All the same, he'd better make sure. He'd ring up Command HQ – there would surely still be someone on duty there – and pass on what Hamish had whispered into his ear. Shaking his head like a sorely troubled man, he made his way hurriedly down the dark corridor towards the duty telephone. Outside some drunken soldier was singing in slurred tones, *'Kiss me good-night, Sarnt-Major... tuck me in me little wooden bed... We all love you, Sarnt-Major...'*

CHAPTER 5

*RAEDER ROLLEN FUER DEN KRIEG!** the letters proclaimed in bright red from the banner strung across the exit to
Munich station. *Hauptmann* Karl-Heinz Pintsch sniffed. At
this particular moment, nothing much was moving at all.
Still the station was packed. Soldiers burdened with packs
and rifles; girlfriends clutching them desperately, not far from
tears; hard-eyed chain-dogs in pairs on the look-out for
deserters; whores lurking in the shadows cast by the pillars;
old peasants humping heavy rucksacks and smoking curved
pipes – all of them filled the platform, waiting for the
midnight train to take them away.

Pintsch, elegant in his *Luftwaffe* uniform, smart brief-case
clutched in his grey-gloved hand, wondered what the end of
his particular journey would bring. Somehow, as he stood
there under the domed glass roof, which had been blacked-
out in 1939 so that the station interior could be illuminated,
he had always known that one day he would have to make
this midnight journey. Ever since his boss had taken up flying
from Augsburg Field again, he had suspected that it was more
than just a hobby, that there was something important
behind those secret flights he had taken against the Führer's
specific order.

Each time his boss had taken off in the prototype
Messerschmitt, leaving him and the boss's private detective
to wait behind in the black official Mercedes, the boss had
solemnly handed him the sealed letter. His instructions had
always been the same. 'Synchronize your watch with mine,
Pintsch,' he had commanded, and when that had been done
he had rasped, 'If I'm not back within four hours, open the
letter. It contains certain instructions. Then take this letter' –

* Wheels roll for victory.

thereupon the other sealed letter had been given to him – 'to the Führer, *in person*. Understood?'

Obediently he had always nodded his understanding, although he had been puzzled beyond measure.

'*He* will want to know where I am.'

Time after time he and the bodyguard had sat for hours in the car, smoking and chatting, eyes flashing to their watches constantly, wondering if *this* time he wouldn't come back after the four hours were up.

Then it had happened, about three months ago. It had been a bitterly cold afternoon, with the fog creeping in across the field like a soft grey cat. Pintsch had looked at the bodyguard, who had looked back but had said nothing. So he had wet his lips, which were suddenly very dry, and said a little hoarsely, 'The weather, Karl. Let's give him another fifteen minutes, *ja*?'

The other man had nodded his agreement.

So they had continued to wait, the only sound the sad drip-drip of the wet fog from the bonnet of the big black car. Finally Pintsch had known he could wait no longer. Outside it was already pitch-black. Taking his torch, he had opened *his* letter and read it, gasping with shock as he did so. '*Jesus-nach!*' he croaked.

The bodyguard asked urgently, '*Was ist los, Pintsch? Sind Sie krank?*'

Pintsch had shaken his head. 'No, I'm not sick,' he had declared thickly. 'It's this letter.' The torch shook as he focused it on the piece of paper with its familiar crested heading. 'The Deputy writes he's flying . . . to England – '

'What?'

'Yes,' Pintsch had croaked wildly, 'flying to England – *to make peace!*'

The bodyguard had crossed himself in the Bavarian fashion and had choked, '*Himmelherrje!*' He had grabbed the letter and forgetting all about the blackout regulations, he had turned on the car's interior lighting to read the letter for himself. In that same instant the two of them froze. For to the

west they could hear the first familiar drone of the Me 110.
Their boss had not gone after all.

'*But why, sir?*' Pintsch had asked almost desperately after
they had returned that January night. 'Why were you flying
to England without the Führer's permission? I know you
must have done because you wouldn't have left the letter for
me to deliver to him otherwise.'

His boss, one of the few who had followed Hitler right from
the beginning, and had suffered for it too, took his time
answering, as they had sat together in the bare attic room, the
green-tiled *Kachelofen* crackling merrily in the corner. 'I am
not a spy, Pintsch,' his boss had said finally. 'Nor am I a
traitor to the cause, if that's what you think. I was to fly to
England to make peace between our countries. It is the
Führer's most fervent wish to have an early peace with
England.' He had hesitated and then said darkly, 'For he has
other plans and wishes to have the war with England settled.
Von Ribbentrop's* Foreign Office and the gentlemen of the
Abwehr† have already tried, indirectly, to make contact with
the English. But they have failed. I' – his boss had puffed out
his big chest dramatically, as if he were standing on the
platform at the annual party rally at Nuremburg about to
make a speech to the excited throng – 'decided that the only
way to succeed is to make a *direct* approach to them. They will
listen to me, the Führer's own deputy.'

It was then that Pintsch had decided that his boss was
slightly crazy.

Now he had done it and he was left holding the baby.
Grosse Scheisse! he cursed to himself as at last the overhead
loudspeakers started to crackle into harsh metallic life,
announcing '*der planmässige Zug nach Berchtesgaden fährt jetzt
am Gleis Eins ein.*' Soon the shit really was going to hit the fan.
Hardly aware of what he was doing, he waited for the first-
class coach which would take him to Hitler's headquarters to
draw to a halt...

* Nazi Foreign Minister.
† German Secret Service.

CHAPTER 6

The news from London was bad. Nearly a thousand German heavy bombers had been raiding the capital for nearly two hours. Apparently the whole of the city centre was virtually cut off. Every main line station, save Marylebone, was out of action. All the central tube stations had been hit or closed and yet again the Houses of Parliament had been struck. In her wooden cubicle, just off Ditchley House's main hall, the duty secretary's pretty face grew ever more solemn as call after call, bringing dire tidings, came flooding in. Already she had a whole pile of them typed out on separate slips to hand to the Prime Minister, once the midnight film was over and he began working once more into the small hours. They made unpleasant reading. This Saturday night it seemed that after four months of constant bombing, the Jerries were really attempting to wipe London off the map once and for all. As she typed yet another message from the Air Ministry reporting that from the building's roof there was nothing to be seen but flames, and that one observer had counted at least *eight* Wren churches ablaze, she thanked God that she and the PM were safe in the heart of rural Oxfordshire this terrible weekend.

Now and then in the breaks, she could hear the rumble of muted laughter coming from the film room, where the Prime Minister and his guests, all well supplied with fine cigars and whisky, were enjoying the Marx Brothers' latest film *The Marx Brothers Go West*. Like his great enemy Adolf Hitler, far off in Berchtesgaden, Mr Churchill did enjoy a midnight movie, especially a funny one. Miss Shearburn smiled fondly at the thought of the Great Old Man, dressed in a florid silk dressing gown, big cigar tucked between lips, taking sips of his whisky (with his false teeth by now probably in the other glass to his side) roaring his head off at the antics of the three crazy

American comedians. And she knew just how much the Prime Minister needed his relaxation. Ever since he had become Prime Minister, exactly one year ago this very day, he had known nothing but defeat after defeat. He definitely had earned an hour or so of pleasure.

Suddenly the phone started to buzz again. She forgot her beloved boss and the Marx Brothers and picked it up. Was it London once again with more dire news of the blaze there, the worst since the Great Fire of three centuries before?

No, it wasn't. It was the guard room rigged up for the weekend outside. These days the Imperial General Staff insisted that Mr Churchill be guarded at all times. Inspector Thompson, his sole bodyguard, was not enough. He had to be guarded by at least a company of infantry, just in case the enemy tried to take the Great Man in a surprise paratroop attack.

Hurriedly she scribbled down the information the guard commander was passing to her. 'Wing Commander his grace the Duke of Hamilton wishes to see the PM at once, if possible. It is of the greatest national importance. . . . No, Miss, he won't say what it is. He says the information is for Mr Churchill's ears only. . . . Right, I'll hold him here, Miss. Tell him you'll see. Christ, Miss, London is really catching a packet. It was just on the news and we guessed it had to be London.'

But Miss Shearburn was no longer listening. Already her slim fingers were slipping back and forth across the keyboard. Hurriedly she rose and half-ran across the hall. Carefully she opened the door of the film room, nostrils assailed by the smell of whisky and cigar smoke, catching the self-important laughter of hearty men who knew that they were the people who ran things – and you'd better damn well learn that! 'For Mr Churchill,' she whispered, as on the screen Harpo with his outrageous blond wig chased a big-bosomed, middle-aged lady, hooting his horn crazily, *'urgent!'*

'Got it,' the messenger at the door whispered back. He crouched low so as not to block the screen and crept down the aisle to where Churchill sprawled in a big armchair looking like a pink toothless Buddha.

She waited, wondering why the Duke of Hamilton wanted to speak to the Prime Minister. Of course, Churchill knew him well. They had met many times when the Duke had been a conservative MP in the House and they had socialized elsewhere, too. But after all, she sniffed, he was only a wing-commander, and wing-commanders were ten a penny in the Churchill entourage.

But be that as it may, the Prime Minister appeared a moment later out of the glowing darkness, clad in his startling mandarin dressing gown, embroidered with red and gold dragons, the belt pulled tightly about his ample girth. 'Well?' he demanded, plump face half-turned to the screen and the crazy chase between Harpo and the big-bosomed lady. 'Spit it out, Mary.'

Swiftly she filled him in, giving him more details of what the guard commander had related to her over the phone from below, while the Prime Minister's smiling look gave way to one of bewilderment, perhaps of annoyance too that he was going to miss the rest of the comedy. In the end, he waved the big cigar at her like an offensive weapon and growled in that magnificent voice of his, which still sent shivers down her maidenly spine. 'All right, then have his grace sent up to the damned study. I'll see him.'

Five minutes later the Duke was telling the great man his amazing story: how he had been summoned by Intelligence to a Home Guard post to be confronted with a tall, imposing German pilot in his early forties who had claimed that he knew him, the Duke, through mutual friends and had flown to England to make an offer of peace with Germany that he, the Duke, must convey to the Prime Minister.

'But on what basis can a middle-aged *Luftwaffe* captain maintain that he has the authority to make such an offer, pray?' Churchill asked.

The Duke hesitated. In the grate a sudden breeze made the dying fire flicker up again, casting their shadows on the wall behind them. The Prime Minister leaned forward to hear the nobleman's answer. 'Prime Minister,' he said slowly, weighing his words with great, very great care. 'He is not just a simple *Luftwaffe* pilot, although he is using the rank and name of *Hauptmann* Horn as a *nom de guerre*.' He swallowed. 'In reality, he is, if we are to believe his words, no less a person than Hitler's own deputy, Party Leader *Rudolf Hess*!'

Churchill nearly dropped his cigar. 'What – what did you say, Hamilton?' he stuttered. Then he recovered himself swiftly, as was his wont. 'Will you please say that again?'

From outside came the stamp of the sentries' hobnail boots on the gravel and harsh bark of orders. It was midnight. They were changing the guards. The Duke of Hamilton licked his dry lips and spoke so quietly that Churchill had to lean forward in his chair to hear him. 'He says, Prime Minister, that he is Hitler's deputy and that he has come to England to make peace between our country and Nazi Germany.'

Churchill sat back as if someone had just slapped him across the face. Slowly, almost as if he were thinking aloud, he whispered, *'The worm is in the apple.'*

Sunday, 11 May 1941

CHAPTER 1

Carefully, *Parteisekretär* Martin Bormann opened his desk safe and ignored the well-thumbed pile of pornographic pictures he had had Heim, his assistant, buy him last summer when he had visited Paris with the Führer. This morning the square-headed party official, who had the look of a run-down seedy boxer about him, was not concerned with sex, but with food. It was going to be a long day with the Führer and he needed something more substantial than the Führer's vegetarian muck inside 'his ribs'. He wanted some good spicy meat to start off the day properly.

Licking his fleshy sensual lips in anticipation, he sliced off a thick chunk of the salami and swallowed it, a look of pleasure flushing his sallow face. Outside, the sun had already risen above the Alps and was casting its rosy hue over the great complex of houses, air-raid shelters and barracks he more than anyone else had been responsible for building here on the Obersalzberg. Virtually single-handed he had created the Führer's favourite retreat, the *Berghof** up here in the mountains on Germany's border with Austria. But of course others had taken the credit for it. Naturally that fool of a boss of his, Hess, with his occult mumbo-jumbo, his food fads, yoga, and all the rest of that unrealistic crazy twaddle that kept him occupied these days instead of attending to his duties here with the Führer, had made it appear he had done the thinking, while his subordinate Bormann had merely carried out his orders.

Bormann's pugnacious face darkened at the thought. Without realizing he was doing so, he cut off another hearty slice of the spicy, garlic-laden sausage and swallowed it whole. One day, he promised himself as he replaced the

* Literally 'Mountain Court'.

salami in the safe next to the picture of two Eton-cropped, naked women doing something delightfully filthy to one another, he'd rid himself of Hess. Then he alone would be the power behind the throne, the 'Führer's brown eminence' in reality. For that was what some of Hitler's toadies were already calling him, naturally behind his back.

He strode towards the full-length mirror that adorned one wall of his otherwise spartan office and studied himself in the glass, tugging at his breeches and tunic, which bore the single ribbon of the rare Blood Order, granted to those who had shed their blood for the party in the old days before the takeover of power. He frowned. Well, he hadn't exactly shed his blood, but he had damn well spent nearly two years in prison for having helped to beat the communist traitor to death back there on the farm in his native Mecklenburg. Yes, he had done his bit for the holy cause of national socialism when some of those toadies and fawning courtiers who now surrounded the Führer still looked down their long aristocratic noses at the 'common, upstart Nazis'.

Bormann took one last look at his burly image in the mirror and was pleased with what he saw. In truth he was running a little to fat, but he could carry the extra weight. He was a real *Mannesbild*, as the Bavarians said, 'a fine picture of a man' the women found irresistible. *Grosser Gott*, that little secretary last night, for instance! She had had her fingers inside his breeches fumbling for his thing before he had hardly sat down on the office couch. Later she had been stretched out on the sofa, legs in the air in complete abandon, writhing and twisting as if she couldn't get enough of the old salami. He grinned evilly at the thought. Yes, there was no doubt about it, Martin Bormann was a cocksman of the first order.

Then Hess's second-in-command forgot the sausage and his amorous experience of the previous night and concentrated on the day ahead. In two hours the Führer would awake – as usual he had stayed up till two – and would commence his daily audiences and conferences. By that time he wanted to have everything in first-class order, ready to meet any and every request the Führer might make. Already the Führer consulted him on virtually everything. One day he wanted to make himself totally indispensable. Then it would be good-bye Herr Hess!

He picked up his brief-case and stamped to the door. Carefully he locked it behind him, as though the office contained some priceless secret. It didn't, of course, but the knowledge that of all the offices in the *Berghof*, including those of the Führer, his alone was locked (Why should they be? The place was guarded by a whole battalion of the SS), impressed the toadies and courtiers.

Now he started to march up the great staircase, flooded with the light from the mountains, his booted feet echoing in the heavy silence. Although the household was awake – the servants, the clerks, the typists and the like – they went about their duties on tiptoe. The Führer still slept and his sleep was holy.

Suddenly the door to his right opened. It was Eva Braun, the Führer's mistress, followed by her two black dogs, Negus and Stasi. Bormann frowned and then forced a fake smile as he saw she was turning to look at him. *'Heil Hitler!'* he barked and shot up his right hand.

The mistress looked at him coldly and said, *'Guten Morgen, Herr Borman.'* It was a deliberate slight, of course. He knew that. She hated him because of his success with the women here at the *Berghof*, that was the reason. Perhaps she fancied a bit of what the others were getting herself, he mused. Aloud, he said, *'Schläft der Führer noch?'*

She shrugged carelessly and answered, 'How should I know?' And with that she swept off down the corridor, followed by her damned dogs.

Bormann watched her go for a moment, telling himself that the Führer must be a fool to allow himself to be dominated by that vain, empty-headed, ex-photographer's assistant. Why only the other day he had heard Hitler plead with her, 'Dear Effie, will you allow poor Blondi to join us for half an hour?' He had meant his Alsatian bitch. Bormann shook his head.

How could the man who ruled half of Europe allow himself to be dominated by that stupid slip of a girl. What she needed was to be thrown on her back, her pants ripped off her and a good piece of Mecklenburg salami slipped inside her! He warmed to the thought and passed on, feeling pleased with himself again.

At the head of the stairs he paused, as if he were about to admire the view from the great picture window. In fact, he was out of breath. The mixed diet of *Schnitzel und Sauerkraut*, washed down by half a dozen *Korns*, and followed by the session on the couch with the nubile secretary, had obviously taken it out of him. He needed a breather. Thus he pretended to survey the view, the sun tipping the still snow-capped peaks of the Austrian Alps a delicate pink. Suddenly he frowned. Down below, a little car was drawing up before the main entrance to the Führer's refuge, the driver coasting the last few metres in order not to wake the leader. But it was not the car that caught his attention.

It was the familiar blond head of his fool of a brother Albert, tarted up in the uniform of an SS officer, complete with pistol holster at his gleaming belt, though his younger brother had never fired a shot in anger in his whole life. Why in three devils' name was *he* poncing down the great steps, where once the Führer had received Neville Chamberlain back in 1938 when he had 'come to save the peace'?

He frowned. Albert had bent to open the car's door as if he were a shitting lackey instead of one of the Führer's adjutants. The figure which emerged was familiar. It was Captain Pintsch, his boss's *Luftwaffe* adjutant. His frown deepened. What was he doing turning up at this time of the morning without the *Stellvertreter*,* and in such a silly little car instead of the usual big black Mercedes?

Martin Bormann pressed his nose closer to the huge window like a naughty schoolboy who had been expelled from his classroom for misbehaviour and was now wanting to

* The Deputy.

return inside. Suddenly he dearly wished to know just what the two of them were saying to each other. Very much so!

In fact, a weary and not a little apprehensive *Hauptmann* Pintsch was revealing only the bare essentials of his reason for arriving at the *Berghof* this early in the morning. 'What makes you so anxious to see the Führer this morning?' Albert Bormann had asked, smiling at the visitor in his usual happy fashion, for they had known each other for several years now.

But for once Pintsch, who was normally relaxed and easy-going, was solemn, even secretive. 'I'm sorry,' he snapped, 'but I can't tell you. As I have just said, I have a sealed letter from my chief for him.'

'How is he these days?' Bormann asked, as he began to lead Pintsch up the steps past the sentries standing rigidly to attention, their rifles raised in salute. 'Still keeping up his flying, eh?' He winked knowingly, as if the great secret had been known at the *Berghof* all the time.

'Yes,' Pintsch agreed in a non-committal fashion, telling himself the damned Gestapo had its nose in everything. 'He's still flying.'

The footmen opened the great bronze door and Bormann, very business-like now, said, 'I'm off to my office. I'll see what I can do for you, Pintsch. But I don't hold out much hope for you seeing him this morning. There's always a crowd waiting to see him, even on Sunday morning.'

Pintsch's expression did not change as he handed his cap, pistol belt and gloves to the footman. 'He'll see me,' he said. 'Of that I'm sure.' What he didn't say was, *'I'm damned scared of what he'll do when he does!'*

CHAPTER 2

The ancient truck screeched by the guard room, brakes squeaking, tyres howling in protest. One minute it was there this quiet Sunday morning; the next it was gone, tearing down the damp, glistening *pavé* road back to the rabbit warren of Calais's working-class suburbs, just off the docks. Behind it, as the startled Wotan sentries ran heavily from their red-and-white striped boxes, an ugly, scarlet-coloured bundle lay awkwardly on the cobbles.

'God in heaven!' the Vulture gasped five minutes later, as he pushed his way through the mob of soldiers gawping down at the open bundle, 'They've – they've – '

Behind him Sergeant Schulze supplied the words he was too shocked to express, and for once there was no humour in his thick Hamburg voice, 'They've shortened his dick a piece!'

The unknown assailants had. The unfortunate young *Sturmmann*, one of the young green-beaks who had just joined SS Assault Regiment Wotan from the Hitler Youth as a volunteer, had been shot in the back of the head. Then his killers had gone to work on him with barbaric cruelty. They had gouged out his eyes, and for good measure had severed the boy's penis and inserted it between his poor dead lips in a kind of gruesome, perverted joke.

Hastily von Dodenburg, his face a deathly white, eyes glistening with outrage, elbowed a shocked and immobile Vulture to one side and quickly slipped off his overcoat. Gently he draped it over the poor kid's outraged and tortured body. 'Sergeant Schulze,' he snapped, only keeping his voice under control with an effort.

'*ZuBefehl!*' Schulze bellowed, clicking to attention and trying to ignore the green-beak who was now vomiting helplessly at his side.

'Take a detail – all old hares – and bring the poor devil to
the MO. And quick about it!' he added, iron in his voice. 'All
right, you troopers, back to your quarters. They'll be serving
breakfast in fifteen minutes.'

'*Los, los!*' Matz took up the chant. 'Back to your quarters.
You've seen enough. Hurry up, the hash-slingers are waiting
for you. It's fart soup and turds for breakfast this morning.'
He meant pea-soup with sausage. But his crude attempt at
trying to defuse the situation didn't help much. Most of the
green-beaks looked green, as if they wouldn't be eating
breakfast anyway; perhaps even the midday meal either.

The Vulture took out a cigarette from his gleaming silver
cigarette case with fingers that trembled, as Schulze doubled
off to find a stretcher. He lit the cigarette, puffed out a
grateful stream of blue smoke and taking a waiting von
Dodenburg by the arm, led him away from the grisly sight.

When they were back in his office, he croaked, 'Von
Dodenburg, that is the second attack on my regiment this
week. First the sergeant who was foully stabbed in the back on
Wednesday night – pay-day – and now this.' He spread out
his well-manicured hands a little helplessly. 'Why? For over a
year we have lived in perfect harmony with the civvies.
Indeed they seemed to welcome us here. We paid excellently
for everything. The troops are well-disciplined. Indeed I have
heard from the local prefect that our chaps are far better
behaved than the Tommies who looted the place before they
fled last year. Now they are killing my young soldiers. *Why?*'

Von Dodenburg, tired and a little red-eyed after a night on
duty, licked his dry lips and wished he could down a cup of
scalding hot black coffee. He felt awful. 'Do you think it is the
communists, that they've got wind of what is, er, to come in
the East? I mean up to now they have regarded us almost as
their allies because we have a pact with the Soviet Union.'

The Vulture pondered the suggestion, while at the gate
Sergeant Schulze commanded the squad taking the mutilated body on a stretcher to the regimental medical officer.

'You might well be right. But right or not, those wretches

down in Calais will have to be taught a lesson. I will not tolerate my young men being murdered. They must learn that for every one of my soldiers killed, ten of them will be made to pay the supreme penalty.' He got to his feet and strode to the big map of Calais and its defences pinned to the wall of his office. 'Tonight we strike,' he snapped curtly, adjusting his monocle and slapping the map angrily. 'Here, where the dockers and that kind of rabble live, just here behind the *Gare Maritime*. They'll be communists, I am sure. That kind of rabble always is.'

'But will you obtain the permission of the Corps Commander, sir? von Dodenburg asked quickly, realizing suddenly what the Vulture intended to do.

The Vulture looked at him scornfully and tugged at the end of that monstrous beak of a nose of his. 'Since when has the commanding officer of SS Assault Regiment Wotan asked for permission to avenge his own. I am one hundred per cent sure that *Reichsführer* SS Heinrich Himmler will back me right up to the hilt.' He gave von Dodenburg one of his wintry smiles. 'Why, Himmler will probably signal his congratulations at my prompt action. It might even mean promotion. But no matter. Tonight we surround this area here with the whole regiment. The assault carriers will take up their position on the fringes, then we go in on foot and search each single house. If we find weapons, things of that nature, all to the good. If we don't,' he shrugged carelessly. 'But when we come out, *mein Lieber*, we will be taking with us twenty French civilians, ten for each of our dead.'

Von Dodenburg nodded his understanding and for once he agreed with the Vulture's decisive action. 'And if there is any armed resistance, sir?' he asked.

'Let us hope that there *is*, von Dodenburg. Then we can shoot – *to kill!* But I can promise you this, after this day no Frenchman will ever dare to lay a finger on any member of *my* regiment. Now off you go and get on with it.'

CHAPTER 3

Slowly Hitler removed the cheap nickel-framed spectacles from his nose (the fact that the Führer wore glasses was a state secret; no one dared photograph him wearing them) and slowly folded the letter that Pintsch had brought. He seemed very calm. No rage, no outbursts, no tantrums. Later Pintsch realized that he had been too calm. But that had been later. Very quietly he asked, 'And where is Hess now?'

Pintsch, standing rigidly to attention, gazing at a spot just beyond Hitler's right shoulder as regulations prescribed, barked as if he were on the parade, 'Yesterday evening, *mein Führer*, at eighteen hundred hours, he flew from Augsburg to Scotland to meet the Duke of Hamilton.'

Hitler nodded. 'At this particular point in the war that could be a very hazardous escapade,' the Führer said gravely and waved for Pintsch to withdraw.

Gladly the *Luftwaffe* captain did so, hardly daring to believe his luck. Nothing had happened!

Mouth open, lips moving, as if he were a small child learning to read for the first time, Hitler re-read the Hess letter.

'And if this project – which I admit may have only a small chance of success – ends in failure and Fate decides against me, this can have no negative result either for you or for Germany. It will always be possible for you to deny all responsibility. Simply say that – I was crazy!'

Hitler's dark, hypnotic eyes brooded as he considered what to do next. Outside the courtiers and lackeys waited, including Bormann, who now sidled up to a relieved Pintsch and asked out of the side of his mouth like a cinema gangster, 'What's happening in there?'

Pintsch did not take his gaze off the great door to Hitler's study. He, too, lowered his voice and whispered so that the others couldn't hear. 'The Deputy has flown to Scotland.'

Bormann looked at him as if he had suddenly gone crazy. *'What did you say?'* he gasped.

Pintsch repeated his words.

'Nach Schottland!' Bormann breathed incredulously. And then. 'Understand, this has nothing to do with me. I know nothing about it, *klar*? Don't try to involve me.'

Pintsch looked at him contemptuously but said nothing. He knew what a bully and an intriguer Bormann was. Undoubtedly, once he had recovered from his fright, he would make capital out of the fact that his boss had embarked on this crazy peace mission to the English. As always, Bormann would land on his feet!

Five minutes later in the solitude of his office, booted feet on the desk, savouring another slice of the salami from the safe, Bormann's mind began to clear. Already the Führer relied upon him almost totally for keeping the party machine working perfectly. It was he, Bormann, who kept control of the *Gauleiters*, ensuring that they worked efficiently in their *Gaus*, spread through the length and breadth of Germany and the German-speaking occupied territories, such as Alsace-Lorraine and the east cantons of Belgium. Up to now Hess had been in nominal charge of the party *apparat*.

Now, however, Hess appeared to be out of the way. That would mean that the Führer would rely upon him one hundred per cent, especially as soon he would be too occupied with the new campaign in the East to have time to concern himself with affairs at home. Bormann decided he could eat another slice of his beloved sausage, his broad brutal face brightening at the thought that perhaps now he would probably take over Hess's position. Of course he knew the old party leaders, such as Goering and Himmler and all the rest, would not allow Hitler to appoint him, Bormann, as his official deputy, he was too young for that. But for all intents and purposes that was what he would be, the Führer's Deputy, the third man in the Reich, after Hitler and Goering.

He swallowed the sausage in one gulp, carried away by a sudden excitement, his heart pounding.

By God, tonight he'd celebrate, once this business was over. He'd have a big plate of his favourite goulash, red cabbage, mashed potatoes and all the trimmings, washed down with a litre of beer and a couple of ice-cold *Korns*. His stomach began to rumble in anticipation. Then he'd summon the new girl from the typing pool. She couldn't be more than eighteen, and had a pair of breasts on her like ripe melons. And her thighs and flanks – like a Flemish mare! He swallowed hard at the thought. Heaven, arse and cloudburst, he'd have her right on this very desk!

He stopped suddenly, the delightful picture of the half-naked typist sprawled across his desk, her white thighs wide open, vanishing as swiftly as it had come. What if that damn fool Hess actually pulled it off and did achieve a peace with the English? Bormann could have moaned out loud. Then the crazy swine would return to the Reich, laden down with honours as the man who had ensured that Germany would not be involved in a war on two fronts. The thought was unbearable.

Bormann sat, agonizing over the problem. But then suddenly the answer came to him. He sat up and dropped his booted feet to the floor. Why, of course. That was it. Hess could not be allowed to return to Germany – ever. Somehow, today he had to convince the Führer of that.

Abruptly he remembered that summer evening so long ago back on the farm when they had got the communist informer drunk. They had plied him *Steinhäger* straight from the stone bottle all evening long, until he was no longer suspicious. The others had drunk, too. Only he, Bormann, had kept sober. He knew already what had to be done, but he was careful enough to let the others carry out the deed. Later they had loaded the Red on the farm cart. They were going down to the village for more drink. That had been his idea, though by now all of them had been too drunk to know it.

'*Stop for a piss here.* Everybody out for a piss!' he had called as they had rumbled through the thick oak wood. Laughing and reeling, all of them, including the Red, had stumbled out of the cart and lined up to urinate. It was then he had given the Red a push and cried, 'Watch him, comrades. He's trying to make a break for it! *Hit him someone!*'

That had started it and he had stepped back into the shadows and watched as they had beaten him to death with clubs and flails from the back of the cart. In the end his face had been an unrecognizable red mess with the blood oozing out of the myriad cuts like the sticky juice of an overripe squashed fig.

That's how he had done it then and although their crime had been found out, he had escaped with a two-year jail sentence because, as his defending lawyer had stated at the trial, he was really only a bystander and had not laid a finger on the murdered man. The knowledge that he had committed a murder and got away with it had cheered him during the long months in that grim Saxon prison. He had been pleased with his own cunning and the manner in which he had committed a crime by using other fools to carry it out for him.

Now, somehow, he had to do the same. He must remain in the background, a humble and loyal servant only giving advice when called upon to do so, but all the while *indirectly* ensuring that he achieved his private objective.

The buzzer on his desk broke into his reverie. It was the Führer. He was being summoned. He sprang to his feet and checked his features in the mirror, ensuring that there was no trace of sausage on his lips. Then he smiled at himself, but there was no corresponding warmth in his dark eyes. Very simply, he addressed the glass and said softly, 'Rudolf Hess, I am afraid I must pass the death sentence upon you. *You must die!*'

And with that he was gone, running clumsily down the corridor to Hitler's office.

CHAPTER 4

''Morning, sir.' Foreign Minister Anthony Eden, as handsome and as debonair as ever, rose to his feet as Churchill entered the room at Ditchley Hall. He had slept late, as was his wont, but as usual he had worked half the night. Now he gleamed a scrubbed pink and he was actually dressed though the Foreign Minister noted, slightly embarrassed, that he had forgotten to do up all his buttons in his haste.

'Good morning, Anthony,' Churchill said cheerfully, waving his cigar in welcome, obviously undismayed by the bad news from London, where nearly two thousand innocent men, women and children had died under the hail of German bombs the previous night. He stopped short at the look on Eden's face and grunted, 'What is it?'

Eden cleared his throat. 'Sir, your guard room door is open.'

'My what?' – Churchill looked down and saw that his flies were still open. With surprising agility for such an old man, he laughed and quipped, 'And was the sentry standing at attention, my dear Anthony? ... *Or was he lolling on a couple of sandbags?*' He laughed and started to do up the buttons, while Eden actually blushed, telling himself that the old man had absolutely no shame. More than once he had caught him capering around clad only in a short silk vest and twice he had actually interviewed his Foreign Minister, sitting naked in his bath, with his teeth out, looking like a naughty, pink Buddha.

Then, suddenly, Churchill became business-like as he sat down in the big Victorian chair. He barked, 'Well, is it him or isn't it?'

Eden knew exactly whom he meant. 'Yessir, it's him all right. Kirkpatrick, who knew Hess before the war, flew up to Scotland during the night to meet him. He telephoned to say that he is one hundred per cent certain that the man we now hold prisoner is Hitler's deputy, Rudolf Hess.'

Churchill looked pensive and sucked on his cigar for a moment. 'Is he mad?'

Eden shook his head. 'Not that I know of, sir. Kirkpatrick reports that he seems in good health, not excited, and that he, Kirkpatrick, could not detect any ordinary signs of insanity. If he is to be believed, he came here to contact certain members of what he calls the "peace movement".' Eden laughed delicately and smoothed his clipped military moustache, as if somehow embarrassed. 'With their aid he believes he can oust your government and ensure a peace between Germany and Great Britain.'

'He has come too late,' Churchill snorted. '*Peace movement*, indeed! If he had come last year, just after Dunkirk, with the Army demoralized and the bombing just started, I don't doubt he would have found takers. Then he could have frightened the pants off us, threatening what the Nazis would do to us if we didn't give in. Now we know the bombs, the U-boats, his threats cut no ice.'

'Exactly, sir,' Eden agreed. Hadn't he personally presided over the top secret conference in York that terrible summer when the generals had told him that most of the Army would desert if the Germans invaded? That wouldn't be the case now. The generals had full control of the troops. 'But still Hess might well be an important source of intelligence and information about the present state of Nazi Germany. He can be pumped, I am sure.'

Churchill waved his cigar at the other man hastily. 'No, no one of any standing like yourself should meet with him. That would be politically embarrassing. You see I am scared of the effect of his arrival here on the USA.'

'What do you mean, sir?'

'Roosevelt is no fool, Anthony, nor is he naïve. He knows there was – and *is* – an important minority here who still wish for peace with Hitler, those who believe that Europe is lost and that it is more important to preserve our empire. We all know those among our own party who subscribe to that particularly treacherous philosophy?'

Eden nodded gravely and wondered for the first time if Hess already had contacts with the traitors within the Tory Party who would get rid of Churchill at the drop of a hat in order to do a deal with Hitler. Surely Hess had not come merely to see the Duke of Hamilton, who was a serving officer and had no political pull to speak of?

'Roosevelt knows our true position,' Churchill continued. 'How short we are of food due to the U-boat blockade, how desperately we need new weapons to replace the ones we lost at Dunkirk. Since then we have lost battle after battle in Greece, the Western Desert, and the like. Might Roosevelt now conclude from this damned Hess business that we *are* prepared to make a deal with the Nazis?' His early mood of good cheer seemed to desert him now and he looked black. 'And we both know that we are not going to win this war without the active assistance of our cousins beyond the sea.'

Eden nodded his agreement. He could see what Churchill meant and once the story broke in the American papers there would be nothing London could do to stop speculation there. America was a neutral country; they could not censor or muzzle its press as they could that of Fleet Street.

'So what are we to do?' Churchill answered his own question. 'First, we must quash any talk that Hess has come here to discuss peace with us. Second, we must place him immediately under the care of a psychiatrist and let it be understood – the gutter press can see to that – that Hess is not altogether quite there.' He tapped his bald forehead. 'Hopefully, on both sides of the Atlantic he will be dismissed as a harmless lunatic.'

'I am sure that can be taken care of, sir,' Eden agreed hastily, though he could see Churchill wasn't really listening. He was really speaking aloud to himself. 'My only real worry,' Churchill went on, 'is what Herr Hitler might do. He is unpredictable. Did he know that Hess has made this flight, for example, and is he therefore awaiting results?'

'Hess told Kirkpatrick no.'

'But surely the third most important man in Germany

can't just fly away like that without Hitler knowing? It would be like you flying off to see Mussolini in Rome without my knowledge.'

Eden frowned. He didn't particularly like the comparison between himself and the Nazi leader, who was undoubtedly of a poor background, probably even working class. But he held his peace. For he knew the old man, he could soon make a fool of him if he so wished.

Churchill sucked on his cigar. 'Yes, Hitler is the problem,' he grunted and then suddenly he had made up his mind in that lightning way of his which brooked no opposition. 'Ensure that Hess is moved from Scotland to the south, somewhere exposed.'

'Exposed?' Eden echoed, surprised.

'Yes, like London, where he might get killed by one of his own bombs. No, that wouldn't do. We can't have him in the capital. No, somewhere remote on the south coast, where he can be cut off from the world. Perhaps Herr Hitler might oblige us by coming and fetching him when he sees we are not prepared to talk peace.'

Eden gasped. Here was the old man calmly hoping for a German commando raid on the shores of the embattled island. Or was he?

For in the very next breath, Churchill said, 'And if Herr Hitler does not oblige us by ridding us of the nuisance that Hess poses, then perhaps,' – he looked challengingly at Eden and the Foreign Minister quailed under such a direct gaze – 'we must take care of Rudolf Hess ourselves . . . '

CHAPTER 5

At the *Berghof* the *Prominenz* had been coming and going all day, as the Führer decided what must be done about what was now being called 'The Hess Case'. Goering, his appointed successor, was first to arrive, straight from France where he had been directing the great raid on London. As usual he was dressed in one of the fantastic uniforms he designed himself. This day his gross three hundred pound body was squeezed into a dove-blue uniform, heavy with decorations, while on his legs he wore bright red boots made of soft Russian leather. His face was made up with powder and rouge, to disguise his paleness; and Bormann standing in the background told himself that he looked like an ageing warm brother trying to pick up some professional male pavement pounder.

'Immediately I was informed that a plane was flying within our air space,' he told Hitler excitedly, fumbling his uncut diamonds (he always carried a handful of the precious stones) from one hand to the other like Greek worry beads, 'I ordered a red alert for the whole of the coast.' He shrugged. 'Unfortunately I couldn't attend to the matter personally as I was fully engaged in the Battle for London and the Messerschmitt slipped through.'

Soothingly Hitler said, 'No one is accusing you, my dear Goering. My question is, since the English have made no announcement that Hess has arrived in that country,' – he leaned forward, giving Goering the full benefit of his fetid breath – 'did he ever get there? Could he do it with this new type? I mean, would it have enough petrol?'

Goering blanched and wished Hitler would give up his vegetarian diet. All that fart food was no good for him; his breath smelled horrible and he broke wind all the time. Hastily he slipped another paracodeine tablet between his painted lips – he took a hundred of the drug tablets a day – and said hastily, 'No, *mein Führer*, the Messerschmitt 110 does not have the fuel capacity* to reach Scotland. It is my guess that Hess, the damned fool, crashed into the North Sea. We will hear no more of the Deputy, I am confident.' He gave his fake hearty laugh and his jowls wobbled disgustingly.

Thereafter General Keitel, the great, ramrod-straight, wooden-faced chief of staff had made his appearance. Keitel could never keep still so he and Hitler had marched up and down the study, with Bormann trotting behind them, notebook at the ready, discussing Hess's motives for having attempted to fly to Scotland. 'Of course, he must have been mad, completely *meschugge*,' he used the Yiddish word without thinking. 'First the flight and then the letter he wrote me. Completely deranged,' he tapped his forefinger to his temple significantly. 'I couldn't recognize my old comrade in that letter. It seemed to be from a totally different person. Couldn't be Hess at all. Something must have happened to him.'

Behind them Bormann stopped an instant and sucked his lips thoughtfully, then he moved once more, head cocked a little to one side in his typical manner, eyes small and shifty, like a boxer advancing upon an opponent for a knock-out.

Some time in the afternoon von Ribbentrop, the Foreign Minister, and his entourage arrived. Hitler ordered tea. There were ham and sausage sandwiches, coffee and wine for those who wished. But Bormann refused. 'I never take the flesh of dead animals,' he told the waiter firmly in a loud voice so that the Führer standing nearby would hear. 'Just a cup of peppermint tea, without milk and sugar, and a small cake, please.'

Obediently the giant SS waiter, in his gleaming white jacket, served him the tea and passed him one of the awful, super-sweet Viennese cakes the Führer preferred. Miserably

* Unknown to Goering, Hess had had two extra fuel tanks fixed to his plane.

he nibbled at it, while close by a huge fat man, who was Ribbentrop's official interpreter, greedily wolfed down a large sausage sandwich.

Von Ribbentrop, the ex-champagne salesman, was as vain and opinionated as ever. 'If anyone could have arranged a peace with the English, it would have been me. During my time there as ambassador I made literally hundreds of contacts in the very cream of society. *Mein Führer*, at this very moment I could give you the names of half a dozen leading British politicians who would be prepared to discuss peace terms with me at the drop of a hat, yes, at the drop of a hat!' He breathed out hard, face full of self-importance and righteous indignation at the thought of that blundering amateur Hess trying to do *his* job.

'Yes, yes, *mein Lieber*,' Hitler said soothingly. 'But we must think of our allies. I am sure the Italian Embassy in Berlin, as well as the Japanese, must already know that Hess has disappeared. Mussolini is no fool. If it comes out that he attempted to fly to England to discuss a separate peace with the English without their knowledge we are in trouble. Can you take care of it?'

'Of course, *mein Führer*, I will fly to Rome to see Ciano this very day.'

'And what will you tell the Italian Foreign Minister, pray?'

'I shall make it all very simple and remove all doubts about our good and loyal intentions.' Von Ribbentrop smiled coldly. 'I shall tell Ciano that Hess has gone crazy, absolutely crazy.' He tapped his forehead.

Bormann paused with his cup of peppermint tea held just below his sensual lips. Again madness, he told himself, thinking quickly. Of course, that would be one sure way of discrediting Hess, if he had ever reached England. But what if he *had* and then pulled off a deal with that drunken sot Churchill? Then nobody would dare say he was mad and he'd be back in office, the hero of the day, while he'd be relegated to the back room once more, without a hope in hell of ever reaching the top, next to Goering, Goebbels and the rest. He started to think and think hard, very hard. *How was he going to work this one out?*

Towards evening Himmler, the last important visitor of the day arrived. He had been visiting the new concentration camps they were setting up in East Poland for what was soon to come out there and he looked tired and sickly. Indeed Bormann standing to the Führer's rear thought the *Reichs-führer* SS looked quite absurd in the uniform of a full general in the SS, the only decoration adorning his skinny chest the Sports Award Bronze he had won for having managed to run a hundred metres in five minutes.

· This time it was Hitler who did most of the talking, for a weary Himmler had little to contribute to the great debate that had been raging at the *Berghof* all this long Sunday. 'Just in case, my dear Heinrich,' Hitler told the sallow-faced head of the SS, 'I am going to issue a statement on the morrow. Something on these lines.' He put on his glasses and looked down at the scrap of paper on which he had scribbled down his own thoughts. 'Party Member Hess, because of an illness of many years standing that was becoming worse, and who had been forbidden by the Führer to do any flying, went against this order and obtained an aeroplane on Saturday 10 May. At 6.00 a.m. he left Augsburg in the plane and has not been heard from since. A letter he left behind shows from its confused writing the unfortunate traces of mental derange-ment and it is feared that somewhere on this trip he has crashed and probably perished. The Führer has ordered the immediate arrest of Hess's adjutants,' he looked at Bormann. Bormann nodded quietly, 'who alone knew of the flight and the fact that such flights had been forbidden by the Führer.' Hastily Hitler whipped away his nickel-rimmed glasses, as if he were ashamed to let even Himmler see them. 'Now then, what do you think of that, Heinrich?' he asked.

For once Bormann decided he was not going to remain in the background, for he knew Himmler would not be offended if he broke into the conversation. Himmler, the weak little ex-chicken farmer, knew a coming man when he saw one. He had already made him a major-general in the SS. So he spoke before Himmler had time to speak. '*Mein Führer*, your decision to release that statement to the press is naturally an excellent idea. But it too could rebound upon us.'

Hitler frowned at him. 'How do you mean, Bormann?'

'Well, *mein Führer*, with all due respect, what will the German public think when they realize that your Deputy was slightly mad? More important, what will they say when they learn that we *knew* he was mad and tolerated his madness? Won't Mr Otto Normal-Consumer* ask: are we ruled by madmen then?' He paused and let his words sink in.

Hitler frowned and Himmler tugged at his pince-nez, which made him look like some provincial grammar school teacher. Neither said anything.

'There is also the question of the coming operation in Russia. Hess knows of it. What if the English use one of those truth drugs upon him, of which the *Reichsführer* SS knows?' He nodded to Himmler.

Himmler gave a careful smile. 'Yes, my fellows say that those things will make even a mummy speak. It's a joke, you see,' he added nervously.

Hitler wasn't amused. 'But Goering thinks that the plane he flew off in could never have made it to Scotland,' he objected.

Bormann played his trump card, but he did so modestly in that unassuming manner that made him appear to be no threat to the other members of the Nazi *Prominenz*. 'When I questioned *Hauptmann* Pintsch after his arrest two hours ago, he told me something of interest, *mein Führer*.'

'What?' Hitler barked.

'That Herr Hess had had two supplementary fuel tanks fitted to the plane. They would have ensured he reached his destination with petrol to spare, but of course not enough to return to the Reich.' The last bit of information he knew was

* *Otto Normalverbraucher.* The German equivalent at that time of the 'man in the street'.

not necessary, but he gave it to soften a little the impact of the original statement.

'What did you say, Bormann?' Hitler snapped.

Bormann repeated what he had just said.

Hitler whistled softly and Himmler looked nervous, as if he half-expected one of the Führer's notorious and frightening tantrums. But when he spoke he was quite calm. 'You mean then, Bormann, that he *could* well have reached his destination?'

'Yes, *mein Führer.*'

'Then why haven't the English issued a statement? Surely this is a great propaganda coup for them – a leading national socialist flying to their country on such an impossible mission?'

Bormann, who had never set foot on English soil in his life, though his dead father had once played in a brass band there, said, as if he were a complete expert on the island people, 'Decadent they are, of course. Why, they have soldiers who dress in women's skirts and eat meat stuffed into sheep gut.' Both Hitler and Himmler looked disgusted and the latter muttered, *'Pfui!'* 'They are a very cunning race. We must not underestimate them. They are up to something with Hess, playing for great stakes.'

'What, for example?' Hitler demanded.

'*Russia*! They want Russia in. If Hess tells them what he knows about our plans, and Stalin is informed before we are ready, all hell will be let loose.'

Himmler looked at the Führer. He too knew the great drive to the East was planned to start in another six weeks, on 22 June 1941 to be exact. If Stalin, the Russian dictator, had advance warning, the whole tremendous surprise attack might fail. It was a thought that made his skinny little legs suddenly begin to tremble. Hastily he held onto the back of the nearest chair in case he fainted.

Hitler, for his part, looked stern and unyielding. 'Would Churchill do that?' he asked, as if speaking to himself.

Bormann didn't hesitate. 'I am one hundred per cent sure

he would, *mein Führer*. He would ally himself with the Devil himself, as long as he did not have to shed English blood in Europe. Let the foolish Russians and Germans kill each other, he would tell himself, while he waited on the side-line to grab the spoils of victory. That has always been English policy in Europe.'

Hitler nodded his agreement. 'Yes, you are right there, Bormann. But what is to be done?'

Now Bormann hesitated. Cautious as ever he told himself he must not overplay his hand. If anything went wrong with his scheme, it must not appear that it originated with him. 'I am sure that it would not be too difficult to ascertain where the English are keeping Herr Hess,' he suggested softly.

Hitler nodded. 'Admiral Canaris, the head of the *Abwehr*, assures me he has his spies and traitors at every level of English society. Yes, that could be taken care of. Go on.'

'Well, *mein Führer*, would it be beyond the bounds of possibility to attempt,' – he hesitated over the word – 'er, to rescue Herr Hess from his captors?'

Hitler frowned. 'Hm,' he said, 'but a mission of that kind would be virtually suicidal. Where do we find troops prepared to take tremendous casualties?'

Bormann looked at Himmler.

Like a big soft trout rising to take the bait that will soon land him on a plate, Himmler rose to that look. He clicked to attention and barked as if he were on the parade ground at Bad Toelz, inspecting his blond young giants.* '*Mein Führer*, where else but in the Armed SS?'

Bormann could have slapped him on the back and cheered out loud. Instead he said carefully, 'Do you think they could, *Reichsführer*? What we need is a group of experienced, battle-hardened troops who are on the spot and who are trained in amphibious operations on the Channel coast, such as those that have been taking place all this winter for the invasion of England. Do you command such men?'

* Bad Toelz, the cadet-officer training school of the SS.

Himmler didn't even hesitate. 'Most of my brave soldiers have already moved East for Barbarossa, *mein Führer*,' he barked, sallow face flushed with pride. 'But there is still one elite unit, trained and experienced, in position on the French coast.'

'Its name, Himmler?'

'Wotan, *mein Führer*,' he announced proudly. 'SS Assault Regiment Wotan.'

'Tell me more,' the Führer commanded.

Bormann smiled to himself. The plan was working. For the moment he was not needed. Later the two of them would believe they had dreamed up the whole thing themselves. 'Please excuse me, *mein Führer*,' he said and clicked to attention, right arm raised in the 'German greeting', 'I know nothing of military matters. I beg to be excused.'

Casually Hitler flipped up his own arm in reply. The two of them did not even notice as he went, they were too excited.

Five minutes later, Bormann was locked safely within his own office, booted feet on the desk, a bottle of good Munich beer in one hand and a large slice of garlic sausage in the other, the picture of absolute happiness. Tonight, he told himself, he would celebrate. He would make some excuse – probably the Hess affair – so that he need not go home early to Gerda and the children. Instead he would summon the new clerk with melon breasts to his office 'for dictation'. By God and all His Triangles, he'd give her some dictation! He'd have her pants off her in zero comma nothing seconds, and then –

In front of him the special red phone started to buzz. It was the call he had been expecting. Hurriedly he swallowed the rest of his sausage and picked up the receiver. '*Hier* Bormann!' he barked.

'*Hier* Mueller,' the harsh Bavarian voice at the other end snapped.

It was the head of the feared secret police himself, no less a person than 'Gestapo' Mueller.

'*Danke für den Anruf*,' Bormann said carefully to the other man, who was in far-off Berlin, 'I have a special request for you – on behalf of the Führer himself,' he added for effect.

But as usual Gestapo Mueller was not impressed, he never was. '*Schiessen Sie Los*, Bormann,' he said quite casually. 'Fire away.'

Hastily Bormann took a swig straight from the bottle. 'I need a member of your Death Squad, but a very special one.'

Monday, 12 May 1941

CHAPTER 1

A red flare, the night sky suddenly colouring the upturned faces of the waiting troopers.

Schulze nudged Captain von Dodenburg. 'It's party frocks on, sir. Ready for the ball.'

Von Dodenburg tightened his clutch on his machine-pistol and began to sweat. He nodded. 'Wait for the green,' he hissed.

'*Jawohl!*' Schulze grunted and from his tone, von Dodenburg could tell he didn't like this mission. None of them did, except the fanatics and sadists.

For the last four hours they had been gradually sealing off the working-class dock area of Calais. Tanks had taken up position at all crossroads. The bridges over the various canals and waterways that criss-crossed the quarter had been placed under guard and then, once curfew had fallen, loudspeaker vans had toured the area warning everyone to remain at home. Anyone now leaving a house ran the risk of being shot on the spot without being challenged. As the Vulture had told von Dodenburg icily an hour before, 'Let's hope that someone does attempt to make a run for it, then we can shoot and get it over with. I hate this kind of business. It's so messy.'

Von Dodenburg had not said anything, but he knew what was going through the CO's head. He didn't want trouble with Corps HQ. He wanted armed resistance, to show that his unauthorized action had been justified. As soon as he saw the green signal flares he was to take his company into the rabbit warren of one-storey workers' houses and systematically search them. If he found any weapons, or anything of that nature, he was to arrest the occupants. If he didn't find anything, he was simply to select a certain number of hostages, who would be shot at dawn in retaliation for the two murdered Wotan men. Von Dodenburg prayed there would be resistance; he hated this kind of thing.

A soft whoosh. A dry crack. To their immediate front a green flare, followed instantly by another one, exploded and bathed the houses in a glowing green. Von Dodenburg rose to his feet. Next to him, Sergeant Schulze shrilled his whistle. Suddenly all was controlled chaos, as the non-coms barked, '*Los, los, Manner!*' and the heavy nailed boots clattered across the damp *pavé* towards the nearest houses, followed by the stretcher-bearers – just in case.

At first everything went well. Tamely the sullen and often frightened civilians allowed themselves to be pushed out of their shabby houses, which smelled of stale fish and poverty, to be lined up outside in the glare of the searchlights. Inside the blond young giants tore everything apart in their search for weapons or anything suspicious, flinging beds out of the windows, strewing the street with personal linen, smashing up chairs, slashing the interiors of sofas with their bayonets. Although they didn't like the job, two of their comrades had been savagely murdered by these frogs and so they were taking their revenge in the only way they could.

The company had crossed one of the stinking little waterways that were everywhere, sending the rats scuttling for cover in the dirty undergrowth, when a single shot rang out from a two-storey house to their right. One of the young troopers cursed, dropped his rifle and sat down suddenly, as if he were too tired to go on. Sergeant Schulze followed by Matz doubled towards him while the rest of the company simply stood there stupidly.

The youth's left trouser leg was torn, revealing the lacerated flesh, pulpy and glistening like fresh meat. The youth groaned and Schulze patted him on the shoulder. 'It'll get you a medal, son,' he consoled the youth, whose face was now contorting with waves of pain as the shock began to wear off. '*Sanitater!*' he bellowed. 'Come on you bed-pan plumbers! At the double, we've got a wounded man here!'

The stretcher-bearers ran heavily towards the little group, as von Dodenburg shouted angrily at his men, 'Get down, you bunch of horned-oxen! Get down!'

His men dropped to the wet cobbles, bringing up their weapons to the aiming position in the same instant that a crackle of ragged fire erupted from the upper storey of the house to their right.

Von Dodenburg dodged into a doorway, nerves jangling electrically as they always did in action. His mind remained ice-cold as he judged the situation, trying to figure out what to do next. He fired a quick burst at the house. The tracer raced towards it like lethal morse. Windows shattered. Angry little spurts of red flame erupted where the slugs struck the masonry. Almost immediately, a burst of fire came his way. The unknown Frenchmen inside had spotted the source of the tracer. The bullets hit the doorway to his left and stone fragments rained down on his helmet.

At least he had established one thing – or he hoped he had. The resistance was coming solely from the two-storey house. His men would be able to flank it on both sides without risk to themselves.

He cupped his hands to his mouth and shouted above the snap and crackle of small-arms fire from the house, 'Sergeant Schulze, take your platoon round the left! I'll take the right!'

'Yessir,' Schulze bellowed back and grinned at Matz. 'Just like the Old Man, eh, Matzi?'

His running mate nodded. At their side the stretcher-bearers slit the wounded youth's trousers and the blood began to run down the cobbles to gurgle down the nearest grate. 'Yes, the Captain is not one to let us poor old hairy-assed stubble-hoppers do the dirty work for him.'

'Three blasts on my whistle and then we go in, Schulze. *At the double!*' von Dodenburg yelled.

'At the double it is, sir,' Schulze echoed and snarled, 'All right, you bunch of pregnant penguins, prepare to foxtrot!' He grabbed his own rifle and rose to his feet, careless of the enemy fire.

Once, twice, three times. The whistle shrilled and then with a great cry they were doubling forward, bent like men beating their way against heavy rain. Another man was hit.

He flung up his arms melodramatically and slammed to the cobbles. Von Dodenburg sprang neatly over the corpse, cursing furiously, machine-pistol chattering angrily at his hip.

A civilian came running out of the house, hands thrust into the air, yelling with fear. *'Nicht schiessen, nicht schiessen, bitte nicht sch – '* He fell, riddled by bullets, his plea for mercy unheard.

Von Dodenburg ripped a hand-grenade from his boot and pulled the pin. Automatically he counted off the seconds and threw it in through the open back door. Next moment he flung himself against the wall. A tremendous roar. The hot blast-wave slapped him across the face. Smoke streamed out, muffling the cries of pain and anger from within. He rushed in, firing wildly.

A smoke-blackened face appeared on the stairs. He caught the gleam of a butcher's cleaver and fired instinctively. The Frenchman reeled against the wall and slid down it slowly, trailing bright red blood behind him.

'Vive Moscu!' someone screamed hysterically just behind. *'Vive Marechal Stalin!'* The slug hit the wall inches from his face. He stumbled and fell to his knees with the shock of the close call. Shit! He had made a hash of it. Now he was for the chop.

But von Dodenburg was not fated to die just yet. As the Frenchman took careful aim at the Boche crouched in the rubble in front of him, the other door burst open, splintering instantly, and Schulze came stumbling into the corridor.

He didn't hesitate. With a great roar he crunched forward over the debris. His 'Hamburg Equalizer' flashed yellow in the gloom and the Frenchman screamed shrilly, hysterically, as those cruel brass knuckles that had won Schulze many a fight on the waterfront connected with the side of his jaw. The impact of the brutal blow lifted him straight off his feet. Something in his neck snapped audibly and he was dead before he hit the ground.

Gratefully von Dodenburg rose to his feet, his hands

shaking slightly. 'Thank you, you big rogue. I thought I was for the meat wagon just then.'

Schulze gave him a broad smile. 'The frogs'll have to get up earlier in the day if they're gonna catch Frau Schulze's handsome son with his knickers down, sir,' he said with his usual modesty. 'Come on, sir, there are more of the shits upstairs!'

Five minutes later it was all over. Von Dodenburg's company had lost one trooper killed and one wounded. Three of the French were dead and now the victorious attackers were busy herding the survivors down into the yard where the Vulture, now that it was safe and all resistance broken, was inspecting them, staring at the prisoners through his monocle as if they were a strange form of life he had not encountered up to now.

With his Schmeisser slung over his shoulder, von Dodenburg searched the place. It was clear that the Vulture was right. The civilians who had fired at them, and who had probably assassinated the Wotan men, were communist. There were communist leaflets in every room, neatly stacked ready for distribution; flags too, red banners complete with gold hammer and sickle; and in one room they even found a highly idealized portrait of Stalin. It was obvious this place had been the headquarters of the local communist cell and the communists had been prepared to offer armed resistance when they thought they had been discovered.

Von Dodenburg heard the Vulture outside rasp, 'Line them against that wall! Come on you men, look lively now. Line them against the wall. Machine-gunner, get in position!'

Obviously, von Dodenburg told himself, the CO was not going to waste any time.

Schulze appeared. He was taking hearty swigs from a bottle of rum he had looted somewhere or other. He saw von Dodenburg staring at the portrait of Stalin and cried, *'Heil Moskau!'* He indicated the bottle. 'It's good stuff, sir. I made Corporal Matz taste it first in case the frogs had pissed in it.

They have nasty habits like that. But they hadn't.' He tendered the bottle towards the pensive officer.

Von Dodenburg shook his head. Outside he could hear the machine-gunner fitting the long belt of ammunition into his MG 42.

'I used to be in that lot,' Schulze said easily, indicating the pile of communist leaflets. 'The Red Front, I mean.'

Amused, Von Dodenburg looked at him. 'You a pillar of the Armed SS, a former member of the Communist Party. Tut-tut. Better not let the powers that be know.'

'In Hamburg-Altona, all of us were in the party in them days, sir. Even my old lady was a fully paid-up member.' He stopped short and put the bottle down carefully. With a nod, he indicated the little door at the far end of the room – it probably led up to the attic. Von Dodenburg followed the direction of his gaze and started.

From beneath the door was coming a bright-red trickle of blood, slowly forming a little pool on the floor next to the bust of Marx that the troopers had smashed with their rifle butts.

Von Dodenburg carefully unslung his Schmeisser and clicked off the safety-catch. Below the Vulture was urging the guards to line their prisoners up more quickly. The executions would start soon, he told himself.

Very lightly for such a huge man, Schulze crossed to the door. One big hand grasped the handle. With the other he reached in his boot and pulled out a stick grenade.

Von Dodenburg indicated he shouldn't pull the pin yet, but to be prepared to fling open the door. He mouthed the word 'three'.

The big non-com indicated he understood.

Von Dodenburg raised his machine-pistol and pointed it straight at the door. At that range he couldn't miss. He started to mouth, 'One... two... *three*!'

Schulze flung open the door and von Dodenburg gasped as if someone had just punched him in the stomach.

A woman – no, a girl – was leaning weakly against the side of the narrow stairs that led up to the attic, which smelled of pigeon droppings. Blood dripped from her left shoulder. Schulze could see the jagged wound and torn cloth quite clearly. In her other hand she had a kind of toy pistol with an ivory butt of a type that he had only seen in the cinema up to now. But the look on her deathly pale face indicated she did not think it was a toy. Through gritted teeth, her eyes watering with the pain of her wound, she cursed them. *'Sale Boche. Sale con d'un Boche. Vive Moscu.'* She raised the silly little weapon.

'Watch out, sir!' Schulze cried in alarm.

Von Dodenburg seemed paralysed by such naked hatred, perhaps fascinated. Never, in two years of war and combat had he ever seen anyone express so much hate as that reflected in the beautiful pale face of this young French communist.

Her knuckles tightened on the trigger. He could see them go yellow and white. It was going to be now.

'SIR!' Schulze yelled.

The trigger clicked.

A dull empty sound. *Nothing!* She had no more slugs left.

For what seemed an age, the three of them stood slightly crouched, panting as if they had just run a great race.

Schulze broke the spell. His big hand reached out, palm open.

Wordlessly she dropped the useless pistol into it, not taking her gaze from the harshly handsome face of the SS officer.

Schulze licked his suddenly dry lips and looked a little helplessly from the girl to his CO. Von Dodenburg knew what he was thinking. The girl had suffered enough already. With a bit of luck a surgeon might save her arm. Let her go. She'd escaped the search. Let her go back into the attic and hide until Wotan had gone. After all, she was a mere slip of a girl, perhaps not much older than eighteen. She had the look of an idealist about her, some university student perhaps who had been seduced into the communist movement because of a guilty conscience about the workers. She certainly didn't belong to the working class with those clothes and those pale smooth hands, now wet with her own blood.

Von Dodenburg hardened his heart. She had shot at German soldiers; perhaps she too had taken part in the mutilation of the Wotan trooper. She was one of them. She was a communist, an enemy of the state. He nodded to Schulze. 'Take her downstairs, sergeant – to the rest.'

Schulze hesitated, then he took the girl's unwounded arm quite gently for a rough man and said softly, 'Come with me, M'selle.'

She didn't resist. Standing there weakly, feeling all energy draining from his body, as if someone had opened a tap, von Dodenburg heard the clump of Schulze's boots on the stairs and lighter sound of the French girl's high-heel shoes. Schulze snapped something to the Vulture. There were several cries of surprise. A moment's silence. They would be pushing her into the ranks of the others lined up against the wall.

'Feuer frei!' The Vulture's harsh incisive voice cut into him like a sharp knife.

'Vive la France. Mère de – '

The rattle of machine-gun fire made him start. Someone screamed. Another cursed. But the bullets put an end to cries, screams, curses. Carefully, too carefully, von Dodenburg lit a cigarette. Then slowly he began to descend the dark stairs.

CHAPTER 2

Carefully Major Carruthers MC read through the top secret instructions that had brought him to this remote coastal village, and that he had been ordered by the GOC to keep sealed until he reached it with his company of Grenadiers. All about him men of the King's Company, each one of them over six foot two as regulations prescribed, descended from the three-ton trucks that had brought them here from London and gazed at the desolate scene: the evacuated sea-front, now covered with rusting barbed wire from the year before, with at regular intervals the notices proclaiming the dangers of minefields. For whoever had laid the wire had also mined the shingle beach.

'Prisoner X is to be strictly isolated. Every endeavour should be made to study his mentality and get anything worth while out of him,' the tall handsome major read, while at the regulation six paces away CSM Douglas waited patiently, pacing stick clasped under his arm. 'Prisoner X should have adequate food, books, writing material, etc. and recreation should be provided. He should have no contact with the outside world. No visitors will be allowed except as prescribed by the Foreign Office. He should see no visitors and hear no wireless. He should be treated with dignity, as if he were an important general who has fallen into our hands.' The directive was signed, 'A. Eden.'

Carruthers rubbed the still livid scar made by the German bullet just outside Dunkirk last year and whistled softly to himself. So that was who it was they had come here to guard. He didn't need to know who 'X' was after hearing the news this morning on the BBC that Hess had flown to Britain.

CSM Douglas, immensely tall and broad, with an old-fashioned waxed moustache sticking out like two pieces of liquorice at the end of his nose, clapped his pacing stick more firmly under his arm and judged it was time to speak. The men had to be kept busy. God had no time for idle Guardsmen; neither had he. 'Permission to speak, sir?' he barked, as if he were on the square at Caterham.

Carruthers grinned. He had known the CSM for years, ever since he had joined the Grenadiers as a subaltern and Douglas had been a corporal. Still the CSM kept up the traditional formality, even after they had drunk out of the same mug of tea at Dunkirk and helped each other to go to the *pissoir*, he hopping on his shattered legs and the CSM with both his arms swathed in bloodstained bandages. 'Yes, permission granted, Sar'nt-Major.'

'What's the drill, sir? The lads are a bit put out at being whipped down here from the Big Smoke. I hope it's important, I mean this detachment duty?'

'It is, it is indeed, Sar'nt-Major,' Carruthers answered. 'You heard the news this morning on the wireless. We've been delegated to guard *him*.'

Even Douglas showed surprise. 'You mean – *his nibs*, sir?' he gasped.

Carruthers nodded. 'His nibs indeed! We've got exactly forty-eight hours before he arrives from the Tower to turn that hotel into a prison.' With his stick he indicated the empty hotel that lay right on the beach next to the low tarred, wooden huts that had once been used by the local fishermen. 'There'll be trenches and machine-gun posts to be dug, trip-wires and the like, and this afternoon the sappers and signals wallah are coming up to conceal mikes under the floorboards' – he grinned – 'just in case his nibs talks in his sleep and gives away any secrets, though I doubt if any of our lot speak German.'

'With all due respect, most of our shower can't even speak English. They're Geordie to a man.' Douglas returned the grin.

''Spect they'll send us some university don masquerading as a NCO in the Intelligence Corps to do the job, Sar'nt-Major. No matter. I think we ought to set up a Bren post to cross that crossroads.' Carruthers indicated a little road behind him that led to Ipswich.

Douglas nodded his approval. 'Yessir, that'll cover any problems coming in, but, sir,' he hesitated and frowned, 'we're only a company, just over a hundred men. As you know, that's not much to guard such an important bloke as his nibs, especially in such an exposed spot like this – right on the ruddy coast, if you'll pardon my French, sir,' he added hastily.

Carruthers grinned. Douglas never let up. He was the traditional Guards NCO right down to his cotton socks, bless him. 'Yes, Sar'nt-Major, I've thought of that, too. It's almost as if we're offering his nibs to the Boche on a silver platter, isn't it.' He glanced at the ugly green swell of the North Sea, as if he could already see the German assault force sailing in to rescue the Deputy Führer. Then he collected himself. 'But then we've always got the Home Guard, haven't we, to back us up?' He indicated the portly middle-aged major, wearing a steel helmet and gas mask for some reason, who was marching towards them proudly, swinging salutes to left and right in grand style to acknowledge those of the Guardsmen.

Douglas allowed himself a slight smile and then stiffened to attention himself, crying, 'Permission to get on with it, sir?'

Casually Carruthers touched his cane to his cap. 'Permission granted.' Then he turned and waited for the Home Guard major.

Five hundred yards away, up on the high ground that overlooked the seaside village, Doyle put down his binoculars. He had seen enough to know why this company of Guardsmen – the King's Company at that – had left London so hurriedly to set up their camp in this remote place, which had no military value whatsoever. They were going to quarter the Deputy Führer here, taking him from the Tower of London where he might well prove an embarrassment for that damned murderer Churchill. He wouldn't want Hess in the capital. It might cause the Americans, fools that they were for supporting such a corrupt, cruel organization as the

British Empire, to ask too many leading questions. Yes, it was only too clear. They were bringing Hess here.

Doyle lit a Woodbine – he knew a tobacconist in Kilburn who kept him supplied with the fags; he couldn't stand those damned Pashas most tobacconists supplied to casual customers – and breathed out hard. This one definitely warranted buying ten gallons of petrol on the black market in order to drive the old Ford to London. He knew his main job was to watch Folkestone and particularly Harwich to report on the comings and goings of the bloody Royal Navy. That was what Miguel paid him for. But ever since Miguel had alerted him to the fact that Hess had been reported imprisoned in the Tower of London, every *Abwehr* agent in the country, including himself, had been on the lookout for the place where the British would finally imprison the missing German leader.

Doyle smiled to himself. With his twisted, scarred face, the result of a razor fight back in the 'thirties when he had been working for the Movement in the Gorbals, it wasn't a pleasant sight. Miguel would pay him well for this afternoon's work, enough for a bottle or two – and a woman as well. He licked his lips at the thought. He hadn't had a woman for nearly a month now and even though he knew it was a deadly sin to do so, he had been forced to touch himself. He really needed a woman!

Quite excited at the thought the mean little Irishman got into the battered Ford with white-painted wings and blacked-out headlights and let out the clutch. He started to roll down the hill to the main road to Ipswich and London, saving petrol because it was a long way to the garage where he knew he could buy the black market stuff. It would cost him a bob or two, he knew, but it was worth it. The Spanish Embassy would pay through the nose for the information he would now give them. *Rudolf Hess was going to be imprisoned at the hamlet of Little Saxton.*

'*Little Saxton, mein Führer!*' Bormann reported excitedly, face flushed and unhealthy-looking from having run all the way from the teleprinter office. He had not even had time to rinse his mouth to remove the smell of sausage and *Korn* when he had been summoned so hurriedly. 'Admiral Canaris has just reported that Comrade Hess is to be taken to that place. It's on the coast of England, in Suffolk.'

Hitler, followed by his Alsatian bitch Blondi, stalked to the huge wall map, put on his glasses, and traced a line with his finger on it until he found the hamlet. 'Here it is,' he said, while an out-of-breath Bormann peered over his shoulder, keeping his face turned to one side, however, just in case the Führer could smell the drink on his breath.

Hitler frowned. 'Strange that the English will place him in such a place,' he murmured thoughtfully, a little puzzled.

'How do you mean, *mein Führer?*'

'Well, it is very exposed, directly on the coast like that, very vulnerable.'

'But ideally suited to our needs and plans,' Bormann said.

Hitler nodded his head slowly, still staring thoughtfully at the map. 'I suppose so,' he said in the end. 'And looking at it from an English viewpoint, the place is within the fortified and defended area of Harwich and Ipswich, here and here.' He pointed at the map.

Bormann nodded his agreement, though he had not the slightest idea of how that part of England was defended, for he was totally uninterested in military matters. His sole concern was the *Reich* and how to gain control of the party machine, which, in its turn, controlled Germany. 'So then, sir, –' he said cheerfully, 'I can give the green light to the assault force?'

Hitler did not answer immediately. Instead he continued to stare at the big map.

Bormann frowned. Why was the Führer wasting time? According to the *Abwehr* report, the English were fortifying Hess's future place of imprisonment. Time was of the essence. The English would not be allowed to make another damned *Westwall** out of the place.

Finally Hitler broke his silence. He took off his glasses and stared at Bormann, while Blondi rubbed her pelt against his boot. She wanted to be taken for her afternoon trot. He sighed and said, 'Party Member Hess has always been a loyal and devoted comrade, Bormann. Do you know that his party number was sixteen? Mine was seven. You can see how long we have been together.'

Bormann looked suitably solemn, wondering what all this was leading up to when time was so important.

'I well remember the time he saved me from serious injury, Bormann. Back in 1921, the Red mob tried to break up one of our meetings – we were hopelessly outnumbered. There must have been a hundred or more of the gutter rats and one of them threw a beer mug at me. Bravely Hess took the blow for me and suffered a bad head injury. He bears the scar of that incident to this very day. Then we were in prison together at Landsberg, as you know, for over seven months. It was there that I dictated my *Mein Kampf* to Hess.' He shook his head, moved by the memory.

Bormann decided it was time to speak – the conversation was taking a very unhealthy direction for him. '*Mein Führer*, every care will be taken, once you have given the order for the operation to commence, to ensure that nothing happens to the *Stellvertreter*. I have already made that point quite clear to *Reichsführer* SS Himmler. He agrees with me that we have a ninety-nine per cent chance of bringing out our beloved comrade without injury,' he lied gibly.

Hitler nodded his head, still looking sad. 'And the other one per cent?'

---

* *Westwall*, the line of fortifications running the length of Germany's frontier, also known as the 'Siegfried Line'.

'It is being taken care of, *mein Führer*. If the situation arises that we cannot take Hess out, then . . . ' He let his words trail away into nothing.

Hitler frowned and said, 'I understand. All right, Bormann,' his voice rose, 'you can signal Himmler that the operation is on. SS Assault Regiment Wotan is to be informed of its role and is to start planning immediately.'

Bormann clicked his heels together and saluted smartly. 'I will attend to it immediately, *mein Führer!*' he cried, startling Blondi, who growled a warning.

'Good,' Hitler said. 'And now I shall take Blondi for a walk in the grounds and think of old times. Come on, Blondi.' Sadly he left the big room, with the Alsatian trailing behind, leaving Bormann standing rigidly to attention, his dark eyes gleaming in triumph. Once Hess was out of the way, he knew now, he would be the sole controller of the party *apparat*. Already the Führer had admitted to him that he had 'totally lost sight of the organizations of the party'. Now only Hess stood between him and the control of the greatest administrative system the world had ever seen since the days of the Romans. But the key to everything was Hess. The old fool, with all his occult mumbo-jumbo, fads, and bone-rattling, must never be allowed to return to Germany.

He waited no longer. Hurriedly, breaking out in a sweat of excitement, Bormann returned to his office and reached for the red telephone. First he'd instruct Himmler to alert that celebrated Wotan regiment of his. Then he would call in Gestapo Mueller's man. He wanted to give the Death Squad specialist specific instructions. Thereafter he would have to work out some little scheme of his own to ensure the specialist never talked.

Too excited even to think of the sausage still resting in the safe, Bormann picked up the phone and bellowed to the operator, who was one of the many he had 'enjoyed', as he always phrased it, over the last few months, 'Get me, *Reichsführer* SS Himmler at once. *Dalli, dalli.*'

CHAPTER 4

Clear the streets, the SS marches.
The storm columns stand at the ready,
They will take the road...
Let death be our battle companion
For we are the Black Band...

Lustily the hoarse young SS troopers burst into Wotan's marching song as they started to enter the camp, bringing the cooks from the mess halls and the clerks out of their offices. This afternoon the Vulture had deliberately paraded the regiment through Calais and down the streets of the dockers' area where they had shot the hostages at dawn. It had been a deliberate provocation. But nothing had happened. The workers in the *bleu de travail* had watched the blond young giants, each man well over one metre eighty-five sullenly. Not a shot had been fired, although the tight column of marching men was a tempting target. There had not been as much as a single boo.

Standing next to von Dodenburg in the regimental orderly room, the Vulture screwed his monocle more tightly in his eye and rasped, 'We have broken the back of that Red rabble, von Dodenburg. I wager we'll have no more trouble with them, as long as we remain in Calais. A little judicious slaughter of civilians always does the trick. They have little stomach for much blood-letting.'

As much as he disliked the CO von Dodenburg had to admit he was right. The news of the shooting of the hostages had spread right through the Pas de Calais, although the censors had ordered the local newspapers not to print anything about the incident. Now the locals knew they couldn't go shooting German soldiers, especially if they were from the SS, and expect to go unpunished. The innocent and the guilty would both pay – tenfold.

The long column came to a halt with an impressive crunch of hobnailed boots, the officers and NCOs bellowed orders, hands slapped the butts of the rifles in immaculate precision and then the order to fall out was given. Von Dodenburg beamed and felt proud of his young men. Green-beaks and old hares alike they were exceedingly smart; they all looked as if they had spent years in Berlin before the war parading for the Führer – real asphalt soldiers.*

The Vulture saw the look on the younger officer's face and sniggered. 'Just mere cannon-fodder, my dear von Dodenburg, just mere cannon-fodder. The Reds can kill them just as easily as they can Rifleman Arse of the Tenth Shit-shovellers' Regiment!'

Von Dodenburg flushed and bit back a hot retort. He knew the Vulture and his attitude to the Armed SS. Instead, he attempted to get his own back by asking, 'Any static from Corps HQ, sir? About the unauthorized shooting of the hostages this morning?'

The Vulture looked at him and then said casually, 'Not a peep, von Dodenburg, not a single solitary peep, though those fat-bellied rear echelon stallions must know by now what happened here. Oh yes,' he chortled happily. 'I don't think we'll have any trouble from that particular quarter.'

As if on cue, 'Papa' Hein, the regimental clerk appeared at the door. 'Papa' Hein, who was reputedly the oldest serving soldier in the Armed SS and who dyed his hair with a mixture of cold tea and henna so that his head looked like that of a chow, was startled out of his usual composure. He had actually buttoned up the top button of his tunic, which he wouldn't do normally even for the Vulture.

'Well,' the Vulture demanded in high good humour, 'where's the fire, Hein?'

Hein swallowed hard. 'It's him,' he choked. 'Him!' He gestured at the other officer, his drinker's face turning purple.

'Who's him, man?' the Vulture snapped. 'Out with it!'

* The name given to the pre-war SS who had guarded Hitler.

'The *Reichsführer* SS personally... on the phone!' the orderly stuttered. 'And he wants to talk to you.'

'*Himmler? Me?*' Now it was the Vulture's turn to stutter. 'Is that what you said – *Himmler?*'

Hein nodded wildly.

The Vulture bolted into the other office, while von Dodenburg remained at the window, grinning slightly. The Vulture was going to get a rocket after all and from the head of the SS *höchstpersönlich!*

'*Jawohl, Reichsführer... Geier am Apparat.*' He could hear the Vulture speaking and through the open door he could see that the CO was standing rigidly to attention, as if Himmler in far-off Berlin could actually see him.

'*Jawohl, Reichsführer, streng vetraulich... Geheime Reichssache... Verstehe vollkommen...*'

The rasped phrases floated out and von Dodenburg frowned. What was top secret about a rocket, he wondered.

Suddenly the Vulture kicked the door with his heel. It slammed shut and the conversation was cut off. Next to the desk, Hein, who had been listening too, head cocked to one side in the manner of old people who are hard of hearing, breathed out hard and said, 'Captain, believe me, I could have pissed down my right leg when I heard Himmler wanted to speak to the Chief. Though I did know him in the old days when he was a' – he corrected himself in time – 'when he wasn't very important.' He clasped a hand dramatically to his chest. 'Still, shocks like that ain't no good for the old ticker when you're getting on in years.'

Von Dodenburg's grin broadened. 'Go on with you, you old rogue. I hear you're still bedding a nineteen-year-old down in Calais.'

Hein smiled nervously. 'Just the simple pleasures of a humble soldier, sir,' he wheedled.

'Be off with you. You'll have me crying in my beer next, Hein,' von Dodenburg said and then stiffened to attention, as the Vulture reappeared, beaming all over his grotesque face. 'Tremendous news, von Dodenburg!' he burst out and then caught sight of Hein. 'All right, take yer hind legs in your hands, Hein, and trot off.'

Obediently Hein 'trotted off' and closed the door with a petulant bang behind him; he hated to be left out of things. The Vulture waited till he had gone and then he said, 'All very important. Himmler told me to keep it to myself, my senior company commander and, for the time being, you.'

'But what is it, sir?' von Dodenburg could not contain himself any longer.

'We've got exactly twenty-four hours, von Dodenburg.'

'For what, sir?'

At last the Vulture seemed to realize that von Dodenburg didn't know what he was talking about. 'We're moving east,' he exclaimed. 'We've got our marching orders at last!' He actually rubbed his hands together like a hungry man in anticipation of a great feast. 'To Poland. The balloon's going up, von Dodenburg,' he cried gleefully, 'and I can assure you, *mein Lieber*, this time there is going to be glory, medals – *and promotion* – for everyone!' He stared at the younger man happily, eyes glowing. 'Now then this is the drill. We load the heavy weapons and tanks at the goods station tomorrow morning precisely at zero five hundred hours, while it is still curfew. The fewer civvies that see the tanks go, the better. The railway transportation company will do the rest. I want all companies paraded in full field service marching order by twelve hundred. I will inspect the men personally. This afternoon they will be allowed to attend to their own affairs. Last letters to be delivered to their officers for censorship by seventeen hundred hours. Supper one hour later, with one bottle of beer from the wet canteen per man. Haversack rations for three days to be collected at the same time. We get on the troop train at twenty hundred hours . . . ' The Vulture rapped out the orders while von Dodenburg as senior company commander scribbled them down. 'Oh and by the way, Berlin is sending down some sort of special guide, a *Rittmeister* von Skalka. God only knows why. The chap appears not even to belong to the SS. Cavalry by the sound of it. Himmler was quite adamant about him. But no matter. Now about the men's personal weapons.'

But even as he wrote, von Dodenburg's mind was elsewhere. Ever since he had been a boy, wearing the black short pants of the Hitler Youth, the Führer had been promising them that one day he would deal with the 'red rabble' that had infected Europe with that deadly disease – communism. Now finally the time had come to reckon up with Moscow. His eyes glittered fanatically as he scribbled. It would be a great crusade. One final great blood-letting and then there would be peace and Europe would be German from the Channel to the Urals. The German century had dawned and he would be part of that holy crusade against the Bolshevik that would bring lasting peace to the world. He could have shouted out loud with joy and happiness. Instead he noted, 'All firing pins will be personally inspected for dirt and rust by platoon commanders.'

DAY FOUR

Tuesday, 13 May 1941

CHAPTER 1

It had been a hectic morning for SS Assault Regiment
Wotan. Self-important young officers had run up and down
the regimental lines carrying check-boards and followed by
harassed, anxious non-coms, urging the sweating young
troopers to ever greater efforts. Red-faced, angry sergeant-
majors and senior sergeants had shrilled their duty whistles
constantly, threatening terrible punishments to the laggards
if anything went wrong. For, as was well-known throughout
Wotan, the wrath of the Vulture was terrifying.

At ten hundred hours there had been a 'short-arm'
inspection by the grey-haired regimental surgeon, known as
the 'Pill', or sometimes as 'Number Nine', for it was number
nine, the laxative pill, notorious and feared throughout the
whole of the *Wehrmacht*, that he seemed to prescribe for
virtually every disease known to medical science.

In turn each company was paraded on the square and at
the command 'trousers down!' each man lowered his slacks
while the Pill, short-sighted and greying, waited. Standing
rigidly to attention and looking slightly absurd, the troopers
responded to the next command barked at them by the
sergeant-major, which was 'Raise shirts. *Shirts up!*'

To the accompaniment of the non-coms calling 'Shirts up,
one, two, three,' green-beaks and old hares alike, virgins and
lechers, raised the tail of their shirts to reveal their naked
loins.

Followed by his medical orderly, armed with his clipboard
and pencil, the Pill proceeded solemnly down the rigid line of
troopers, pausing briefly at each man and raising his penis
disdainfully with his pencil to stare at the disgusting object for
a moment before usually declaring over his shoulder,
'Negative'. And yet another man would heave a hidden sigh
of relief. For the Vulture saw in VD 'a personal affront', a

'deliberate attempt at sabotage', which he punished with the utmost rigour.

Fortunately the regiment had passed the muster with the minimum of 'casualties', save for an old hare who, it was discovered, had 'the whole house', both the clap and the pox, and a blushing seventeen-year-old whose comrades had thought a virgin, but who had in fact been 'sabotaged' by those 'loathsome frog whores', as the Vulture called them, to the extent of a mild case of the clap.

Now, with the heavy weapons and tanks gone and the medical inspection over, the green-beaks packed frantically, filling their packs with the cheap junk they had collected over the last few months – the Eiffel tower in tin; cheeky Mannekin Pises in bronze, holding up his willy and urinating for all the world to see; pornographic pictures; silk stockings; and all the rest of it – tossing out of the windows into the yard the surplus kit they would not be taking to Russia with them.

Schulze and Matz, old hares that they were, disdained such activity. They sat behind the shelter of the cookhouse, sipping the real bean coffee, well laced with rum, Schulze had bullied out of the hash-slingers. Matz, a benign smile on his face, declared that he was at peace 'with God and the world'. Schulze for his part was disgruntled.

'I'm packed,' he declared to no one in particular. 'A spare pair of knickers, my foot-rags,' (old hare that he was, Schulze disdained socks and stuck to the old-fashioned foot-rags) 'a bit o' porn and me flatman.'

'Very important, the flatman,' Matz agreed. 'I've got two in my monkey.' He meant his pack. 'They say it's frigging cold in Popov-land. Me, I'm taking no chances.'

A morose Schulze didn't seem to hear him, for he continued, 'So I've got my monkey packed, while those green-beaks yonder are still fart-assing about. But what good does it do, I ask yer, what good in-frigging-deed?' He looked at the May sky, appealing to God on high to rectify this appalling injustice being done to him. 'It's inhuman, Matzi, I tell yer. Men who are expected to do their all for their

Fatherland – soon to die like heroes – should be allowed their last little bit o' pleasure before they set off into the unknown, before they start looking at the taties from two metres below in some foreign country. One last chance to dip the wick into the old honey pot.'

Matz smiled secretively and said nothing. He continued to sip the real bean coffee appreciatively.

'Old Papa Hein let me nip in the orderly room and call the twins,' Schulze continued miserably, putting down his mug to flick away the dewdrop that hung from his nose like an opaque pearl. '*Nix!* Not even a nooner. Not even a knee-trembler against the back wall of the signals building. They said they were still on red alert. A likely story. I bet they know we're going and one of them rear echelon stallions is already slipping the old salami to 'em. Some fat quartermaster bastard nicking the troops' rations.'

'To them both?' Matz asked mildly.

Schulze didn't seem to hear. Instead he moaned, clutching his crotch, as if in the last throes of sexual passion. 'Christ on a crutch, I've got so much ink in my fountain pen, I don't know who to write to first, I swear it!'

'There always Slack-Arse Susie's place,' Matz suggested with deceptive casualness.

Schulze shot him a dark look.

Matz had pulled out his bayonet, now his coffee was finished and was neatly excising the thick dirt from beneath his nails like an expert manicurist.

'Have you got air in yer teeth, you little yellow turd?' he demanded angrily. '*Bei dir piepst wohl?* And where, pray, are we gonna get the *marie* to pay for Slack-Arse Susie's gash, I ask you? It's still two days to pay-day.' He spat angrily. 'Oh hell, I might as well go into the thunderboxes and have a good frigging wank.' He half-rose as if to do so.

But Matz laid a hand on his big brutal shoulder and said softly. 'Not so hasty, Sergeant Schulze.' Solemnly, almost dramatically, he reached into his pocket and, like a conjuror producing a white rabbit out of a high silk hat, pulled out a thick wad of greasy French francs. '*Voilà!*' he said. 'That's frog, you see, for get yer mitts off my tits, I'm a nun!'

Schulze's mouth fell open and he gasped. 'Well, I'll be a frigging piss pansy! Where in three devils' name did you get all that frog *marie*?'

'While the chain-dogs was looking the other way this morning, I siphoned off most of the petrol out of the Vulture's command car. Half an hour later I was flogging it on the frog black market.' He sucked his yellow teeth thoughtfully. 'Imagine there's enough there for the two of us to dance the mattress polka, don't you think so, Sergeant Schulze?'

'You can bet yer frigging life there –' Schulze stopped short suddenly, his delighted smile vanishing as swiftly as it had come. 'But what about Parisians.* Neither of us have any Parisians. You know how poxed-up Slack Arse Susie's gash is and if we catch a dose now, the Vulture won't let our feet touch the ground. It'll have us in Torgau† in zero comma nothing seconds. He'll say it's a self-inflicted frigging wound!' He spat miserably at the ground.

Matz took it in his stride. 'Never fear, Sergeant Schulze. I have taken care of that, too.' With a flourish, he produced a bright little packet of contraceptives from his boot. 'None of yer frog rubbish. This is *Volcano* brand, made in Solingen, – officially certified by a professional tester, or so it says on the packet, *to withstand the outpouring of Vesuvius*!' While Schulze stared, he opened the packet, took one of the little rubber devices out and placed it to his lips. When he blew hard the contraceptive expanded to become a long pink sausage which had strange rubber horns running its length like the jagged back of a crocodile. 'Joy through strength,' he proclaimed, punning the Nazi slogan of 'strength through joy'. 'German thoroughness and frog piggery.'

'A French tickler made in Germany!' Schulze breathed wide-eyed. 'Bullshit baffles brains. Now why didn't I think of

* SS slang for contraceptives.
† A notorious military prison.

that? After all, you're only a crappy corporal and I'm a sergeant.'

Matz beamed at him. 'It was one of yer off-days, perhaps Schulzi. Now come on, let's not waste time. Papa Hein's lent us a couple of the orderly room bikes. Only for an hour. So it's gonna be in, out and wipe it!'

Schulze did not need a second invitation. Clutching his already bulging crotch, he chortled, 'Lead me to it, Matzi. For Chrissake, lead me to it.' He thrust out a big paw like a blind man trying to find his way and staggered after his little friend. 'I don't care if I do go blind, *lead me to that lovely grub.*'

CHAPTER 2

'*Turn out the guard! Officer* – ' Even before the sergeant of the guard could finish his order, the big white open *Horch* tourer roared by at eighty kilometres an hour, swung round in a tremendous turn with a squeal of protesting rubber and screeched to a halt outside regimental headquarters. Papa Hein, lounging outside enjoying the midday sun, coughed and spluttered as he was engulfed in thick white dust. 'By the great whore of Buxtehude,' he began, 'where the dogs piss out of their ribs, what the shitting hell – ' He stopped abruptly, as a lean figure vaulted neatly over the door and landed at his feet, crying in a thick Viennese accent, '*Servus, Herr Unter-offizier.* Bit of a hurry, you know.' He threw back the elegant, fur-collared coat that was draped about his tall figure like a cloak and declaimed in front of an astonished Hein, '"The enemy comes in gallant show. The bloody sign of battle is hung and something to be done immediately."' He beamed at Hein. 'Shakespeare, you know.'

Hein didn't know. All he could do was to pull himself together the best he could and raise his hand to his woolly old head in salute.

Casually the young officer returned the salute, his cool, jaunty face revealing little, though Hein told himself that this particular cool customer was not like any SS officer he had met in his time in the Armed SS. '*Rittmeister* von Skalka, First Austrian Cavalry,' he announced. 'I am to see your delightful commander *Obersturmbannführer* Geier – what an apt name for an SS officer – as soon as it is humanly possible. Is it?'

'Yes – yes. I suppose, sir,' Hein stuttered, telling himself that the Vulture would make a sow of this one.

'Oh, excellent,' *Rittmeister* von Skalka tossed his car keys to the old sergeant. 'Park the old chariot, will you? See that it gets food and water. Burning oil, you know, what?' And with that he had passed by Hein straight into the orderly room. He

barely even knocked on the Vulture's door. Hein winced and
waited for the explosion to come.

Nothing happened!

Inside, standing framed in the doorway, von Skalka stood
to attention and announced himself with none of that
Prussian rigour the Vulture expected from his own officers,
but there was something in the Viennese's style that made the
Vulture desist from bellowing at him in one of his feared
rages. Besides von Skalka was straight from Berlin and
Himmler's HQ. Instead he said, somewhat puzzled by the
Austrian's presence, 'Welcome to the Regiment, *Herr Rittmeister.*'

Standing next to the window, von Dodenburg, who had
just been discussing the last few details of the night's move
with the Vulture, noted the newcomer was about his own age,
tall and handsome, with a lean, trained athletic figure. Yet
apart from the startlingly white star of a bullet wound on his
right hand, raised in salute, the Austrian was totally void of
decorations. Even the black medal for having been wounded
in action once was absent from his tunic. He frowned. What
was an obviously very fit cavalry officer doing, after two years
of total war, without a single medal? He shot an inquiring
look at the Vulture.

But there was no response from that quarter. The Vulture
was obviously as bewildered as he was. 'Would you like
something to drink, *Herr Rittmeister?*' he ventured, obviously
realizing that it was important to treat any visitor, however
silly-looking, from Himmler's headquarters with kid gloves.
He indicated the bottle on the side table. 'We have a passable
cognac.'

The *Rittmeister* shook his head. 'At any other time, my dear
Obersturmbannführer!'

Von Dodenburg did not know whether to smile or grin. No
one, as far as he knew, had ever called the Vulture 'my dear'
before.

'In any other circumstances, of course.' He stretched out
one hand and declaimed beneath the Vulture's astonished

gaze, '"If I were fierce and bold and short of breath, I'd live with scarlet majors at the Base. And speed glum heroes up the line to death."' He grinned suddenly. 'A poor translation, but my own. I'm afraid there is no time for base details. Ha, ha, a pun. There is a great deal of work to be done.'

'Work to be done?' both von Dodenburg and the Vulture exclaimed in unison.

'Yes,' the other man said easily, 'there has been a change in plan. Our Führer, in his infinite wisdom, has decided upon it personally.' Smartly he whipped out a large sealed envelope from the coat slung casually around his shoulders and handed it to the Vulture with a slight bow. 'Beware of Greeks bearing gifts, what? For you personally, *Obersturmbannführer*, from *Reichsführer* SS.' He nodded to von Dodenburg. 'Senior Company Commander *Hauptsturmbannführer* Kuno von Dodenburg, I presume. I recognize your photograph. You, too, Captain are to be privy – a strange word that – to the great secret.'

Von Dodenburg told himself that the newcomer was definitely a card. Aloud he said, 'I am flattered you recognize me.' Then he fell silent while the Vulture broke open the seal and began to scan the directive, which bore a black and gold letterhead: *'From the Office of the Reichsführer SS'*. Stamped below it in a bright red was 'Top Secret. To be conveyed by officer courier only'.

Softly he whistled as he read the first line. . . .

Ten minutes later, the Vulture was facing the two of them. Freshly pinned to the wall behind them was the map of England that they had been using these last months when the *Wehrmacht* had seriously contemplated invading Britain. 'Well, gentlemen,' he commenced as soon as Papa Hein who had brought the map had left the room and von Dodenburg had dutifully locked the door behind him, 'there has been a complete change of plan for Wotan.'

Von Dodenburg frowned and the *Rittmeister*, idly swinging one gleaming, elegantly booted leg quoted Kipling, 'I'm old and I'm nervous and cast from the service'.

'We shall still commence the move east tonight, as scheduled, but not *all* of the regiment will reach the assembly area in Poland. In fact, your company, von Dodenburg will be leaving the train at Hazebrouck – '

'What did you say?' von Dodenburg interrupted, no longer able to contain himself.

'Your company is to leave the troop train under the cover of darkness and in the greatest of secrecy.' Von Dodenburg opened his mouth, but the CO raised his hand for silence. 'All will be explained in due course, von Dodenburg. Bear with me, *please*!' It was a command, not a request.

Obediently von Dodenburg shut his mouth, while next to him, the young debonair Austrian seemed to be whistling silently, as if he were not part of the whole business.

'According to these new orders from Berlin, your company, von Dodenburg, is to be placed on detachment, with *Rittmeister* von Skalka here as your official guide. He will ensure that you are taken by truck to the naval base of Zeebrugge during the hours of darkness to arrive there before dawn. There you will be briefed on your further employment.' He hesitated a brief instant and then it came out in a rush. 'You and your company, Captain von Dodenburg are to be given the great honour of being the first German soldiers ever to land on English soil. Indeed, the *Reichsführer* SS writes that in the short history of the Armed SS, the Führer's own black guards, there has never been such an honour awarded them.'

Von Dodenburg's mind raced electrically. 'Detached duty... Zeebrugge... the first German soldiers to land on English soil.' The wild thoughts flashed through his brain without making any sense whatsoever. Everyone knew that the invasion of England had been called off. Now it was up to Goering's bombers to bring the perfidious English to their knees. Now the new enemy was to be the Ivans. What were they doing landing in England – and a mere company of them at that? *What in three devils' name was going on?*

A moment later the Vulture enlightened him. 'Captain von Dodenburg,' he said very formally, 'the First Company of SS Assault Regiment Wotan has been given the task of rescuing *Reichsleiter* Rudolf Hess!'

Von Dodenburg turned on *Rittmeister* von Skalka, for he knew instinctively that the latter knew more of what was to happen than the Vulture whose ugly face reflected surprise and bewilderment, just as his own did. 'Well, *Rittmeister*, what have you to say about all this . . . ' He couldn't find the right word and ended lamely with, 'this strangely bloody business?'

Rittmeister von Skalka laughed easily and said, 'I am under orders, too, just as you. As the Bible says, "For I am under authority, having soldiers under me; and I say to this man, Go, and he goeth; and to another, Come and he cometh; and to my servant, Do this, and he doeth it."' He smiled, but von Dodenburg could not overlook the fact that there was no real warmth beneath the Viennese charm. 'So, my dear fellow, we are ordered to do something by higher authority and to the best of our ability we will do it – *without questions!*'

He let that final phrase sink in before saying, 'Now with your permission, *Obersturmbannführer*, I should like to take a bath and get some of this ghastly frog dust off me. Do you think one of your chappies could show me the way to the bath-house?'

The Vulture was so startled by the Austrian officer's directness that instead of barking, as he would normally have done, 'What do you think I am, a damned bath-house attendant?' he said, quite tamely, 'Oh yes, yes, Sergeant Hein outside will show you the way.'

Rittmeister von Skalka saluted casually, bowing slightly at the waist in the Viennese fashion as he did so, and left, leaving the two SS officers staring at each other in complete bewilderment.

Hess had been depressed for twenty-four hours now. Immediately after his flight to Scotland he had been supremely arrogant, feeling himself the most significant person in both England and the Reich. After all, wasn't he the only person in a position to make peace between the two countries: a peace which would allow the Führer to strike a decisive blow against the Bolsheviks without fear of having to conduct a war on both fronts? That had been at the beginning. Now he was slowly starting to realize that the English were not prepared to begin talking peace with him. So far not one single leading English politician had come to see him, even when he had been in the Tower. Now he had been transferred to this remote seaside hotel, completely cut off from the centre of English power in London.

Admittedly the English had done him the honour of guarding him with their Grenadier Guards. Indeed the giants in khaki who surrounded him were, he had learned from their officer, from something called the 'King's Company', which he assumed was the one that protected the safety of the monarch, King George VI himself. Still, he reasoned, that was a mere courtesy without any political significance.

He crouched in the big leather armchair provided by the Ministry of Works, listening to the thunder of the waves outside, pondering his situation. Everything had gone wrong with his mission right from the start, he realized now. To all intents and purposes it had ended in failure. Churchill, he knew, couldn't talk with him. If England made peace with Germany, that drunken sot realized he would have to go into exile. But the others – Eden, Halifax, and the like – they could have talked with him about his mission. Even their poor, stuttering, sick King had refused to see him.

Now, too, he was beginning to suspect that some of his

polite uniformed guards were not as harmless as they appeared. A couple of them, he was sure, were members of that notorious Secret Service of theirs, with instructions from Churchill to do away with him. Their task was to murder him and make it look like a suicide. He suspected, too, that they were already putting things in his food, perhaps even poison. For the last twenty-four hours, to make sure, he had refused to eat or drink anything before one of his guards had tasted the substance.

His supper cooling untouched on the table next to the miserable fire, he brooded over the piece of paper, wondering just how he ought to phrase the last letter he would ever address to the beloved leader. He had commenced it well enough with a verse from Goethe: *'According to eternal iron great Laws Must we all Complete the cycles Of our being'*. That, he felt, would make it quite clear to the Führer what his intention was right from the start.

He frowned and listened for a few moments to the hiss and slither of the shingle, punctuated by the steady tread of the evening sentry's boots on the gravel path outside his blacked-out room. That, of course, couldn't be the way. They'd stop him before he reached the water, even if he did manage to force open his window. Suddenly he wished almost passionately he had hidden an 'L-pill' about his person before he had left Augsburg, of the kind the *Abwehr* agents bore with them when they were on a dangerous mission. That would have been the easiest way out of all.

He forced himself to concentrate on his letter. In the corner, the old-fashioned clock ticked away the moments of his life with grave metallic inexorability. 'I die,' he wrote slowly, 'in the conviction that my last mission, even if it ends in death, will somehow bear fruit.' He sucked at the end of his fountain pen and stared hard at the words he had just written. They were not great or memorable like those the Führer had dictated to him so long ago in Landsberg Prison, but he was sure his old comrade would be able to decipher the depth of feeling behind them. He continued slowly. 'Perhaps my flight will bring, despite my death, or indeed partly because of my death, peace and reconciliation with England . . .' He lowered the pen and listened to the sounds of the night for a moment.

The weathered timbers of the old house were creaking audibly, the noise from the officers' mess, located beyond the stairs, came to him muted by the thick walls and the hiss of the sea. Once he, too, had been a carefree young soldier like they were and had laughed and drunk with the best of them. But that had been before he had joined Hitler and become part of that holy crusade, national socialism, to bring order and new faith to a shaken, beaten Germany. He sniffed and felt tears well up into his eyes at the thought of those brave great days when a handful of national socialists had set out to shake the world, with, seemingly, every man's hand against them. But they had won through, all the same. Oh yes, that they had!

He rose to his feet, stretched to his full height, and stared at himself in the old fly-blown mirror. Even its poor-quality glass could not detract from the fine figure he cut in his smart *Luftwaffe* uniform, complete with his World War One Iron Cross on the breast. Yes, if he had to die for the cause in this remote foreign place, he would do so in the uniform of the service to which he had belonged so proudly as a young man.

He looked at his watch. It was nearly ten o'clock. He knew that they had already padlocked him in his room. Outside a guard armed with a tommy gun would be sitting on a chair, his feet in rubber shoes so that he would not make any noise and alert the prisoner that he was there. But last night Hess had discovered the man's presence when he smelled cigarette smoke in the small hours before dawn. Like soldiers the world over, his guard had risked smoking on duty in the belief that no officer would do his rounds of inspection at that unearthly time.

Hess bit his lip. It was now or never. Once the door had been opened he had to act – and act fast. If he failed the first time, they would never allow him another chance. More than likely they would make him sleep in handcuffs, or even in a terrible strait-jacket like they used in lunatic asylums. He whimpered aloud at the very thought. He would never be able to stand that. He licked his suddenly dry lips and advanced to the door on tiptoe, hoping the creak of his elegant, polished boots wouldn't give him away.

He tensed and then moaned out loud, as he had planned. In his excellent English he called out, as if in dire pain, 'I want to see a doctor. I'm hurting. I just can't get to sleep. A doctor, *please*!'

He heard the creak of the chair outside and someone called out, the words muffled by the thickness of the door. He crouched behind it expectantly, every muscle tensed, his breathing coming in short harsh gasps. Would they fall for his trick?

'Doctor coming, Sarge,' he heard someone say. He gulped and tried to control himself. This was it.

There was the sound of a padlock being opened. The door handle turned. With a creak, it began to open. For one moment he took in the scene outside in the poor light of a single bulb: the giant guard with his tommy gun standing to one side, a sergeant coming down the great stairs, balancing a tray laden with mugs, the fat doctor struggling into his dressing-gown, carpet slippers on his feet. Then he darted forward, face contorted, dark eyes wild and crazed.

The guard leaped for him. He side-stepped and the man slammed against the opposite wall with a clatter, his tommy gun falling to the floor. 'Stop him!' the doctor yelled urgently. On the stairs the sergeant let the tray fall and grabbed for his revolver. 'Don't shoot, man!' the doctor shrieked wildly.

Hess grinned wolfishly. *'Heil Hitler!'* he gasped. Next moment, he dived forward right over the ornate banisters and smashed into the floor in a crazy heap, howling with pain. An instant later all was panic and chaos.

CHAPTER 4

Churchill listened intently, the ash on his cigar getting longer and longer, while C, who had been his sole guest this night sat hunched and passive, seemingly not at all interested in the fact that the Prime Minister had been so rudely disturbed at this hour. But then C, that grey little man, had experienced many such shocks at late hours in his particular business.

'Well,' Churchill growled finally, 'what is the sawbones' diagnosis?' He waited a moment. 'An uncomplicated fracture of the upper left part of the left femur, eh? Can you handle it down there yourselves? I don't want him sent to hospital if it can be helped ... You can? Excellent. And tell the officer in charge that more care will have to be exercised in future. We can't have Herr Hitler's number two committing suicide upon us. What are you doing with him now?'

He listened to the unknown speaker's answer, while C finally moved, brushing the dandruff off his skinny shoulder with a hand like a grey claw.

Suddenly Churchill burst into laughter and said, 'Let us hope, doctor, that you can do as good a job with his leg as you have with his outside plumbing. Thank you. Good night.' He put down the phone and took a quick puff at his cigar, scattering ash everywhere, before turning to the head of the Secret Service. 'Hess attempted to commit suicide an hour ago, Stewart,' he announced. 'But he didn't pull it off – thank God. Broke his leg, that's all.'

C remained unmoved. 'Chap in charge ought to be given a rocket,' he croaked in his crusty, upper-class voice. 'Grenadier, isn't he? Never much good the Grenadiers.'

Churchill grinned, in spite of his mood. C. was running true to form. 'Spoken like a true Life Guard, Stewart. Now apparently he's having trouble with his water. Can't pee, or couldn't until the MO told him to stop behaving like a baby and inserted the catheter. That did the trick.'

C looked at his well-manicured nails. They were as grey as everything else about him. 'He's very young to be having trouble with his waterworks?' he commented without any apparent interest.

'Shock, I suppose,' Churchill said and then dismissed the matter. He sat down at the other side of the fire, dipped the end of his cigar in the glass of brandy that stood on the table next to his chair, and said, 'The reason I have called you here tonight, Stewart, apart of course from the pleasure of your stimulating company, is this. What are we going to do with Hess?'

C didn't even hesitate. Without the slightest trace of emotion in his voice, he replied, 'Hang him in the Tower, as soon as his leg heals.'

Churchill shook his head in wonder. C was living up to his reputation for being absolutely one hundred per cent cold-blooded. The head of MI6 must have ice-water running in his veins, he told himself. Nothing ever seemed to startle or shock him. Even when his whole continental organization had been smashed by the Nazis back in November 1940, he had accepted the fact quite calmly with, 'Hm, that's rather unpleasant news, isn't it?' What a blessed relief it would be sometimes to be a man like C, without nerves and imagination!

'Can't do that, Stewart. What would the charge be? And we can hardly try him as a war criminal at this stage of the war.' He took a huge puff at his cigar and chortled. 'Why, we might damn lose the thing and then *we'd* be in the dock ourselves as war criminals. No, that's not the way.'

'I see!' C said and took a tiny sip at his tiny sherry.

'Naturally I would dearly love to be rid of Hess. He is already prejudicing our cause with the Americans. Roosevelt is being very cagey at the moment. Then there is Russia. I am afraid once the balloon goes up out there, Stalin, the old bear, might well think that Hess has been sent over here by *Herr* Hitler to cook up some deal so that Germany would have a free hand with Russia.'

'Not a bad idea after all, Prime Minister,' C said. 'Let 'em finish each other orf – and good riddance to them both. But Stalin is highly suspicious of us. We've told him already on the QT – not revealing our sources, of course – that Germany is going to attack him. But he doesn't believe us. Thinks we're trying to set the cat among the pigeons to save our own bacon. A provocation he called it. Impossible chap.' He took another sip of his drink.

Churchill looked sharply at C. He couldn't remember a time when the head of the Secret Service had said so much in one go. Surely the sherry – beastly stuff that it was – couldn't be that strong, he asked himself. 'Well,' he continued, 'the Germans don't seem to want to come and fetch him back. We can't have him committing suicide. So what in Sam Hill's name are we going to do with the chap?' He took a deep breath and attempted to answer his own question. 'It would, of course, Stewart, be best to get rid of him – *quietly.*'

C nodded, but said nothing.

'The problem is, of course, that it would get out sooner or later. Someone would blab, the press would be after the story.' He shrugged. 'One of the problems with democracy is that you can't stop people talking. So, Hess must seem to be there even though he isn't there, if you follow my meaning?'

Surprisingly enough C did. In spite of his wooden appearance, his moneyed background, Eton, Sandhurst and the Life Guards, Major-General Stewart Menzies was nobody's fool. 'You're talking of what I believe the Hun calls a *dopplegänger*, Prime Minister?'

Churchill nodded. Far away to the east of the great sprawling city, the first sirens were beginning to sound, being taken up by others, coming ever closer by the second. The Germans were returning yet once again to attack the hard-pressed capital.

'It would be damnably difficult,' C said, his grey face not revealing whether or not he had heard that stomach-churning howl. 'The person in question would have to look like him, speak fluent German, and know a great deal of the Nazi past.'

'Hess could conveniently lose his memory, once he has recovered from his broken leg,' Churchill said softly, toying with his glass. 'Slowly, progressively, of course. The doctors who have examined him report that he is already in a highly neurotic state, not far from outright madness.'

C didn't seem to hear. Now, far off, they could hear the first drone of the attackers winging their way. Down in the city the shelters in the tube would already be packed, with more and more people frantically trying to get in, paying money to the spivs for any piece of the platform to shelter from what was soon to come.

'What we want really,' Churchill tried to sum up his feelings, 'is a tame replica of Hess – and C, it's to be your task to find one.'

C drained the last of his dry sherry, an impulsive gesture for him. 'But where in heaven's name do I start, Prime Minister?' he asked a little testily.

Churchill gave him a wintry smile, as the first bomb of this new night of terror came whistling down. 'What about a Jewish lunatic asylum,' he suggested, 'a German-Jewish lunatic asylum? There must be one.' Then he rose from his chair with remarkable speed for such an old, portly man. 'And now we really must depart for the shelter. The Hun appears to be after my scalp tonight.' They fled.

CHAPTER 5

It was like all the departures von Dodenburg could remember since September 1939. A blacked-out station; chain-dogs planted in the shadows in twos, hard-eyed and suspicious, looking for deserters; cheerful or despondent soldiers, returning or going on leave, kits packed with goodies for the Homeland; a few shrunken 'grey mice' seeing off boyfriends, clinging to them as if they wouldn't let them go, sniffing into their grey regulation handkerchiefs at regular intervals; drunken soldiers taking swigs out of their 'flatmen' and not giving a damn if anyone saw them doing so – what the hell, they were cannon-fodder heading for the new battlefield anyway! And then the train, blacked-out and expectant, the flak gunners already in position around their gun, sinister in their leather face masks, with officious RTO sergeants striding up and down its length, checking off things on their clipboards, waiting, waiting, waiting.

Von Dodenburg sighed and huddled deeper into the collar of his greatcoat, for it was cold in the compartment – the heating had not been turned on – and wondered how many more of these midnight partings he would experience. His new mission had unnerved him a little. It seemed so unorthodox, so daring, yet very vague. All he knew was that he and his company would leave the train, head for Zeebrugge and then set about the rescue attempt. But how?

A little annoyed, he stared at where von Skalka slumped in the corner. He, too, was huddled into his elegant greatcoat with its real fur collar. But his eyes were closed and he appeared to be asleep, his face revealing nothing. Von Dodenburg frowned. The Austrian puzzled him. An officer without decorations after two years of total war, yet his delicate right hand bore a definite bullet wound scar. Despite his somewhat effeminate Viennese manners and charm, which were anathema to a Prussian like von Dodenburg, he could sense the steel and fierce determination beneath. Von Skalka was not a man to be trifled with. Yet when all that was said and done, what role was he to play in the mission to come? Why had he been sent by SS HQ like this? God in Heaven, he wasn't even an SS officer!

'*Alles in Ordnung*, von Dodenburg?' the Vulture's harsh voice broke into his reverie.

He started to his feet and touched his hand to his peaked cap. 'Everything in order, sir. Half my company's drunk, but no matter.' He forced a grin. 'It'll keep them tame and quiet for what is to come?'

'They know?'

'Only the senior non-coms and subalterns, sir,' von Dodenburg replied. 'I thought it wise to inform them so that the switch will go smoothly.'

The Vulture nodded his approval. 'I think you'll be able to cure your throatache in this one, von Dodenburg, if things go well.' He touched his skinny neck above his collar to indicate that the other officer might well win the Knight's Cross of the Iron Cross, which was carried around the neck.

'I don't know, sir,' von Dodenburg said uneasily. 'The whole thing is very vague. I'd prefer to stay with the regiment.'

'Don't be foolish, my boy,' the Vulture chortled with fake bonhomie. 'It's the chance of a lifetime. The honour of being the first German troops on English soil, a good decoration to be won, promotion even perhaps. Why, I'd jump at the chance to lead the mission, if it were offered to me.' He touched his riding crop to his cap. 'Now I must be off. *Hals und Beinbruch*. Happy landings, von Dodenburg.'

'Thank you, sir,' von Dodenburg said and sat down again, as the Vulture stamped off, the leather gusset in his enormous riding breeches creaking audibly.

Listening to them, von Skalka, his eyes firmly closed, told himself that if he had his way there'd be no medals or promotion for the tough-looking young SS officer in the opposite corner. But with a bit of luck, there *would* be another five thousand Swiss francs winging their way from Gestapo Mueller's own private slush fund to the numbered account he kept in a discreet little bank in Zurich.

A shudder. A hiss of wildly escaping steam. The clatter of steel wheels trying to get a grip on the rails. A great trembling swept the length of the long blacked-out troop train, jerking kitbags and packs out of overfilled racks. Drunks clutching their flatmen slammed against doors. In the *abort*, a greenbeak, drunk but still obeying the rules, gulped with relief before throwing up the lid and beginning to vomit into the toilet. 'We're moving!' someone cried, as if in wonder. And another voice yelled scornfully above the sudden noise and confusion, 'What d' yer fuckin' think we're doing, pissin' in the frigging thundermug!'

Gathering speed by the instant, smoke trailing back and filling the carriages, the train began to leave the station, its whistle sounding a shrill farewell. With a sigh of relief, Sergeant Schulze, who occupied the best seat in his overcrowded compartment, pulled off his boots to the accompaniment of 'Gas alarm everybody!' and 'Shit on the shingle, who opened the door to the cheese factory?' and the like.

Schulze, his two flatmen, ring of salami, and dirty book already lined up for the long journey ahead, remained completely unmoved by the protest. 'Rank hath its privileges,' he declared to the compartment. 'If Sergeant Schulze wants to take off his dice-beakers, Sergeant Schulze takes 'em off – and that's that.' He massaged his big feet, clad in the footrags, gratefully. 'Or does anybody think otherwise?' He paused in the massaging of his feet and clenched a fist like a small steam-shovel threateningly.

No one thought 'otherwise'.

Next to him Matz dabbed his brow with a pair of still warm red silk frilly knickers and said, 'By the Great Allah and all His whirling dervishes, that was some gallop back there!

Going at it like a fiddler's elbow, I was!' He licked his lips fondly at the thought of the pleasures of Slack-Arse Susie's place.

Schulze looked down his big nose at his running mate disdainfully, 'You mean with that little *Wiener Würstchen* o' yourn,' he remarked scornfully. 'That poor miserable little thing couldn't even make a nun come! Now, when even a fully grown, experienced knocking shop assistant sees mine,' he said grandly puffing out his big chest, 'she turns white with fear, absolute naked fear.' He grabbed hastily for his precious flatmen as the train clattered over a level crossing and jolted them loose. 'Phew,' he breathed, as he caught them just in time. 'That was a close call!'

Matz licked his lips significantly and said, insult forgotten, for he was suddenly exceedingly thirsty, 'Ought to get rid of them here and now, I suppose, in case there is a tragic accident, don't yer think, Schulzi?'

Sergeant Schulze ignored the comment. Instead he pulled the cork from the first flatman, flung back his big head and took a tremendous slug of the fiery gin, his Adam's apple racing up and down his throat like an express lift. 'Arr,' he grunted and wiped the back of his paw across his gleaming lips, 'that was good!'

'Greedy sod!' Matz said and then he forgot Schulze and his flatman. He leaned back against the hard wooden boards of the fourth-class compartment and closed his eyes, suddenly very tired. One by one the others did the same, lulled into an uneasy sleep by the chatter of the wheels. It had been a long day.

As the long troop train clattered through the May night, across the dull, flat French plain, von Dodenburg was unable to sleep. He found himself continually opening his eyes to check the time (noting as he did so that in the opposite corner the Austrian officer seemed to be fast asleep). There were so many imponderables facing the regiment now. A year ago it had swept through France to what had appeared to be final victory and now it was to be thrown into battle against a new enemy, while he and his company were to set out into the unknown on what seemed an impossible mission.

He frowned in the poor yellow light, afflicted by those doubts that attack even the most resolute in the middle of the night. Was the Third Reich vulnerable after all, in spite of the fact that Germany seemed to dominate the whole of Western Europe? Could things go wrong even now and snatch that tremendous victory away from the Fatherland? Was it possible?

Von Dodenburg swallowed dryly and longed for something hot and strong to drink. His throat was abruptly parched, although it was cold inside the compartment.

'"Soldiers are citizens of death's grey land,"' von Skalka's soft voice cut suddenly into his gloomy reverie, '"drawing no dividends from time's tomorrows."' Von Dodenburg opened his eyes, startled, to find the Austrian grinning at him. Still, however, his grey eyes revealed nothing.

'And what is that supposed to mean?' he asked icily, containing his anger.

'Not much, I should imagine,' the Austrian said easily, taking out a silver cigarette case and politely offering it to von Dodenburg. 'Just showing off my university education, I expect. We Austrians, as you know, are great show-offs – and we *do* dearly love university titles.'

Von Dodenburg refused the cigarette and snapped, 'Well, since you're going along on this Hess thing, perhaps you would be good enough to tell me what exactly your role in the affair is supposed to be?'

The Austrian looked down at his gold-rimmed cigarette as if he had never seen one before and sniffed. 'Oh, just a sort of general guide and assistant,' he said slowly. 'You see, I know England well. I was at university there – Cambridge to be exact.' He grinned winningly. 'See, there I go again, boasting about my university education.'

Von Dodenburg was not going to be fobbed off. 'A guide, eh. But there might be some action.' He leaned forward.

'People might get killed – and you *seem* to have seen little action in this war so far.'

Von Skalka shrugged easily. 'I expect I shall get by somehow or other,' he commented. 'I'll let you know if I fill my pants.'

Von Dodenburg flushed angrily. A hot retort sprang to his lips, but at that very same moment, the long train started to shudder to a halt and he could just make out the first thin wail of the air-raid sirens, the agreed-upon device to keep the civvies tucked away in their cellars. In a few seconds the flak guns would begin firing at non-existent Tommy bombers, all part of the plan to cover the fact that a whole company would be soon leaving the train, heading for a completely different place than Eastern Poland.

Hastily von Dodenburg forgot the *Reittmeister*'s mysterious behaviour. He seized his pack, his helmet strapped neatly to it. '*Los!*' he snapped. 'The trucks are waiting.'

Von Skalka stubbed out his cigarette. His languid easy-going manner vanished. He, too, grabbed his pack, his greatcoat falling open as he reached up for it, and for the first time von Dodenburg noticed that the rather useless little cavalry pistol he had worn before had vanished. It had been replaced by the great wooden holster of a Luger, the sort that could be used as a butt to turn the weapon into a sharpshooter's rifle. But why?

As the startled, sleepy troopers of the First Company were turfed out of their compartments by their non-coms and the flak guns started to bark at the sky, he had no further time to wonder about the transformation. Besides, the trucks were beginning to switch on their engines under the trees that lined the track at this lonely spot. It was time to be off.

Five minutes later the little convoy had vanished into the darkness leaving the train to continue its long journey to the East.

Wednesday, 14 May 1941

CHAPTER 1

Bormann belched happily. His stomach was distended by a huge Munich pig's knuckle, heaped mashed potatoes, and a mound of *sauerkraut*, all washed down with several litres of excellent beer. He felt at ease with the world. He did not even have the energy to summon one of the female duty clerks from down below in the teleprinter room, to tumble on the big couch in the corner.

All was silent now in the *Berghof*, save for the soft tread of the giant SS guards in their black uniform who at night prowled everywhere, carrying drawn pistols. The Führer and his toadies and cronies had watched one of those forbidden Hollywood musicals (at least for the German public) filled with the long-legged blondes he doted upon, had stuffed himself with cream cakes and *Enzian*, the only alcohol he tolerated, and had then staggered off to bed with Eva Braun. Not that he'd be much good to her, Bormann told himself contemptuously. Everyone knew the Führer couldn't get his pistol up. Why he kept a mistress in the first place was anyone's guess. It must be years now since that cocky bitch Braun had had something up her knickers – and it served her right. She was far too damned full of herself.

Lazily, Bormann, his tunic unbuttoned, braces dangling, tie ripped to one side now that there was no chance of his being summoned by the Führer, reached over for the stone bottle of *Steinhager*, a fierce northern schnapps that he preferred to the muck they brewed down here in the south. He poured himself half a water glass full and took a drink. He gasped with pleasure as the fiery stuff burned the back of his throat. '*Ach du Scheisse,*' he mumbled to himself, '*das schmeckt!*'

He looked at his watch, blinking and trying to fight off the sleep that was now threatening to overcome him. It was nearly two. It couldn't be much longer now before he received his call from Berlin, providing everything went well, of course. Gestapo Mueller was very reliable. He had to be – with what Bormann had on him in his own secret files on the *Prominenz*.

He ran over the Hess business again. Everything seemed to be working out splendidly. The English appeared not to have made any great fuss about his arrival there, and so far there had been no peace soundings at their embassies in such neutral countries as Portugal, Spain and Sweden. For his part, the Führer was relieved that his statement about Hess's mental problems seemed to have been believed. All in all, Hess was slowly disappearing from the limelight again, though the Führer *had* asked a couple of times about progress in the rescue mission. Naturally he had obliged Hitler with the information that everything was moving at a cracking pace; it wouldn't be long before he hoped to report that Party Comrade Rudolf Hess had been successfully rescued.

He grinned to himself wickedly at the thought. If he had his way 'Party Comrade' Hess wouldn't have a chance in hell of ever seeing the Fatherland again. Only a fluke – no, *a damned shitting miracle* – would ensure that Hess ever returned, the way he had set it up. His plan was foolproof like all his plans and intrigues.

Then, when the deed was done, it was only a matter of tidying up, covering up the traces. Himmler was a fool and a pawn. That skinny ex-chicken clerk with his book-keeper's mentality wouldn't even *know* that he had been used. Gestapo Mueller, who in his days as a Munich cop before 1933 had been a leading persecutor of the local national socialists, would keep his mouth shut, if he didn't want trouble. All that remained was to deal with the Death Squad man. That would be Mueller's task.

Suddenly the telephone started to shrill on the big desk in front of him. Bormann removed his feet and picked up the thing. 'Bormann,' he rasped.

He recognized the voice at the other end immediately.

There was no mistaking that thick Bavarian accent. It was Gestapo Mueller speaking from his HQ at 10 *Prince Albrecht Strasse* in Berlin. 'Well?' he demanded curtly.

Virtually every German lived in fear and trembling of Gestapo Mueller. They all knew what went on in those bloodstained cellars below No. 10. Even top men in the party suddenly turned pale when Mueller's name was mentioned. Not he. He would show the cruel ex-Munich cop that he, Bormann, was in charge, right from the frigging start. He waited.

'It's just come through from France,' Mueller answered. 'The assault company has left the troop train and is now on its way to Zeebrugge.'

'Excellent. And the Chief?' he meant Himmler. 'Has the old fart left Berlin already?'

Mueller chuckled at the reference to the 'old fart'. He, too, had absolutely no respect for the *Reichsleiter* SS Heinrich Himmler. 'No, he leaves by plane from Templehof at first light tomorrow morning. Presently he's in bed – according to my spies – with that secretary of his, Dorothea, the one with the size forty woollen knickers!'

Bormann allowed himself a smile. 'Well, you know what they say, Mueller? If you want to keep a good secretary, *screw* her on the desk. Ha, ha!'

Mueller guffawed. His humour, too, was of the same basic, crude kind. 'That's good, very good!' He choked. 'With the pick of the most beautiful women in Berlin, he goes to bed with that big-flanked Rhenish mare.'

Bormann was business-like again. 'Right then, Himmler will brief the assault company in Zeebrugge personally. But he must be made to understand that your man is *really* in charge of the attack and that his orders are paramount. Is that clear?'

'Absolutely. He's a strange fellow. Typical Viennese aristocrat. "Have the honour", "kiss your hand, madame", and all that Austrian crap,' Mueller rasped. 'But he's the best man I have.'

'Soon to be the best man you *had*!' Bormann emphasized the past tense.

There was a sudden silence at the other end. Bormann could almost feel Mueller's brain racing as he digested that one word. 'You mean he's got to go ... *afterwards?*'

'Naturally,' Bormann said easily, as if this was the most natural thing in the world. 'We want no one who might blab afterwards. It's got to be N and N for your chap.'*

'N and N, it is then, *Reichsleiter*. Leave it to me. I'll take care of it personally. Is that all?'

'That is all,' Bormann announced firmly.

'Also, dann, gute Nacht.'

'Gute Nacht, Mueller.' Bormann hung up. He poured himself another *Steinhager* and raised the glass to the picture of himself and Hess that hung on the wall opposite. It showed the Deputy as a witness at his wedding to that muddle-headed wife of his back in '29. How confident and full of himself Hess had looked then; while he had remained in the background, humble and appreciative that Hess had done him the honour of attending his wedding, an ex-jailbird who was little more than a clerk in the party hierarchy. Now the boot was on the other foot, well almost. *'Gute Nacht, Herr Hess*,' he toasted the picture. *'GOODBYE!'* He drained the spirit in one gulp and with unusual demonstrativeness for a man who was always so careful to keep his emotions under control in public, he threw the empty glass with all his strength at the wall. It shattered into a myriad pieces, as Bormann's head slumped to the desk in a drunken sleep.

---

* *Nacht und Nebel*, literally 'night and fog'. A Gestapo practice of making an opponent of the regime vanish without trace.

CHAPTER 2

'*Ordnung ist das ganze Leben,*' his father had been wont to proclaim at regular intervals. 'All life is order.' It was the creed that he had lived by ever since he had left the cavalry after the collapse of the monarchy back in 1918 and he had taken over the family estates and the sugar factory that was the von Skalkas' main source of income. Slumped there now in the swaying truck, packed with Wotan troopers, smelling of diesel and sweaty feet, von Skalka smiled fondly at the memory.

How bourgeois the old man had really been! Everything was done by the clock – eight o'clock arrival at the office, letters completed by nine, conference with the works manager at ten, tour of the plant by eleven; and then the midday meal, always taken in the same café at the same *stammtisch*, with the same companions, and the same servile waiters mouthing their '*Herr Doktors*', '*Herr Direktors*', '*Herr Rittmeisters*' at the drop of a hat. Week in, week out, month after month, year after year. Everything had its time and its place. *Ordnung ist das ganze leben!*

But in the thirties, after his mother had died, things had begun to change radically. In neighbouring Germany Hitler had come to power and at his *stammtisch*, wreathed in cigar smoke, sipping his *Kapuziner*, sweeping cavalry moustache dripping with yellow cream, his father had proclaimed in disbelief. 'But the chap was an NCO. A corporal as a leader, that's not right. Besides he's not normal, not married, no children, a vegetarian. Why the fellow even likes dogs!'

A year later, his father's world had really begun to crumple when the *Sozis*, as he called the socialists, had revolted in Vienna. They had barricaded themselves in their housing estates in the capital and had begun firing at the police. In the end the dwarf-chancellor Dollfuss had been forced to bring in the army and heavy artillery to root them out. There had been an indiscriminate slaughter of the prisoners taken afterwards. '*Sozis*, they may be,' the old man had declared at the *stammtisch*, 'but they are still Austrians. You don't shoot your own chaps just like that!' He had shaken his greying head, as if he didn't quite understand the world any more.

Dollfuss had been murdered. Open warfare broke out in the streets of the big cities between communists, socialists, and the Austrian nationalist socialists, plus the members of a dozen other smaller parties. Anarchy was in the offing. And so it had gone on, blow by blow, with public order slowly breaking up: strikes, street battles, the ever-present threat of revolution from left or right, while he had been studying Coleridge and Wordsworth in the cloistered calm of Cambridge, in what was really another world.

The old man had shot himself six months before the *Anschluss*. The three-month long strike by the *Sozis* had ruined him. The estates had vanished, sold to American–Jewish investors (and his father had always hated Jews) in a last attempt to keep the sugar factory running. But it had all been in vain. Rather than be declared a bankrupt, he had very neatly blown his brains out.

And that had been the end of the English eighteenth-century poets for the future *Rittmeister* von Skalka. His dream of becoming a *Herr Professor* at a university were over. He had left Cambridge to return to a depressed, strife-torn Vienna, just waiting to be taken over by the New Order across the border, penniless and without a job, and with little hope of ever finding one. The unswept streets of the capital were full of similar penniless, jobless ex-students.

That month he had shot his first victim, Deutscherle, the union leader who had led the strike which had ruined his father. Filled with bitterness towards what he was wont to call the 'ruling class', after von Skalka's death Deutscherle had boasted to his union friends, 'So what? Another of those aristocratic swine has killed himself? Well, what am I supposed to do? Cry for those who grind the face of the poor?'

Von Skalka had shot the union leader in his favourite café at ten o'clock in the morning, when the place had been full of similar comfortable, middle-aged men drinking the first of the dozen cups of coffee that would see them through the day and reading through the papers in their wooden holders that the café provided. He had walked up to him in an apparently hesitant manner, though in reality he had burned with suppressed rage. '*Herr* Deutscherle?' he had asked, twisting his cap in his hands as befitted a young man speaking to an important union official.

'*Ja,*' Deutscherle had answered, hardly deigning to look up from the *Wiener Kurier, 'Was ist's?*'

Von Skalka had brought up the gun he had bought with the proceeds from the gold watch his father had given him on his eighteenth birthday. Quite calmly he had begun to squeeze the trigger, while the fat-faced union leader had stared up at him in total, absolute disbelief, his jowls quivering, but unable to speak. The bullet had caught the older man squarely between the left eye and ear. It had exited in a gout of deep red blood that had splashed all over his right hand. With a soft moan Deutscherle had slumped face forward, squashing the cream cake he had been about to eat, dead before he had hit the table. Quite deliberately while the guests had stared at him in horrified silence, von Skalka then blew the back of Deutscherle's shaven skull off with a second bullet.

Around him was complete stillness. No one had dared move, seemingly mesmerized by the body and the gun. The crowd had frozen like the actors at the final curtain of some cheap melodrama. Quite calmly, not even looking back, von Skalka had walked out into the square dominated by the grey gothic bulk of St Stefan's Cathedral and had disappeared into the busy morning throng. No one had followed.

Thereafter he had taken up with the now illegal Austrian National Socialist Party, though he had not had the slightest interest in politics. Working from just over the border in Bavaria it had been his task, and that of a small group of similar Austrian refugees, to bribe or smuggle themselves across the Austrian border to 'take out' well-known socialist or communist leaders. The 'trigger men' they called themselves ironically – after the characters in one of those Hollywood gangster movies of the time, featuring an Austrian Jewish actor Paul Muni. But the others had not been able to stick it very long. Killing soon satiated them. They fell sick, went on prolonged drunks, broke down, or simply refused any more assignments.

He hadn't. The act of murder for him was neither pleasurable nor distasteful. All he had ever felt was a sense of iron purpose as he pulled the trigger. He guessed it was the same feeling that a good bull-fighter must experience at the 'moment of truth'. Once the deed was done, he forgot about it. His conscience didn't trouble him one bit. There were no bad dreams. Anyone who had known him at Cambridge would have thought him the same pleasure-loving, handsome, intelligent Viennese he had been then.

In 1937 Reinhold Heydrich had called him to Berlin. The tall, blond, neurotic head of the SD and Gestapo, whom even Hitler called 'the man with the iron heart', had swung a fencing foil loosely in his right hand: 'So you're the Austrian?' he had rasped. 'Our tame killer.' Suddenly he had lunged forward with lightning speed – for he was a champion – and the foil had sliced the air next to von Skalka's face.

He hadn't flinched a centimetre and Heydrich had obviously been impressed, for he had said, levelling the foil at the younger man, 'We have driven the red rats from the Reich. But now they gnaw at the fabric of the Reich from Paris, Zurich, London, and the like. Diplomatic protests avail us nothing. So we are going to deal with them in our own way.' Again that gleaming blade had lashed out at lightning speed. 'Are you with us, von Skalka?'

'*Jawohl, Gruppenführer,*' he had answered, impressed and yet unimpressed by this neurotic cold-eyed giant who was going to be his new boss, his mind racing as he pondered what terms he could make. He knew of Heydrich. He would use people and then, when they were no longer required, they were quietly 'liquidated' – that was one of Heydrich's favourite words – in one of the new concentration camps. He had to have a safeguard, a key in the back door.

'Your terms?' Heydrich whipped the air with the foil, making it sing like he did with his violin when he was drunk and sentimental, which was often.

He heard himself say, as if listening to someone else, 'So far I have worked for the cause, *Gruppenführer*. Now I think it is time I was paid properly for, er, each job.'

Heydrich had squinted at him, still toying with his foil. 'And what is *properly*?'

'Five thousand Swiss francs in an account I shall open in that country.'

Heydrich whistled softly, impressed. '*Mein Respekt, Herr von Skalka, mein Respekt!* You know of course it is illegal to export foreign currency from the Reich?'

He had kept silent and Heydrich, eyeing him now with new respect, asked softly, 'And what will you do with all this money? *Women?*'

He had shaken his head and said, '*Nein Gruppenführer, Kultur!*'

And with that he had left the baffled *Gruppenführer* to become the first of the Gestapo's notorious 'Death Squad'.

Squatting there in the uncomfortable truck, rolling through flat Belgian countryside, the tyres hissing over the wet cobbles, he smiled to himself as he remembered that little scene at Number Ten. That 'culture' had completely floored Heydrich. He had agreed to the outrageous terms without any further ado and had never mentioned the incident again, though he often referred to von Skalka in a mixture of contempt and admiration. 'Aha, here comes the *Herr Professor*, I see!'

Von Skalka smiled to himself in the darkness. How little did Heydrich, who had now become the governor of occupied Czechoslovakia, realize that this was *exactly* his intention? One more 'job' and he would take a little leave in

Switzerland, never to return. He would head for one of those banana republics in South America where English was the second language. There he would sit the war out in some provincial university, reading, reading, reading, and one day when it was all over he would appear again as the *Herr Professor*, to settle down to carpet slippers, some erudite research – and obscurity.

Silently he quoted Owen to himself, *'Merry it was to laugh there, Where death becomes absurd and life absurder, For power was in us and we slashed bones bare. Not to feel sickness or remorse of murder,'* and told himself one more job and then it would be over. He closed his eyes and fell asleep at once, his breath inaudible, his chest appearing not to move. For all the world he might well have been dead already.

CHAPTER 3

The Tommies caught the little convoy of trucks full of sleeping men completely by surprise. One moment they had been trundling slowly along the blacked-out coastal road, each vehicle well spread as regulations prescribed, the young troopers deep in sleep and snoring their heads off, their dreams filled with rivers of foaming beer and nubile blondes without their clothes on; the next the dramatic green flares were dropping to left and right of the little dead-straight road, that was devoid of any cover.

Almost at once the Spitfires came zooming in at tree-top level, drawn like some lethal metallic insects to the glow of the flares. At three hundred miles an hour they raced in, bright angry lights crackling the length of their wings as they opened fire with their eight machine-guns. Tracer zipped to the suddenly stalled trucks in angry profusion, and in an instant all was panic-stricken confusion.

'Hit the dirt!' Non-coms yelled wildly, slapping the canvas frantically with horny palms. 'For fuck's sake, *hit the dirt!*'

As officers shrilled their whistles and loosed off purposeless bursts of automatic fire at the dark shapes swooping in for the kill, the men, rudely awakened from their sleep, threw themselves out of the trucks, slammed into the ditches and ran squelching through the waterlogged fields, shoulders hunched in anticipation of that first red-hot blow that would send them reeling to the ground.

A whoosh! A dull roar. Next moment the petrol tank of one of the trucks exploded with a thick crump like a shell detonating. Von Dodenburg cursed wildly as the blast buffeted him across the face and made him stagger. The whole damned countryside was as bright as day. Furiously he ripped off a hurst at the silver belly of a Spitfire roaring by only metres above his head. He could see every damned rivet and oil patch on its surface. 'Stop returning fire!' he yelled crazily. 'Get down. For God's sake, get down!'

'You heard the CO,' Schulze bellowed and aimed a tremendous kick at the rump of a young trooper pointing his rifle uselessly at the burning lorry. The youth landed head-first in a pile of manure.

For a few moments more the planes circled, firing with their machine-guns for they did not seem to possess bombs, then from the east came the snarl and roar of fresh engines. *'Messerschmitts!'* someone yelled above the noise. 'It's our lads! Now watch the buck-teethed Tommy buggers run!'

The unknown speaker was right. The Spitfires knew they were at a disadvantage now, with their petrol low and their ammunition running out. They made one last dive, machine-guns blazing angrily, and then curved round in a tight noisy turn to head west for their island bases. Behind them the Messerschmitts pumped their cannon angrily in fury and frustration.

The sky emptied and the only sound was that of the merrily crackling truck. 'Any casualties?' von Dodenburg asked anxiously, machine-pistol slung across his back once more, as the men started to file back to the trucks. 'NCOs report your casualties!'

But there were none, save the one whom Schulze had booted. He had swallowed a large cow turd and was now being violently sick.

Von Dodenburg breathed a sigh of relief. 'Come on,' he shouted, 'get back in the trucks.'

Von Skalka slowly walked by the handsome SS officer to his own vehicle. Suddenly, for no reason whatsoever, an old piece of doggerel he had learned at Cambridge during a weekend drinking session came to him. What was it called now? Oh yes, he grinned. 'The Calcutta Cholera Song'. As he clambered over the tailgate he started to repeat it to himself. *'Betrayed by the country that bore us. Betrayed by the country we find. All the best men have gone before us and only the dull left behind. Stand by your glasses steady. Here's toast to the dead already. And here's to the next man to die.'*

As the driver started the engine and rammed home first gear noisily, *Rittmeister* von Skalka smiled to himself in the darkness and told himself that if anyone was going to die, it wasn't going to be him.

CHAPTER 4

Himmler, looking paler than ever, dark circles beneath his pince-nez, cast a glance around the bare briefing room, its sole decoration a picture of the Führer, dressed in white armour, riding a horse (though he had never ridden a horse in his life), and a large-scale map, heavy with symbols, of the Channel and the North Sea. Very carefully and softly, obviously to lend weight to his words, he said, '*Meine Herren*, this is to be a mission of the greatest moment.' The bearded commander of the Third E-Boat Flotilla, von Dodenburg and von Skalka stared at him. 'You have been given the task by the Führer *himself*' – he looked lovingly at the portrait, pigeon-chest swelling with pride – 'of rescuing dear Party Comrade Hess from the clutches of the perfidious English.' He paused and let his words sink in.

Outside a gale raged over the sea, making the windows rattle, as the seagulls swept by in great effortless curves. The sky was a threatening grey and black. Soon it would rain.

'We know now,' Himmler continued, picking up his pointer, 'that Comrade Hess is being held in what used to be a hotel – here at Little Saxton.' He tapped the map pedantically like the schoolmaster he had once been for a while. 'He is guarded by what appears to be a company of English infantry. As far as we know from our spies, that is the extent of the English defences save for the usual beach obstacles, barbed wire, pill-boxes and the like – perhaps a minefield, too.'

Von Dodenburg's face revealed nothing, but his mind was racing. How easy Himmler made it seem. '*Perhaps a minefield, too!*' God in Heaven, a whole company could be slaughtered by a single machine-gun while trying to get through a minefield!

Himmler nodded to the E-boat commander. 'Well, Lieutenant-Commander?'

THE HESS ASSAULT – THE PLAN

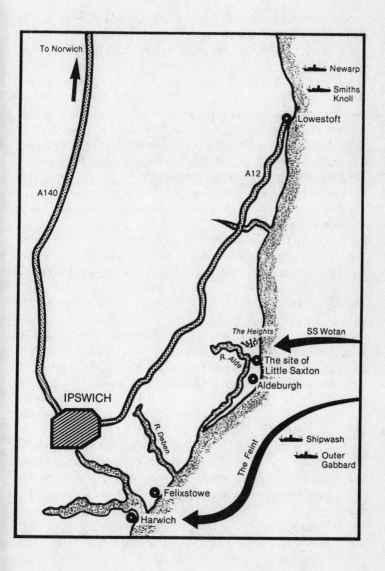

Kapitanleutnant Hansen stroked his black beard which made his skinny face appear even paler. Like all E-boat skippers his stomach had been ruined by the constant pounding of the waves the light torpedo boats encountered at high speed. Most of them could only keep down the lightest foods; they vomited up anything else. *'Reichsführer,'* he said in a thick Hamburg accent, 'the Tommies have several belts of minefields, backed up by heavy coastal defences, in the Felixstowe-Harwich area, which as you know, is a major naval port, responsible for our own sector of the North Sea. However, beyond that area and Ipswich, the closest city in the interior, we think their defences are pretty thin on the ground. Obviously they can't cover everything, though they do have an auxiliary defence force, the Home Guard, made up of old boys. Not very effective, in our opinion.'

'Thank you, *Herr Kapitanleutnant*,' Himmler said and continued himself.

'Because of that defence complex just to the south-west of the place where Comrade Hess is being held, we suppose that the English feel they are quite safe from attack from the sea. On the day they will find out that they are mistaken.' Himmler attempted to smile, but the attempt failed. His sallow, weak-chinned face, with its absurd wisp of a black moustache, was not meant for smiling! *'Reichsmarschall* Goering has promised the full support of the *Luftwaffe* fleets in Holland and France. Thus, on the night of the assault, his planes will attack targets ranging from Bristol to Ipswich.' He tapped the towns on the map with his pointer, obviously enjoying this military briefing. More than once he had pleaded with the Führer to allow him to have an active military command. After all he had over half a million SS troops nominally under his orders. But always the Führer had refused for some reason known only to himself. Now Himmler felt in his element, briefing these fighting men, few as they were.

He nodded to Hansen again and the latter responded promptly to his cue. 'At the same time as the air attacks go in,' he said, 'my flotilla will launch a feint at the Harwich defences with three boats. We know the position of their minefields and we'll sweep a channel free earlier on in the evening, then we'll go in and hopefully alert the whole area. With a bit of luck it will divert the Tommies from the real attack.'

Von Dodenburg nodded his understanding and flashed a quick look at von Skalka. But the Austrian seemed completely bored by the whole thing. He still stared out of the window at the antics of the seagulls.

'Now the actual assault itself,' Himmler went on, beaming at Hansen like a schoolmaster at a favourite pupil. He unrolled the big chart he had placed on the desk beside him and then pinned it to the map.

Von Dodenburg craned his head forward. It was a simple diagrammatic sketch of the coastline and hinterland of Little Saxton, with the defences of Felixstowe and Harwich marked in in red. Just off the coast there were several blue symbols he couldn't identify.

As if he could read the SS officer's mind, Himmler tapped the sketch-map and announced, 'Newarp, Smiths Knoll, Shipwash and Outer Gabbard, all light vessels and the only obstacle – save for a patrol boat of the English Navy – to our assaulting the shore without discovery. It is, therefore, here that *Kapitanleutnant* Hansen and his ships – '

'*Boats, Reichsführer,*' Hansen corrected him patiently, as if he were long used to landlubbers misnaming his craft.

'Thank you. *Boats* then. Well, as I was saying, *Kapitanleutnant* Hansen and his boats will, therefore, sail between Smiths Knoll, here, and Shipwash, here, while the aerial and naval diversion is taking place and will land your company, *Hauptsturmfuhrer*, before midnight on X-day.'

'Radar, sir?' von Dodenburg asked hurriedly, telling himself that it was surely not going to be as easy as that.

Hansen answered for Himmler. 'I'm sure we'll be picked up by their radar, Captain. But the Tommies won't pay too much attention to that. They are used to our craft operating in their waters, especially off Harwich. Besides, once the feint is over and they attempt to follow, they'll be in for a little surprise. Seaplanes are coming in from Kiel to drop mines. They'll run into a juicy new minefield that'll blow their bollocks off if they're not careful.'

Himmler frowned and then thought it better to attempt to smile. He had always hated strong or coarse language, but then, he told himself, these hardy fighting men were used to such talk.

'But what about the land forces?' von Dodenburg persisted. 'Will they be alerted, once we are picked up by radar?'

Again Hansen answered, ignoring Himmler. 'Do we alert the SS when we spot an English motor boat in the Channel?' he asked with a grin.

Von Dodenburg grinned back, taking an instinctive liking to the naval officer. 'No, of course not.'

'Well, I'm sure it's the same with the Tommies. Liaison between the various arms of the service will be no better than between ours, I'm sure.'

'Meine Herren.' Himmler cleared his throat testily and for the first time von Skalka seemed to take some notice of the proceedings. He tore his gaze from the window and whispered out of the side of his mouth, 'Take care, von Dodenburg, you're upstaging the old fart, you know, and he doesn't like it one bit.'

'Right then,' Himmler continued, 'the first task of your company, when it has been landed, von Dodenburg, is to capture and hold the high ground just behind the place, here.' He tapped his map again. 'As you can see the high ground dominates the two roads leading to Little Saxton, Aldeburgh and Snape.' He pronounced the English names with difficulty. 'They in their turn lead to the main highway between Lowestoft and Ipswich. By seizing that high ground, therefore, you will effectively seal off Little Saxton from the outside world.'

Von Dodenburg could see that someone at SS HQ had done some serious thinking. Not only would he cut the road network by seizing the high ground, but he would also have established himself in an excellent defensive position. His right flank would be on the sea while his left flank would be protected by what looked like the flood plain of the River Alde. On the map at least it seemed a fairly broad stretch of water that would be difficult to cross under fire.

His face must have shown his pleasure for Himmler said, 'Well thought-out, isn't it? Now, once you have taken the high ground to the west of the village, you will leave behind as many men as you think needed and assault the house that holds Comrade Hess itself, here.' He tapped the map once more. 'You can see it is fairly isolated, at the northern end of the village, fronting the water, about fifteen metres from the beach itself. Later I shall give you the latest aerial photos for more careful study. It is hoped that you will be able to overcome most of the sentries outside without the use of firearms. All your men will carry sidearms, trench knives, clubs, etc. for that specific purpose. *Klar?*'

'*Klar, Reichsführer,*' von Dodenburg answered promptly, though his mind was racing, trying to take in all these new facts and to assess the problems, which were mounting rapidly.

'The place in which they are holding Party Comrade Hess is, apparently, a rambling rabbit-warren affair and once trouble starts, it is more than likely that whoever is in charge will give the order to have Hess shot to prevent him from falling into our hands. That must not happen, naturally.'

Von Skalka barely prevented himself from giggling at the statement.

'It is therefore imperative that we reach the room in which Hess is imprisoned and free him as soon as possible. Once that has been achieved, you will signal the blocking party to withdraw from the high ground to the beach where you will be picked up, together with the *Reichsleiter*. All in all, it is estimated that from landing to being re-embarked, you will take some hundred and twenty minutes, two hours at the most.' He coughed, took off his pince-nez and rubbed it busily like a self-satisfied schoolmaster who had given his lesson and now expected his pupils to get on with it without any further trouble or attention.

'But sir,' von Dodenburg objected, rising to his feet, while Hansen looked down at his hands, which, unlike his face, were hard and reddened with the wind, as if suddenly embarrassed. 'I think that two-hour limit is unreasonable, if not unrealistic. There are several imponderables, most important of which is that the terrain is completely unknown to us. Yet we are expected to seize three objectives, possibly against opposition and successfully extradite Herr Hess in a mere one hundred and twenty minutes – and that in the blackout!' His face flushed angrily and he clenched his fists. *Kapitanleutnant* Hansen looked even more embarrassed. Outside it had begun to rain at last, the raindrops streaming down the big windows of the briefing room like cold tears.

Himmler gave the red-faced SS officer a wintry smile. 'But you have a guide already, an excellent one, who knows that part of England, er, intimately.'

'A guide?' began von Dodenburg, and then stopped short as he remembered what the Austrian had said to him the day before. Slowly he turned to look down at a cockily grinning von Skalka. *'You?'*

'Of course. Didn't I tell you I'd been to Cambridge in the thirties. Often visited those coastal places, including Little Saxton in the summer vacs. Plenty of tasty little English shop-girls there on day trips. Very glad they were of a piece of charming aristocratic salami – and a few shillings tip afterwards.' Knowingly he winked at the SS officer.

Himmler flushed slightly. He didn't like that kind of talk. But these aristocrats were always like that, a lecherous bunch. Besides, everyone knew there was something slightly decadent about the Austrians.

'But do you really know this Aldeburgh place, *Rittmeister*?' von Dodenburg demanded urgently. 'It is very important for me to know that I can rely on you one hundred per cent. My men's lives depend upon it.'

Von Skalka nodded casually. 'Oh yes, I know the place. Once spent a week there – in that very self-same hotel – with a nice shop-girl from Ipswich Woolworths. Most of it was in bed, but we did go for walks around the place – occasional ones.' He grinned again.

Von Dodenburg overlooked the cocky grin. Instead he said, 'You realize that it will be a combat situation. Somebody might well shoot at you, von Skalka – and shoot to kill!'

The Austrian remained unmoved. '"Let the boy try along the bayonet blade. How cold steel is and keen with the hunger of blood,"' he quoted mockingly. Then suddenly there was iron in his voice. 'I think I shall be able to cope, *Hauptsturmführer*,' he said and returned von Dodenburg's look with eyes that were as cold and as resolute as his own.

Von Dodenburg gave in and nodded to a waiting Himmler. 'We shall do it, sir,' he announced grimly.

Himmler beamed. '*Kolossal!*' he barked. '*Kolossal!* I knew my brave chaps of SS Assault Regiment Wotan would not fail me this time. And I can tell you already, von Dodenburg, that there is going to be a nice piece of tin in this one for you. If you pull it off successfully, you'll cure your throatache all right, this time.'

Von Dodenburg was unimpressed. Instead of simpering his thanks and gratitude, as Himmler undoubtedly expected him to, he snapped, 'How long have we got, *Reichsführer*?'

Himmler consulted his watch – as always he was very methodical – before answering. 'You have got exactly thirty-six hours until X-day. Wotan is familiar with assault landings, that's why you were picked. You have trained all year for the attack on England, so I feel thirty-six hours will be enough to brief yourselves more thoroughly, and then the men.' He reached for his cap, and the three of them sprang to attention. Firmly he placed it on his head and said, 'Gentlemen, your mission is of historic importance. Even to you I cannot explain just how vital it is that Party Comrade Hess be returned to the Reich.' Now it was Himmler's turn to stiffen to attention. He frowned and flipped up a limp soft hand in the 'German greeting'. 'Comrades, I salute you,' he barked in his best imitation of a Prussian parade ground voice.

'Who are about to die,' von Skalka whispered cheekily out of the side of his mouth.

And then the great man was gone.

Hansen grinned and relaxed. 'A royal pain in the ass, what, comrades?' he shot a sly look at von Dodenburg, as if he were testing the SS officer.

Von Dodenburg sat down in his chair and grinned. 'A right royal pain in the ass!' he agreed. 'And that man commands the destiny of the Armed SS!' He shook his blond, cropped head in disbelief.

'All right, comrades.' Hansen was very business-like now, Himmler forgotten. 'There's a lot of work to be done.'

'Agreed, Hansen,' von Dodenburg snapped. 'I'm going to need anti-tank and anti-personnel mines to hold that high ground. Then at least half a dozen cycles to get the men away from the height once the order for withdrawal is given . . . '

Von Skalka left them to it. *His* requirements had already been taken care of. Indeed, all he needed now hung at his belt. Let them talk and plan. His plans had already been made. Softly he walked to the streaming window and looked out at the green heaving sea.

Somewhere out there was England, a country he had not seen for years. Now he would return for one last time and then it would be all over – for good. He shivered suddenly. Von Skalka was a lonely man, without friends. The nature of his work demanded it. But suddenly, for no reason he could explain, he felt the need for company, to have people around him, talking about anything, even about the war, as long as they were talking next to him, exuding human warmth. He turned swiftly and broke into the conversation. 'I say, you two. There's a bar or something just down there – fifty metres to the right of this dull place. What about going down there for a short one?' He laughed a little too forcedly.

Hansen tugged his beard and said, 'Why not? A grog or two wouldn't be out of place on a day like this. What do you say, von Dodenburg?'

The latter picked up his cap, looking curiously at the Austrian *Rittmeister*. What had he seen out there through the window that had made him so friendly? This was the first time he had dropped his flippant, cynical, hands-off attitude. 'Sure, it's all right with me, as long as you're paying, von Skalka.'

'Of course, I'll pay,' von Skalka answered eagerly.

Together, heads bent against the beating rain, they descended to the wind-swept promenade, its length covered by rusting barbed wire and miserable, half-soaked naval sentries crouched in rough shelters at regular intervals, three young men who would soon be leading the most daring mission ever undertaken by the Greater German *Wehrmacht*. The actors were in place. The drama could commence.

Thursday, 15 May 1941

CHAPTER 1

The bitter rain of the previous day had ceased, but the wind had not dropped and the three soldiers walked along the sand-swept road with their hands on their caps to prevent them being blown away, the fat Home Guard major breathing hard.

There was an air of desolation about the village, Carruthers couldn't help thinking, though Little Saxton was substantial enough. But everything was shuttered up and had obviously been thus for some time. The paintwork was beginning to peel. Here and there broken gutters, long unrepaired, dripped mournfully, and the posters on the local cinema, advertising Anton Walbrook in the *Warsaw Concerto*, were peeling and flapping in the wind. Even the beach defences, constructed only the year before, had a definite air of neglect and decay about them, the bunkers slowly being submerged in drifting sand, the barbed wire half hidden by the new dunes and rusting. A dreary place, Carruthers told himself, a real arsehole of the world.

It seemed the fat Home Guard major, with his pepper-and-salt moustache and the florid complexion of a whisky drinker, thought the same. For he paused and pointed the swagger cane he affected at the nearest concrete pill-box. 'Just look at that, Major,' he cried, his refined bank manager's voice barely disguising the native Suffolk beneath. 'Absolutely useless if the balloon went up. Take my chaps half an hour to dig out the sand to get inside the damned place.'

Carruthers looked at CSM Douglas, but save for a slight twinkle in his eyes, his old sweat's face gave nothing away. 'Do you still think they'll come, Major Pettinger?' he inquired. 'The Germans, I mean.'

The bank manager turned part-time soldier stared up at the handsome Guards officer. 'Of course. I mean why are you here otherwise? A company of Grenadiers here, when they are presumably crying out for first-class fighting troops in the Middle East. Of course London must still be taking the threat of invasion seriously.'

'Of course, of course,' Carruthers agreed hastily. He didn't want to have the locals start thinking there was anything suspicious going on in Little Saxton. 'But what is it exactly that brought you down here this morning? I am sure you have your own civilian job to attend to, Major.'

'The old country comes before the bank,' Pettinger proclaimed pompously. 'There's a war on, you know. We've all got to make sacrifices. In fact, I've taken all this week off – part of my annual leave, as well – to prepare for this one. Thought, however, I'd come and discuss it with you before I gave my chaps the green light.'

'Green light for what?' Carruthers asked, as they continued walking again, with CSM Douglas keeping the regulation three paces behind the two officers, swinging his brass-shod pacing stick as if he were back at the depot drilling raw recruits.

'An exercise,' Pettinger puffed. 'The chaps are getting slack, not to say bolshy. It was all right back in 1940. All that fight 'em on the beaches stuff. But that was a year ago. Far too much absenteeism and slacking. Typical working class. All they want now is to make exceedingly good money for doing little in the new war factories and then get their idle feet up at night, sloshing tea and listening to that damn fool *ITMA* programme on the wireless. My God, sometimes I pity poor Mr Churchill having to fight a war with a shower like this!' He sighed, obviously a sorely tried man.

For once CSM Douglas allowed himself a mild grin. Typical civvie, he told himself, always crying bleeding stinking fish.

'Exactly,' Carruthers tried to appease the irate little bank manager, whose face was flushing a dangerous scarlet. 'But what form is this exercise of yours going to take, Major Pettinger?'

Pettinger lowered his voice. 'I'm going to spring a surprise alert on them tonight, just after they've paraded. They'll all be ready for heading for the local public houses in Ipswich, once the parade is over. You know some of them get as much as five pounds a week these days! So they'll be expecting to waste their money on ale. It's Thursday night, you see, around these parts the men are paid on Thursdays – and that kind of improvident person is easily parted from his wages.' He smiled a little maliciously. 'I'm afraid this Thursday night they're going to be in for an unwelcome surprise.'

'I see,' Carruthers said, though he didn't really see what Major Pettinger's plans for his long-suffering company had to do with him. But he was a patient man, brought up to listen politely to the complaints and problems of less fortunate creatures than himself. So he asked, 'And how exactly will this exercise affect us, Major?'

Pettinger stopped, obviously out of breath again, and pointed to the dull wriggling snake of the River Alde to his right. 'Back in 1940, when everyone took the threat of invasion seriously, we always used the Alde as our defensive line – the whole battalion, I mean. With our left flank on the A12 running down to Ipswich and our centre and right flank dug in along the far bank of the river as far as Orford.'

'As a line of defence protecting Ipswich presumably,' Carruthers interrupted. He was not going to take a lecture on infantry tactics from this fat, pompous part-time soldier.

'Why, yes, hm, of course,' the Major said, looking a little flustered at the interruption. Nobody ever dared to interrupt at the bank, it would be as much as their job was worth. 'So my chaps will think when I pull the alert on them that it's the nice old comfy romp. By truck to Orford and then into the positions – trenches, pill-boxes and the like – that we prepared last year. All very cushy.' Again he smiled maliciously and at his side an attentive CSM Douglas thought, I wouldn't like to try and get a five-quid loan from yon bugger. Christ, wouldn't he just make a bloke squirm!

'But tonight they're going to be in for a very unpleasant

surprise,' Pettinger continued. 'I'm going to change the usual drill entirely.' He swung round and pointed to the tree-covered rise some half a mile to their rear. 'You see that height, Major?'

Carruthers nodded warily, wondering when the point would be made. He was getting cold and could do with a nice stiff drink.

'To my way of thinking that would be an ideal defensive position if the Hun ever did land on our beaches around here. From it you can cover the whole of Little Saxton and the length of the beach, too. A couple of good machine-gunners well located and you could hold up a whole German army.'

Carruthers thought of the May morning when the German tanks had started rumbling down the dead-straight road into Louvain and the tracer from the Bren had bounced ineffectually off their thick metal hides like glowing ping-pong balls. What did the bank manager know of the might of the German Army, he and his 'couple of good machine-gunners'? That day the battalion had lost half its effectives. Very quietly, he said, 'I see, Major Pettinger. You just wanted to warn us that you are going to run the exercise tonight?'

'Exactly. I'd dearly love to use ball, but the men are too careless. There could be accidents, and, of course, there would be questions.' He sighed. 'Can't anyone in this country ever realize this is total war? You can't make an omelette without breaking eggs. No matter, my chaps will use blanks tonight, so there'll be a bit of noise.'

Carruthers looked at CSM Douglas. The latter pretended to be studying the sky. He grinned and said, 'What about a drink, Major, before you go back to Ipswich.'

Major Pettinger looked shocked. He pulled out his silver pocket-watch, stared at it, and exclaimed, 'But it is only ten-thirty in the morning!'

Carruthers said nothing. During the long retreat from Belgium they had been drunk most of the time, the men on

Belgian beer, the officers on champagne. Christ Almighty, the mornings they had shaved in champagne! Drunk they might have been mostly, but clean-shaven they had been all the time. After all they were Guardsmen.

'Shall I escort the Major back to the fifteen hundred-weight, sir?' CSM Douglas barked, killing the silence.

Carruthers sighed to himself. Old Douglas was like a bloody old mother hen. He knew the CO was pissed off at this civilian pip-squeak. He wanted to avoid any trouble; he was mothering him again. 'Yes,' he heard himself say. 'If the Major will excuse me, I do have my duties to attend to.'

'Of course, of course,' Pettinger said, 'I understand.' He acknowledged Carruthers' casual salute with a tremendous one of his own, his brown-gloved hand quivering with the effort as he brought it up to his peaked cap. 'Don't be surprised if you hear a bit of firing tonight, then, will you?'

'No, I won't be surprised, Major,' Carruthers answered a little wearily.

As CSM Douglas marched the Home Guard officer smartly towards his waiting Bedford fifteen-hundredweight truck, Carruthers slowly started to walk back through the deserted, forlorn, dripping village towards the prison. Since his attempt at suicide, Hess had become quieter, as if he were resigned to the fact that he was going to be a prisoner for the rest of the war. The MO had told him privately that Hess lived in a state of 'complete hallucination', to which he had replied, 'As long as he is quiet with it, I don't give a tinker's curse if he thinks he's Bonaparte!'

But the fact that Hess had settled down could well mean that he and his King's Company would be stuck out here in this arsehole of the world for the duration of the war.

Carruthers frowned and aimed a half-hearted kick at a rusty can in the gutter. It was nearly a year now since what had been left of the King's Company, virtually everyone of them wounded, had been taken off the beaches by an ancient paddle-wheel steamer from Folkestone. Behind them they had left a burning Dunkirk to the looters, drunks, and defeatists, who had already thrown away their weapons and were just waiting for the Germans to pick them up and put them behind barbed wire for the rest of the war.

But that long killing, fighting retreat seemed to have taken something out of the survivors. Of course, they were smart as ever, their brasses gleaming, creases razor-sharp, blancoed equipment immaculate. They were obedient and loyal enough, too. But somehow he suspected the old spirit had gone from his veterans. The old sweats didn't mix with the nineteen-year-old replacements. In the evenings they sat by themselves in the wet canteen, nursing their pints, talking softly among themselves or more often than not simply sitting, not listening to the radio, staring at nothing.

More than once he had mentioned the fact to Douglas, the old mother hen. 'They haven't gone bolshy on us, Sar'nt-Major, have they? They seem as willing as ever, but somehow they're not the same men we took with us to France in 1939.'

Invariably Douglas would appease him, replying, 'Don't you worry about the lads, sir. They're just taking a bit o' time to recover, that's all, sir. Most of 'em thought they was knackered over there – had it. Takes some time to get over it.' And he would give one of his tight-lipped grins, trying to cheer up his worried CO. 'Don't you worry yer head, sir, the lads'll be all right on the day.'

Carruthers stopped and pretended to be looking at one of the half-submerged pill-boxes on the dreary damp beach, while beyond the grey-green waves tossed and dropped violently. But when would that day be? he asked himself. Were they going to be condemned to stay here for the duration, guarding the crazy German and polishing their damned brasses? What kind of life was that for a fighting guardsman?

Major Carruthers MC need not have worried. Before this weekend was over, half his King's Company would be dead and the other half would be heading for postings that would take them as reinforcements to the furthest outposts of Empire. None of them would ever come back. No one was to know what had taken place in this remote Suffolk coastal village on 16/17 May 1941 . . .

CHAPTER 2

'*Nothing!*' Matz declared miserably, wizened face red with the sea-wind. 'Not one solitary piece of gash in sight.' He dropped miserably into the chair next to Schulze, who had his big yellow feet propped up on the table and was cleaning the nails with the point of his bayonet. 'I've bin all way down the prom – frigging kilometres I've marched this morning, I tell yer, Schulzi – and the only bit o' female gash I clapped my glassy orbits on was two frigging seagulls going at it on the rail.'

'But there must be some tail around, with all them sailors and staff and the like? Look at me,' he indicated his big feet, 'I'm going to all that trouble to make myself look nice for some honest woman,' he simpered in what he took to be a very seductive, feminine manner.

Matz ignored him. Instead he reached inside his tunic and pulled out his precious flatman. He took a hearty swig, apparently not hearing his running mate's sudden murmurs of protest that he was being left out. He pocketed the bottle and said bitterly, 'Of course, the frigging boys in blue have got their gash – at least frigging officers and gentlemen of the staff have.' Outside the wind buffeted the windows of their sea-front billet and made them rattle noisily.

With a clatter Schulze dropped his bayonet. 'What did you say, arse with ears. Come on, you piss-pansy, out with it!'

'Aw, go and piss in the wind!' Matz said morosely. All the same he repeated what he had just said, while outside a small convoy of camouflaged trucks drew up on the mole next to the anchored E-boats rocking in the choppy sea. They'd be bringing up supplies for the mysterious operation upon which the Wotan would soon be embarking.

'So there *is* gash here after all,' Schulze whistled softly.

'Yer,' Matz admitted miserably, 'fancy pavement pounders in frilly silk knickers with nasty sex habits specially imported

from Brussels to keep them naval rear echelon stallions happy
– and we all know sailors are all warm brothers!' He spat on
the floor. 'The sentry on the door told me that they were
inside, though I didn't see 'em myself. If I had, it might at
least have inspired me to go and visit the old five-fingered
widow.' He made an explicit gesture with his right hand, but
Schulze could see his heart wasn't in it.

'A sentry?' he echoed, eyes narrowing to slits.

'Yer, what else? They need a sentry with us lot here. Randy
lot o' buggers, the sentry said we was. Screw anything with
hair on, so they've hidden the brooms.' Matz's face contorted
angrily. 'Thought that was funny, he did, the boy in blue. I
told him what to do with his frigging rifle and that quietened
him down, the bugger, risking a thick lip with me like that.'
He sniffed.

Outside a bunch of the green-beaks were now watching the
trucks being unloaded, talking in a hectic, over-excited sort of
way, as the crates of ammunition began to be carried down to
the sleek, rakish motor torpedo boats. Cynically Schulze told
himself the innocents were going through the usual phases
prior to their first taste of combat: a lot of idle chat, too many
lung torpedoes, half-smoked to be tossed away and another
one lit almost immediately, and then they'd be falling out to
take a piss every few minutes as the tension mounted. Yer,
he'd seen it all before. Then he forgot the green-beaks and
concentrated on the whores. 'Where is this officers' knocking
shop, Matzi?' he inquired with deceptive casualness.

'At the far end of the prom, next to the town hall, or
whatever it is, where the rear echelon stallions have their
Kasino. Fill their guts full of oysters and caviar, and all that
fishy muck that officers eat, and then they're right over there
for a bit of the other. Don't yer love me or is that a revolver
you've got in yer frigging pocket, general? *Officers*, I've shat
'em!'

'And where's the gash?' Schulze persisted. 'Upstairs or
downstairs?'

'Upstairs. All fancy red lights and that kind of crap, so the boy in blue on the door said. Said that if the officers wanted they could have two o' the pavement pounders at one go. Just like you with the twins.'

Schulze swallowed hard at the thought and snarled, 'Knock it off, willya. Don't frigging well remind me.' He flashed a glance at his watch. It was nearly midday. Soon the officers would be leaving their offices for the noon meal. Perhaps some of them might be inclined to take a nooner, but that would be after they had fed their faces, he was sure of that. With a bit of luck, they'd have a full hour before one of the officers decided he'd like to get his leg over and dance the mattress polka.

Schulze bit his bottom lip in suppressed excitement. The very thought of the cunning Brussels whores in their frilly silk knickers made his heart beat faster. Soon other portions of his massive anatomy would be getting out of control if he didn't watch it. He rose gingerly, as if he were afraid he might well knock something off the table top, and reached for a foot-rag.

Matz looked at him suspiciously. 'Where you off to, you big horned-ox?' he growled. 'The hash-slingers won't have got the fodder ready yet. Besides it's only the same old fart soup and a slice of burned old man.' He meant tinned meat, which the Wotan troopers suspected was made out of dead old men collected from Berlin's many workhouses.

'Hold yer water, you perverted banana-sucker!' Schulze commanded roughly. 'Can't hear mesen frigging well think with you rabbiting on like that all the time.' With practised ease he began to fold the foot-rag about his big yellow foot: first the two flaps above the instep, then the third over the toes and finally the fourth end up and about the ankle. 'The foot-rag squadron marches again!' he announced proudly and picked up the other one, preparing to do the same with it.

'And where, pray, is the frigging foot-rag squadron going to be marching off now?' Matz asked sulkily.

Schulze paused momentarily and looked at him as if he were seeing his comrade for the very first time. 'Sometimes, yer know, I think you ain't got 'em all up here – yer know real old funny farm material. Where the frig do you think I'm going?'

'Well, frigging well tell me!' Matz almost exploded.

'GASH!' Schulze cried uproariously. 'We're going to knock off a piece of that gash you've been talking about. Or do you want to stay behind with the old five-fingered widow in the crapper?'

Matz sprang to his feet, face flushing with excitement. 'Not on yer life, Schulzi. If you say we're gonna get some, I'm with you. Here, comrade, knock that one behind yer wing-collar.' He pulled out his flatman and handed it generously to Schulze.

Schulze crossed himself, raised his eyes to heaven, cried, 'Will frigging wonders ever cease?' pulled the cork out of the bottle with his teeth and took a tremendous slug at the fiery gin. He flung the empty bottle to one side and yelled, 'Sling me my dice-beakers.'

Obligingly Matz flung him his two jackboots. He tugged them on and then they were off, linked arm in arm, laughing uproariously like two crazy men, while the gulls whirled and shrieked above their heads in the breeze.

Standing at the long window in the second floor, von Dodenburg watched them go, staggering about, scattering the sailors in their path, as if they were both drunk, and wondered what his two tame rogues were up to this time. To no good, he guessed. He shrugged and told himself that they had every right to enjoy themselves. Time was running out. At fourteen hours precisely, when the men had eaten, he would fall in the company and brief them on what was to come.

Captain von Dodenburg was a bold, daring man, but he was also a methodical one. He did not subscribe to the average young SS officer's belief that boldness and audacity alone paid dividends. He liked to plan his operations carefully, to work out every possibility, ensure that there were no loose ends, if possible. It was the way, in his opinion, to cut down casualties. 'Train hard, fight easy,' was his motto.

Now, however, everything was being done at a rush. The planners in Berlin had obviously dreamed this one in a great hurry. To his way of thinking there were still far too many imponderables, even though he had now the help of an excellent naval team under Hansen and von Skalka to guide him.

Von Dodenburg frowned and walked thoughtfully back to the big table upon which were spread the latest aerial photographs of the English coast. The shore defences around the objective were obviously poor. Sand had drifted across them and there was clear evidence – neat lines of footprints across the wet sand – that the minefield, if there was one there in the first place, was ineffective. But the long sprawl of the ex-hotel at the northernmost end of the village where they were holding Hess revealed nothing, save for a few sandbagged positions that had not been there on the previous photos. 'Damn it,' he cursed to himself, 'you might think the damn Tommies are just aching to get rid of him!'

But if the beach defences were inadequate and the minefield not functioning, the Navy still had not been able to ascertain the depth of water on the midnight tide off Little Saxton. Would his men be jumping out up to their necks in water, heavily laden as they would be, or would they just be tiptoeing through mere wavelets? Surprisingly enough no one seemed able to tell him.

Then there was the question of rubber dinghies. At this very moment, Hansen was signalling every single naval station from Texel to Brest in a frantic attempt to get enough boats for his one hundred and twenty troopers. It was unbelievable. But none of the rear echelon stallions had thought of providing the dinghies in advance. Von Dodenburg shook his head in sheer disbelief. He couldn't have believed that the *Kriegsmarine*'s staff work would be that bad!

The door opened. It was von Skalka, his elegant greatcoat stiff and white with sea salt. He saw von Dodenburg peering at the photos, surrounded by odd bits and pieces of equipment and declaimed, ' "Now thrive the armourers, and

honour's thought reign solely in the breast of every man."'
He grinned and taking off his cap, flipped it neatly on to the
hatstand. 'Shakespeare as translated by Tieck. Think I could
do a better job myself though.'

Von Dodenburg ignored Shakespeare and Tieck, whoever
he was. Instead he snapped, 'What's the situation with the
equipment, *Rittmeister*?'

'All loaded, including a batch of the latest S-mines.
Wooden cases and glass container. Top secret and apparently
can't be picked up by a conventional mine detector.'

'Let's hope that we're not around long enough for them to
start picking 'em up in our presence,' von Dodenburg
commented swiftly. 'The boats, Hansen's boats, you've had a
look at them. What are they like?'

'Fast and furious, forty knots at least, armed with
torpedoes, twin twenty-millimetre cannon and a thirty-seven
millimetre' – he grinned – 'at the pointed end.'

'*At the pointed end.* Ha, ha, very funny!' Von Dodenburg
laughed hollowly. 'They're sending three craft with us, aren't
they?'

Von Skalka nodded. 'Two to carry the company, one as a
general escort.'

'So, that gives us quite some fire power, just in case we run
into trouble when we re-embark. That could be one devil of a
situation. Troops in the water under fire. Sitting ducks.'

Von Skalka looked at the SS officer, sensing for the first
time during this whole business a feeling of apprehension
bordering on fear. Now he had made up his mind, he wanted
nothing to go wrong with his personal plan. 'Do you think
something like that could happen, *Hauptsturm*?' he asked
quickly.

Von Dodenburg shrugged, in a way a little glad that he
had got some sort of reaction from the *Rittmeister*, for he had
noted the look of sudden fear on the latter's face. 'Anything –
everything's possible in an operation like this. A handful of
men landing on the enemy coast.' He dismissed the matter.
'The essence of success is to get in there quick, do our job, and

get out even quicker before the balloon really goes up. I mean the English hunters will be out in full force, chasing us home once they realize what has happened at Little Saxton. That's why I want you at my side, giving me your knowledge of the terrain at all times. Is that clear?'

'Absolutely clear, *Hauptsturm*,' von Skalka answered promptly and this time the usual bantering, cynical note was gone from the Austrian's voice.

Von Dodenburg looked at his face in the big mirror on the wall for an instant. What had suddenly got into the man he didn't know, but he *did* know that von Skalka was more than just a guide who had been picked because he had studied in England back in the thirties; there was more to him than that. But for the life of him he couldn't figure out what it was. Then he dismissed the matter and got on with the planning for the coming raid.

CHAPTER 3

'Parade. Parade, shun!' Colour-Sergeant Higgins, very grey and sporting the small ribbons of both the Great War and the Boer War, did his best though his voice was decidedly shaky now. It was a good twenty years since he'd left the old Suffolks.

'Thank you, Colour-Sergeant,' Major Pettinger announced, cane set rigidly under his right arm. 'I'll inspect the men now.'

'Very well, sir,' Higgins swung him a wavering salute and backed off three paces to let the Major face the company.

They were drawn up in the old church hall that served as Home Guard HQ, local WVS HQ and a Sunday school. Around the hall ran friezes of posters for the WVS, War Department posters explaining the innards of Vickers machine-guns and Stokes mortars, plus a brightly crayoned childish picture of an idealized Christ, bearing the legend in yellow and green crayon, 'Jesus Loves You'. As Pettinger eyed his command of middle-aged warriors, he thought it hardly likely that the Saviour loved this particular bunch of misfits. He sighed and to the tune of 'Run Rabbit Run', which was coming from next door where the vicar was trying out his records for tomorrow night's forces' dance, he began to inspect his command.

He did it systematically, taking his time with each man as though conducting a bank interview for a loan, sizing up the applicant before, mostly, turning him down. He eyed the guardsman's badge first to see if it were polished, then the chin to check whether he had shaved before the parade. After that came the collar – were the twin hooks fastened? After that it was the buttons of the tunic pockets, the belt – had the brasses been polished and the belt itself blancoed? Finally came the boots. They were very important to his way of thinking. A soldier who was shaved and had his boots polished was one hundred per cent more efficient than one who hadn't.

But this afternoon the turn-out was virtually perfect. Even 'Dirty' Jones, the illiterate Welsh stall-holder, who was renowed throughout the company for his filthy turn-out was decent. He was even wearing his false teeth, which he usually kept in a grubby handkerchief in his pocket. 'Allus wear me teeth for the Thursday night piss-up, sir, pardon my French!' And he knew why. As soon as the parade and the usual drill were over, they'd be off, still in their uniforms, straight into the Black Swan, or the Mucky Duck, as they invariably called it. He gave the back of the men's heads under their forage caps a careful scrutiny, but their necks were neatly shaven too, and barked, 'Stand the men at ease, Colour-Sergeant!'

Higgins bellowed out his commands, 'Stand *at ease*. Stand easy!' and there was a shuffling of booted feet, with, invariably, 'Dirty' Jones breaking wind loudly. Pettinger sighed like a man sorely tried. But there was nothing he could do about it. He couldn't even charge 'Dirty' Jones for 'dumb insolence', the standard catch-all. Regulations wouldn't allow him to punish a man for carrying out his 'natural functions', however disgusting.

Pettinger slapped his gloved palm with his swagger cane and eyed his men. Next door, the vicar had now launched into a 'Happidrome' recording of the 'Hokey-Cokey'. *'You put your left foot in... shake it all about...'* He ignored the silly text and told them, 'Tonight after I've dismissed you for an hour to get your supper, we're going out on a surprise exercise. Battalion HQ has agreed to provide lorries...'

From the rear rank there came muttered groans of dismay and all their faces showed disappointment. Even Colour-Sergeant Higgins, loyal as he was, looked a bit downcast.

Pettinger overlooked it. 'We've all got to make sacrifices, men,' he said. 'I, personally, for example, have given up a week's leave and at my own expense have planned tonight's exercise. I know most of you chaps want to be off to the pub tonight, it being Thursday. But you'll just have to forego that pleasure this particular Thursday night. Now when Colour-Sergeant Higgins stands you down, I want you to hurry off home to have your supper.' He flashed a self-important glance at his watch, as if he were about to order them to go over the top in a film about the Old War, and barked, 'I expect you all back at twenty hundred hours precisely.' He looked at them warningly. 'And let there be no absentees, or I shall be compelled to report to the local police, and you all know what that will mean?' He nodded to Higgins.

Loyally the Colour-Sergeant sprang to attention and yelled, '*Tshun!* Officer on parade ... dis-*MISS*!'

As Higgins raised his hand to his cap, the rest turned dispiritedly to their right, slapped their hands against the butts of their rifles in salute and broke up, hurrying to the door, slinging their rifles as they did so.

Pettinger watched them go, noting their haste and telling himself he knew the reason for it. Most of them would take their 'supper' in liquid form at the Mucky Duck, wasting their weekly pay packets as usual. He sighed and forgot the men. He sat down, loosened his collar slightly, and then, checking that no one had lingered in the shadows near the blacked-out door, he pulled out the small silver flask of whisky. Furtively he took a tiny sip and hid the flask again, savouring the warm glow that began to spread through his body. It was his only vice. He closed his eyes for a moment, a fat middle-aged bank manager who dreamed of glory as a warrior on the battlefields, pompous, narrow-minded, absurd – and sad.

Even in 1941 there were plenty who made fun of men like Algernon Pettinger. They had never heard a shot fired in anger in their whole lives, but they took the greatest pleasure strutting around in their new officer uniforms, trying to look more regular than the regulars. 'Bullshit baffles brains,' the regulars would sneer. 'Will you just get a gander at his nibs. Christ, if it moves, salute it. If it don't, paint it white!'

Now forty-one-year-old Pettinger dozed a little in his

chair, plump hands clasped around his even plumper stomach. For a year he had devoted all his energy and spare time to the Home Guard, with no brass bands, no pay, no medals, no glory. Absurd he might be, but there was a little touch of nobility about his devotion. One wonders what he dreamed of on this last night of his life on earth?

CHAPTER 4

'Where in three devils' name have the two rogues got to?' von Dodenburg raged, as he stood the parade down and his men drifted down the wave-lashed, dripping mole, chatting excitedly with one another now they knew what their mission was to be.

Hansen tugged his beard. 'I could send out the shore patrol to look for them.' He indicated the heavily armed naval sentries, guarding the E-boats.

'Thank you, *Herr Kapitanleutnant*,' a worried von Dodenburg answered, 'but I want to deal with the two of them myself. And, by God, when I do catch them, they'll be for the damned high jump.'

Hansen touched his big hand to the battered salt-encrusted brim of his cap. 'We run out eighteen hundred then, *Hauptsturm*.'

'I'll remember,' von Dodenburg answered, returning the salute. 'Never fear we'll *all* be there.' He took another look at the lean rakish E-boats, their crew busy ripping the tarpaulins off the guns, stowing fresh depth charges and what he presumed were reserve cans of fuel on the decks. Up on the bridge of Hansen's own craft, chatting with one of the young E-boat officers, was von Skalka. He had changed. The elegant cavalryman's uniform had gone to be replaced by the camouflaged overalls and helmet of the SS, which made him look just as tough and aggressively military as the rest of the Wotan troopers. But von Dodenburg noted he had kept his own weapon – the big clumsy Luger in its wooden holster. He wondered why. A Schmeisser would have been much more effective for the kind of close-quarter fighting they might be involved in if anything went wrong. Then he dismissed von Skalka from his mind and strode down the mole back to the promenade. Time was running out and he had to find his two rogues before they got themselves into serious trouble. If they missed this mission, the Vulture would have no mercy on them. He'd court-martial both Schulze and Matz on a charge of 'desertion in the face of the enemy while on active service', and there could be only one outcome if that particular charge was proved against them – *death by firing squad!*

Sergeant Schulze and Corporal Matz were, unknown to a worried von Dodenburg now making his way down the long promenade, peering into doorways and windows, looking for his missing men, already in trouble, serious trouble.

At first everything had worked like a charm. Boldly Schulze, (wearing von Dodenburg's overcoat, which he had 'borrowed') had marched up to the youthful naval sentry outside the staff brothel, followed by an apprehensive Matz. 'Well,' he had barked in his best imitation of a Prussian officer, all SS arrogance and contempt, 'is that the way the boys in blue present arms when they spot an SS officer! Great crap on the Christmas Tree, man, hold that rifle straight now, or I'll see my corporal here makes a complete sow of you! Now out of my way, I've only got half an hour and the dirty water is about up to my neck already. Come on, Corporal. *Dalli, dalli ...* '

Trembling at every limb, the ashen-faced sailor had let them through without even a murmur. The helmet, the greatcoat, the pistol belt had come off like a flash and then Schulze towered over the squealing excited whores, most of them in various states of undress, crying, 'I'm in love! I'm in love! Who's gonna be first for the old SS salami?' He had grabbed his bulging crotch dramatically.

'*SS salami, SS salami,*' the whores had tittered and giggled. '*Oh, la la! Quel drôle!*'

In truth, the whores, used to the quicker trade of the young infantry officers they had been accustomed to servicing in Brussels, were sick of these older staff officers and their special 'needs' to restore their flagging libidos. Zeebrugge bored them, too, after the shops and excitement of the capital. Besides, staff officers, with their need for sex once a week, were proving not very profitable, and all of them lusted after that nice little nest-egg that would one day buy respectability and a solid middle-class husband in some provincial town. They welcomed the two bold young men in their dashing SS uniforms with open arms. At least they were good for a laugh. That had been at the beginning.

But neither the two running mates, nor the happy whores, had reckoned with the important visitor who had suddenly descended upon them, 'Just as I was getting into my frigging stroke!' as Schulze would complain bitterly afterwards. 'Slapping it into her at a nice steady thirty strokes a minute, I was, rattling her bones right smartish – *and she was enjoying it*!'

Hardly had the elegant aide thrust open the door to the second-floor brothel imperiously and bellowed, as if he were on the parade ground, *'Der Herr Admiral lässt bitten!'* than the place had abruptly filled with officers, and in their midst was no less a person than *Herr Admiral* Dietrich von und zu Halbach, Chief of Operations, North Sea; and by the look in the eyes of the big, bearded admiral, he had other operations in mind than playing with a rubber duck in his bath.

That had been just before one. Now, virtually naked, save for their 'dice-beakers' (as old hares Matz and Schulze had grabbed instinctively for their boots as the door had been flung open and one of the whores had screamed, *'Out, out, they're taking over the whole place!'*) the two comrades, loins still aching from unrequited love, crouched on a narrow ledge outside the whores' bedrooms, listening to the popping of corks, hearty male laughter, the clink of glasses, and the urgent squeak of bedsprings from inside, while all the while a stiff breeze whistled about their bare buttocks straight from the heaving North Sea.

Below them lay a sheer drop of thirty feet and even if they had been prepared to risk it, the street beneath was packed with important-looking staff cars surrounded by petty officers and chauffeurs smoking idly and waiting for their masters to depart. As Schulze whispered mournfully to Matz, his extremities slowly turning blue in the biting east wind, 'This time, they've really got us with our hooters in the shit. If we go in, the Admiral'll have us strung up at the yardarm – whatever the fuck that is. If we don't, and the Vulture catches us missing them E-boats tonight, he'll saw the arse off'n us *toot-sweet*. Great buckets of flying hot crap, what a mess!'

But there was worse to come. About an hour or so after they had commenced their vigil, the door of the room Matz had vacated so hurriedly was flung open and the room filled with naked, drunken girls, giggling and falling all over the place as they swung their champagne glasses, bearing in their midst Admiral Dietrich von und zu Halbach, stark naked like themselves, save for his ceremonial sword attached to the white-and-gold belt girded around his mighty paunch.

Schulze nearly fell off the ledge and ducked down hastily. 'Matzi,' he croaked, 'do you see what I frigging well see – *the Admiral*! They're bringing in the Admiral for a bit of the other.'

Matz, chattering now with the cold, nose red and dripping, quavered, 'He only need look out of the window and we're sunk, sunk to the bottom of the frigging ocean.' He gulped hard and looked down as if tempted to jump and get it over with. 'Heaven, arse and cloudburst, Schulzi, what are we gonna do?'

'How should I shitting know? D'yer think I'm Jesus Christ, man?'

From inside there came the creak of protesting springs as the massive Admiral presumably collapsed on the bed, and the giggling and simpering of the drunken whores. The two friends racked their brains for a way out of the mess they found themselves in. 'Only three ladies, only three at a time, *please*. I am not as young as used to be, *mesdames*. Ha, ha,' the Admiral chortled hugely as the whores proceeded to work upon him. 'That's the way. You are real snake charmers. Look, look, the snake's beginning to rise and perform! Ah, my dear, what cunning little tricks you foreign ladies know. You're earning the heartfelt thanks of an old sea dog.'

'Aw, go and put yer dog in a wringer,' Schulze snorted. 'Why – ' he stopped short suddenly, a new note of hope in his voice. 'Matzi,' he hissed, 'look down there on the other side of the prom!'

Matz whistled. 'It's the CO. It's Captain von Dodenburg,' he whispered in the very same moment that the latter looked up and caught sight of the two of them crouching naked on the ledge, thirty feet above the ground.

Von Dodenburg's mouth dropped open stupidly and for one long moment he could only gape, hardly able to believe the evidence of his own eyes. Then he understood in a flash. The two of them had been up to their usual bedroom tricks and had been literally caught, as they would have put it, with their knickers around their ankles. Now they were in trouble. For reasons known only to the two rogues they dare not venture back into the house.

Von Dodenburg acted decisively. His gaze took in the circular canvas static water tank, standing ready to be used in case enemy incendiaries caused a blaze on the promenade; then the chauffeurs and sailors hanging about the line of gleaming staff cars.

'You sailors over there,' he barked arrogantly. 'Out with those cigarettes and over here – at the double now!'

The reputation of the Armed SS was such that the twenty or so sailors and drivers stubbed out their cigarettes immediately and doubled over to where von Dodenburg stood, legs astride, hands on hips, the picture of SS arrogance. He looked down at them disdainfully and then snapped, 'All right, ten of you on this side of the tank, ten on that side. When I give the command, I want you to lift. Then we're going to take it over to the other side of the road.'

A burly petty officer, an old hare to judge by the medals on his brawny chest ventured 'And for why, sir, if I may be so bold as to ask?'

'You may be so bold, *Obermaat*,' he replied loftily. 'Because I'm about to rescue those two rogues up there.' He pointed.

All eyes followed the direction of his pointed finger and

then the sailors burst out into wild laughter as they saw the naked men crouching on the narrow ledge. The brawny petty officer slapped his thigh in delight and chortled, 'Well, I'll go and piss in the wind! Did you ever see the frigging like. A couple o' stubble-hoppers without their drawers on. Hey, you the big one,' he called to a red-faced Schulze, 'How cold is it up there, mate. This long . . . or this long?' He narrowed the gap between his fingers to almost nothing and bellowed at his own supposed humour, while Schulze fumed with impotent rage.

'All right, enough of that!' von Dodenburg snapped. 'Let's get on the stick. Get a hold. Now *lift*!'

Five minutes later the red-faced sailors had dragged the heavy canvas water tank to a spot directly beneath the two trapped men. Von Dodenburg didn't give them a chance to hesitate. Cupping his hands to his mouth, while all around him the delighted sailors grinned and jeered, he commanded, 'On a count of three, Sergeant Schulze, I want you to jump first. Then as soon as he's out of the tank, Matz, I'll give another count of three and then it's your turn. Now then, I shall begin counting. *One . . . two . . .*'

Up on the ledge, Schulze gulped hard and cried back, 'Watch my eggs down there. They're very delicate and I don't – '

'*Three!*'

Schulze closed his eyes and, holding his testicles in his big paw, he jumped.

CHAPTER 5

'Understandably they're all emotionally disturbed to a greater or lesser degree,' Dr Levy-Keyser said, as he steered his black Ford Popular down Chapeltown's main street, lined with shabby, run-down Victorian houses. 'They've been turfed out of their homes in Europe and transplanted here in an alien environment.' Neatly he avoided one of the grubby, clanking trams heading for Leeds' city centre, 'They've been dumped here in Leeds and Manchester and the like and it's been a hard blow for them, a very hard one indeed.'

'I'm sure,' C mumbled, telling himself that judging by the way his companion pronounced his 'v's', this was not his native sod either. He wondered if the sharp-faced little doctor in his neat blue pinstripe had been interned himself back in 1940 when Churchill had growled angrily, 'Collar the lot!' and had sent Jews and Nazis, anyone of German origin, packing to the internment camps in the Isle of Man.

'The tailors and the small businessmen have taken it best. They find jobs and get on with it, learning English and English ways as they go along. It's the more intellectual classes who find it most difficult – doctors, artists, writers, and the like.' He smiled at C in the driving mirror, showing his gold teeth.

Flash, C told himself, but then most of the Jews he knew, even those who had been in England for generations and had married into the upper classes, were flash in one way or another.

'A very high rate of suicide among them, especially the German ones. Not only have they lost their country – German Jews were the most assimilated of all of European Jewry – but they have lost their language, too, the writers and journalists, I mean.' He shrugged in what C thought was an un-English way. 'I mean, they can hardly write for the German or Austrian reading public, can they?'

'I suppose not,' C said without interest. He wished he could have let Dansey, or Winterbotham, or one of his other deputies come up here to do this job. He hated the north, although the family fortune had been founded in the Hull shipping business. He only ever came up this grubby depressing region for the shooting. But Churchill had insisted he should carry out the task personally. It was an 'eyes only' job. 'Is it much further, doctor?' he asked, wishing the latter would stop chattering. What concern of his were a lot of crazy continental Jews?

'Not much further, General,' Dr Levy-Keyser said cheerfully, pretending not to see the scrawled notice on the wall opposite. '*You are now entering Little Palestine. Non-Jews Keep Out!*' Anti-semitism was very strong in working-class Leeds. 'As I was saying,' he continued, while C closed his eyes wearily, 'many of these intellectuals can't stand the alienation and the stress. As we say in the trade,' he flashed C his gold-toothed smile at the word, 'a neurotic builds castles in the air; a paranoiac lives in them! And that is what has happened.' He shrugged expressively. 'So the Board of Guardians has been forced to set up this, er, home for them.'

'A lunatic asylum, eh?' C opened his eyes.

The doctor frowned and his good humour seemed to leave him for a moment. 'Well, hardly that. We prefer to call it a *Home*, General, though I am afraid with the limited resources available to the Guardians, it is not much of a home. Ah yes, here we are now.' He changed down and pulled in at the white-painted curb in front of two large terraced Victorian houses, which were as shabby and as unpainted as their neighbours, differing from them only in that recently iron bars had been attached to all the windows and the outside railings were still in place. Evidently the council had not taken them in the great Beaverbrook scrap metal drive of 1940.

Stiffly C got out of the car and looked at the place, its walls defaced by crudely painted swastikas. 'Are there a lot of Huns around here?' he barked, ears taking in the strange variety of sounds and moans coming from the houses.

Dr Levy-Keyser looked at the grey-faced general as if he thought the latter was joking; then he shook his head in disbelief, and said, 'Sister Klara – she's in charge – will show us round.' He pulled the bell. Squeaky boots sounded beyond the door, bolts were pulled back, locks turned, and it opened to reveal a square-faced woman with more than a suspicion of a moustache dressed in some kind of outlandish nurse's uniform that C failed to recognize. A large bunch of keys were attached to the leather belt that encircled her ample waist. *'Der Herr Doktor,'* she intoned in a deep masculine bass, *'Guten Abend.'*

Levy-Keyser said something in German and then followed in English with, 'This is the important gentleman I telephoned you about, *Schwester* Klara. He has come from London to see, er, him.' Suddenly the doctor was strangely embarrassed.

'Yes, I understand,' the head nurse said in heavily accented English. She stepped back and held out her big, heavily knuckled hand, on which C noted with some revulsion, grew long black hairs. 'Please enter.'

The two of them stepped into the dark hall, which smelled of Dettol, ether and stale urine, while she went through the ritual of locking the door once more, grunting stiffly as she bent to shoot home the lower bolt. C heard her corsets creak and told himself he, for one, wouldn't like to be in Sister Klara's heavy-handed care.

'Sister Klara is in charge,' said the doctor. 'We can only afford to have two full-time staff, though we do have volunteers, while I am, naturally, on call at any time. I, too, am of course a volunteer.'

'Of course,' C said stiffly, definitely wishing now he had not come on this mission; the place, with its peeling dark-yellow Victorian wallpaper and the flickering gas jets, was unnerving. Somewhere, too, what sounded like a demented woman was moaning and crying out in a language he couldn't identify.

'Have they been good today?' Levy-Keyser asked brightly, as the head nurse indicated they should follow her formidable bulk down the long smelly corridor.

'Yes, *Herr Doktor*,' she replied, without looking round, 'though we have been forced to place Moses in a strait-jacket. He has been threatening Jesus Christ with the fists all the long day.'

'Mentally disturbed Jews tend to religious delusions,' Levy-Keyser explained a little awkwardly. 'In such places as this there are always a high percentage of Abrahams and Moses. It is due, I am certain, to our history.'

'Of course,' C replied once more, hoping that they could get this thing over and he could get back to the Queen's. He could do with a stiff whisky.

They paused while the head sister opened the door at the far end of the corridor and they passed into a large room where three old men in soiled pyjamas, minus their false teeth, were being fed porridge by a harassed young woman, most of it slipping from their slack, drooping mouths to the floor.

'Tut-tut!' Sister Klara clicked her lips in disapproval. 'Can't you even do a simple thing like feed them?' she snapped and the young woman went red. 'Look, I show you yet again.' She grabbed the spoon from the embarrassed girl, dipped it in the porridge, then with her other hand, she held one of the old men's jaws firmly in her big paw and rammed the spoon deep in his open mouth.

'Swallow, Otto,' she commanded harshly. 'Swallow at once, hear you, Otto!'

It was then that C heard demonic, maniacal laughter that sent a cold frisson of fear down his spine, and a harsh voice declaiming, '*Jüdische Sweinehunde . . . Juden Raus . . . Juden Raus!*' followed an instant later by another insane cackle.

'My word,' C stuttered, 'what was that? And . . . did I hear right? Did he say, "Jewish pig-dogs. Jews out!"? *Here in this place of all places?'*

Levy-Keyser flushed crimson and Sister Klara looked very stern, dripping spoon held in front of her massive starched bosom like a defensive weapon. 'Yes, General,' Levy-Keyser said unhappily. 'You heard right. That is what he said – '

'Ausrotten-sollte man sie!' the unknown inmate shrieked as if addressing one of the huge Nazi Party rallies C remembered from the 1930s. 'Das jüdische Pack!' He cackled crazily again and then burst into the words of the Nazi Storm Troopers' song, banging in time against the door with his feet as he did so. *'Die Fahne hoch . . . die Reihen fest geschlossen . . . Die Fahne . . .'*

C stared pale-faced and aghast at the doctor. Under the impact of the blows on the door the gas jets flickered and shivered, casting their shadows on the dirty wall in grotesque distortion. One of the senile old men began to blubber with fear and Sister Klara mumbled to herself in German, even her resolute face suddenly showing fear at the crazy outburst of national socialist hate.

'Is that him?' C broke his own silence at last. 'The man I have come to see?'

Silently Levy-Keyser nodded. Beyond the door the crazy man stopped singing. Suddenly he snapped to attention – C could hear his heels click together quite distinctly – and roared at the top of his voice, *'Das deutsche Volk – SIEG HEIL . . .'*

Friday, 16 May 1941

CHAPTER 1

Commander Hansen bent down to speak into the voice tube, 'Engine room, dead slow now.'

'Dead slow ahead, it is sir,' the disembodied voice floated up to the bridge and almost at once the leading E-boat's speed decreased dramatically.

Standing next to Hansen on the soaked, dripping bridge, von Dodenburg breathed a sigh of relief as his stomach settled back down once more. They had crossed the North Sea at a cracking pace, the sharp prow of the E-boats slapping into the waves. Von Dodenburg's stomach had been in a constant, surging turmoil. Each time they hit a wave it felt like hitting a solid brick wall. How he had prevented himself from being seasick as most of his poor suffering troopers were he didn't know. Perhaps it was because he had to set an example, he supposed.

'Typical awful weather off the English coast,' Hansen commented, the raindrops dripping off the rim of his battered white cap. 'Rain and fog, but just the thing we need for this one.'

'How far are we away from the English coast now, Commander?'

'About five sea miles, with Smiths Knoll three to our north. Everything seems to be working out all right, *Hauptsturm*, but I'm not taking any chances. Even on an awful night like this, there might be some fool of a fisherman out or one of those colliers that run coal in down the coast from Newcastle to the Thames Estuary. Can't be too careful.' He leaned over the edge of the bridge and called to the two look-outs on the bow, barely visible in the dripping gloom. 'Keep your eyes peeled down there – like tomatoes!'

The two ratings in their dripping black oilskins laughed softly and returned to their watch, while the leading E-boat ploughed steadily through the green heaving sea at a snail's pace. Time started to pass leadenly. Von Dodenburg ran through his plan yet again and the ship's crew tensed at their guns. Even the thickest rating among them knew they were slowly nearing one of the greatest concentrations of British naval strength in the North Sea. It took only one small craft to raise the alarm, and they would find themselves in a virtual hornet's nest if it did.

Just after midnight, when they had safely left Smiths Knoll behind them, they became aware of the sinister drone of heavy bombers coming from the east. Von Dodenburg forgot his plans and raised his night glasses, as did Commander Hansen.

Dark vague shapes slid into the circles of calibrated glass, flying westwards in V-patterns, unaware that they were being observed from below. 'Ours,' Hansen concluded, lowering his glasses with a sigh of relief. 'Thought it might be those damned Sunderland flying boats of the Tommies. Sneaky buggers they are. Come in with their engines turned off and drop a square egg right down yer funnel.' He laughed curtly.

Von Dodenburg laughed with him, his relief obvious. 'They're Fat Hermann's boys, out to bomb the coastal towns. Recognized those twin engines of the Junkers.'

Again the two men on the bridge fell silent, and the E-boat's prow continued to cut the tossing green water at a mere ten knots, the glass plating of the bridge constantly lashed by the storm. Every now and again came the silent flash of spring lightning, illuminating that vast sombre seascape with electrifying suddenness.

About twelve-thirty, the cook, known to the crew as the 'dirty one', in true naval fashion, brought up two steaming mugs. 'Nigger sweat with a dash o' firewater, skipper,' he said cheerfully. 'Yer could stand yer spoon in this one, sir.'

''Bout time,' Hansen growled in a good-humoured manner. 'My tonsils were just about doing flip-flops for the want – '

He stopped abruptly, hand braked in mid-air foolishly as

he reached out for the mug. *'What in God's name was that?'* he asked softly.

Von Dodenburg cocked his head to one side to listen. But he could hear nothing.

Hurriedly Hansen bent and whispered into the voice tube, 'Chiefie, stop both – *quick!*'

The engines died almost immediately. Suddenly they were swaying back and forth in the troughs, with no sound save the hiss of the rain lashed against the craft by the wind. Suddenly von Dodenburg heard it, an odd scraping sound like metal being run along the side of the E-boat. 'I just heard – ' He froze, alarmed by the sudden look on the skipper's face in the green-glowing darkness reflected from the bridge's instruments. 'What – what is it?' He managed to stutter.

'A mine!' Abruptly Hansen threw all caution to the wind. 'You look-outs, keep your eyes skinned. Off-duty men on deck. At the double now. We've run into mines. *Los, los!*' There was no mistaking the urgency and apprehension in the bearded naval officer's voice. Suddenly men were running onto the deck from below, tugging on their overalls and caps, jostling and cursing each other in their haste.

'What an absolute shit!' Hansen cursed and bent to the voice tube again. 'Something I hadn't reckoned with at all, von Dodenburg. Somebody at Navy HQ ought to have a frigging cigar shoved up his arse for not having spotted this one! Engine room – dead slow ahead,' he commanded angrily.

From below the engine room officer repeated the order as slowly, very slowly, the leading E-boat started to edge its way forward, the men on the deck tensed, their long boathooks at the ready.

Next to Hansen, von Dodenburg swallowed hard. He hated mines, but at least on the land you had a hope of finding them, those tell-tale prongs always gave them away sooner or later. But here on the sea . . . He scanned the dark-green water the best he could through the murk. Nothing stirred save the ceaseless toss of the waves. It was hardly possible to believe that down there, perhaps only a couple of fathoms beneath the surface, there was an evil, death-bringing, one-ton ball of high explosive that could split the E-boat apart as if it were made of matchwood.

The minutes ticked by in nerve-racking expectancy. They were crawling through the dripping gloom now and in spite of the coldness of the night, von Dodenburg could feel the sweat breaking out unpleasantly all over his body. More than once he caught himself grasping the bridge rail with sweat-wet hands, body tensed for an explosion. Von Skalka came up on the bridge. Wordlessly, he positioned himself next to the SS officer and began to try to pierce the gloom.

Then, there it was, an ominous grating on the hull of the E-boat. 'Mine to port!' a frightened voice called.

Hansen didn't hesitate. '*Stop both!*' he yelled into the voice tube. '*Quick!*'

As the E-boat stopped and began to wallow in the waves, he cried, 'Take over, Number One,' and without waiting to see if the young, pale-faced *Leutnant* was complying with his order, clattered down the dripping steel ladder followed by the *Wotan* officers.

Already the look-outs with the boathooks were swinging into action. Grunting and cursing, their oilskins crackling noisily under the strain, they had their boathooks lodged against the bobbing evil black ball, carefully avoiding the prongs, and were heaving with all their strength.

Hansen didn't hesitate. He grabbed another boathook from an ashen-faced, bemused rating and cried over his shoulder, 'Give me a hand, you two! Got to push the bugger away from the hull.' He thrust the copper point between the prongs. Metal clanged against metal. Like some demented holiday-maker out for a day on the river in a hired punt, Hansen exerted all his strength, while the two officers took hold of the pole behind him. 'Heave,' he urged through gritted teeth, '*heave with all your strength!*'

The desperate little team fought to bring the mine under control. Even the foot soldiers knew that the slightest slip would bring disaster. The deadly mine was only centimetres away from the hull. There would be no second chance now if they lost control.

'Number One,' Hansen gasped like a man being strangled to death, 'slow, dead slow, both engines.'

Once more the big diesels throbbed into life and the team began to walk the mine along the deck, the sweat dripping down their faces and threatening to blind them, their nerves jingling electrically, praying that they would not stumble over an obstacle in the gloom. Slowly, terribly slowly, they edged the deadly ball of high explosive along the hull, gasping like men running a great race, ears tensed for the first lethal rap of a horn against the side.

Twice the mine was washed against them by the swell and they halted in their snail-like progress like climbers bent on the face of a terrible mountain ascent, shoulder muscles screaming out with red-hot pain and strain as they sought to hold off the mine. Somehow they managed it and von Dodenburg could have cried out with relief. His legs felt as if they were made of soft rubber and he would dearly have loved to let the boathook fall and slump to the deck. But that could not be.

Once, caught by a sudden wave, the mine rolled in the water and they heard another boathook scrape against a prong. 'Holy straw sack!' a frightened rating cried hysterically, *'she's gonna blow up!'* But nothing happened and they continued their dread progress, the blood-engorged veins standing out at the temples of their tormented, sweat-lathered faces like steel wires.

Then it was done. The ball of death was bobbing up and down behind in their white wash and the signaller was flashing urgent warnings to the other two craft behind them. Von Dodenburg let go of the pole, wet with sweat, feeling as weak and as helpless as a newborn babe.

Von Skalka did the same. His face in the gloom was peaked and ashen and he looked ten years older. 'Oh, my God,' he choked, chest heaving frantically. 'Oh, my God!'

'Half speed ahead both,' Hansen called, voice shaky, 'and you, look-out, don't let up for a frigging minute.' He reached into the pocket of his dripping oilskins and brought out a small flask. 'I think we deserve this one, gentlemen, Danish *aquavit*, make yer collar stud rattle. But we deserve it.' He took a deep swig and handed it to von Dodenburg. He did the same, as did von Skalka. Three young men in the middle of nowhere, destined to die early...

CHAPTER 2

The bitter rain had let up now, but the fog still persisted. It rolled in from the damp fields on both sides of the road like a soft grey cat, curling in and out of the trees, deadening the sound of marching boots. But to Major Pettinger's ears, as he led the company on the road to Little Saxon, there was still something disciplined and martial about the stamp of his men's big ammunition boots.

At first there had been resentment and murmured complaints as he had turfed them out of the battalion three-tonners for the three-mile march to the heights. The rain hadn't helped things either, and twice 'Dirty' Jones had threatened to drop out on account of his 'dizzy spells'. But slowly the men had got into their stride, with Colour-Sergeant Higgins, bringing up the rear with an old-fashioned red horse lantern attached to his pack, crying at regular intervals above the hiss of the rain, 'Come on lads, show a bit of swank. Remember the old Suffolks!' *'Fuck the Suffolks!'* was the whispered reply. Now they were really striding out at a regular fifty paces a minute, a good step for men of their age and state of health. Major Pettinger, stick clasped firmly at his side, revolver snug at his waist, started to feel proud of them. They weren't a bad bunch after all.

He turned to Corporal Maltster, who had been in the trenches in the Old War. 'Corporal, have you got your mouth organ with you?' he demanded.

'Yessir.' Maltster, a dogged old boy, who wheezed a little as an after-effect of the gas he had swallowed back in 1917.

'Then what about giving the men a tune? Cheer 'em up on a rotten night like this.'

'What about this one, sir?' Maltster tapped the little mouth organ to knock the damp out of it. He blew a few bars of 'Colonel Bogey'.

'A bit bolshy,' Pettinger said. 'But why not. All right then, men, let's have a bit of a song.'

The corporal blew a flourish on his mouth organ, helmeted head cocked to one side and then they were off, lustily belting out, ' *"Bollocks* – and the same to you.... Where was the sergeant-major when the boiler burst? They found his bollocks – and the same to y-o-u..."'

As Pettinger sang away merrily, feeling a warm oneness with his little command, proud of the way they were bearing up on this rotten night, he planned what he would do next. Once they were within five hundred yards of the heights, he would order them off the road into the fields on both sides. They would attack the height as if this was the real thing, using the dead ground he had already picked. Once they were up there, with their blood roused, he'd get them to dig in and fire five rounds rapid at the 'enemy'. He frowned momentarily. He didn't want any accidents and hoped that Colour-Sergeant Higgins had made a careful check that their old Canadian Ross rifles were loaded with blanks only.

Instinctively he touched his own breast pocket where he always kept six rounds of live ammo for his .38. As he had always sworn to his unfeeling wife, who had made him impotent, 'The Hun will never take me alive, Dora, if they ever come.' Even now with the chances of a Hun invasion receding weekly, he invariably made sure he had those comforting little brass bullets with him on every exercise – just in case. Thereafter he'd whistle up the trucks with the surprise he had paid for out of his own pocket. There'd be hot coffee laced with rum and corned-beef wads for everyone as they were borne back in comfort to Ipswich. Play ball with me and I'll play ball with you, he told himself happily, pleased with himself and the men. The men deserved a treat.

Slowly the music began to falter, and with it the singing.

'What about the "Quartermaster's Stores", Corporal,' he called over his shoulder happily, striding out proudly, 'You know? "There's ham, ham, mixed up with the jam, in the quartermaster's stores. My eyes are dim, I cannot see, I have not got my specs with me – " ' He broke off suddenly, as Maltster ceased playing altogether and a low rumble of comment came from the men behind him. 'What is it, Corporal?' he demanded.

'Look over there, sir,' the corporal said, apprehension in his voice. 'Over in Ipswich.'

Instinctively he stopped and behind him the company faltered awkwardly to a standstill, while he stared to the south beyond the river. Silver searchlights were cutting the night gloom everywhere above the city and by straining his ears he could just catch the rumble of gunfire coming from further afield. Hastily he took off his horn-rimmed glasses and rubbed them free of the mist. Now he could see the stabs of scarlet flame out to sea and hear the faint drone of engines, ships' engines. He frowned. What the devil was going on? Nobody had informed him that there was going to be another exercise tonight.

Battalion should have known from Area Command, he told himself with sudden anger. Why hadn't anyone thought of passing on the information to him? After all, he had spent his own good money and a week of his time –

He stopped short as he realized what was really going on out at sea. A surge of sudden excitement swept through his fat body. Of course, that was it!

'What do you make of it, sir?' Maltster asked in his slow puzzled Suffolk way.

'Make of it, Corporal? Why don't you see? The Hun is attacking Harwich from the sea like Admiral Keyes did at Zeebrugge back in 1917. They're having a crack at the harbour.'

'The cheeky buggers!' Corporal Maltster snorted indignantly. 'Them Jerries ought to – '

'Company,' Pettinger interrupted his protest harshly. 'Company will deploy. Colour-Sergeant!'

'*Sir!*' Higgins bellowed from the rear.

'Get ready to move into the fields. We're going to attack.'

'*Attack*, sir?' Higgins echoed in the darkness in bewilderment. 'Attack who, sir?'

But Major Pettinger was too carried away by excitement for explanation. Inside that portly, pompous, middle-aged bank manager's body was a lean, bold warrior and leader of men, eager to burst out. The Hun was actually *attacking* Harwich with shot and shell. Now his own rather tame show was going to be given some up-to-date realism. He waited no longer. Raising his voice and at that same time drawing the revolver attached to his neck by a lanyard, he gave an order that made his spine tingle with excitement, 'Company A. Company A will fix bayonets!'

There were curses, gasps of surprise, and then the slither of the long bayonets being drawn out of their scabbards. Cold steel, he thought to himself, the small hairs at the back of his fat neck rising urgently, then he bellowed '*FIX BAYONETS!*'

CHAPTER 3

It was pitch black now after the green glow of the E-boat's bridge and there was no sound save for the steady rhythmic hiss of the surf. Slowly, carefully, they paddled towards the shore. Von Dodenburg, in the leading rubber dinghy, bent his head low and then brought it up slowly – an old soldier's trick for seeing better in the dark – and then he saw it, the jagged, stark black outline of Aldeburgh. They were almost there.

'Cease paddling,' he hissed, 'pass it on to the others.'

The tense young troopers, the spray dripping from their helmet rims stopped at once. Behind them the rest of the little invasion fleet did the same, one by one. Von Dodenburg listened, head cocked to one side. Nothing but the distant muted rumble of gunfire to the south. He made up his mind. '*Mir nach!* Stick close, *Rittmeister.*'

'Like glue.'

Together with Schulze and Matz, who had appointed themselves their beloved CO's unofficial bodyguard, the two officers dropped into the water. The cold cut into their bodies like a sharp knife. 'Christ on a crutch,' Schulze cursed as he went in up to his waist, 'this water is knocking hell outa my outside plumbing! Hope my eggs don't fall off.'

'Shut up,' von Dodenburg hissed threateningly, 'or something *will* fall off.'

Weapons held above their heads, the company started to wade ashore, fighting the undertow that threatened to drag them off their feet, while behind them the three E-boats disappeared into the gloom.

Von Dodenburg hit the shore first and was brought to his knees by cunningly concealed barbed wire at ankle-height. '*Kacke am Christbaum,*' he cursed and straightened up again.

'All right, you men,' he warned, 'watch the wire.' The soaked, heavily laden troopers clambered up onto the shingle beach, making what seemed to anxious von Dodenburg a tremendous noise. He hoped the constant hiss and slither of the surf would cover it.

Swiftly he jerked his fist up and down three times. The infantry signal for advance. With von Skalka at his side, he moved forward, body half-bent and tense, gaze fixed on the silent, blacked-out village that lay to their right. The others followed, leaning forward at an unnatural angle like men advancing against heavy rain.

The minutes passed. To their front the skeletal trees swayed in the sea breeze and the raindrops fell from them in a mournful drip-drip. Otherwise nothing moved. They were alone in the world. They were the first German soldiers ever to invade this island in two world wars and they had still not been spotted. New hope surged through von Dodenburg's lean body. Perhaps this crazy mission was going to succeed after all. If anyone *could* pull it off it would be the elite of SS Assault Regiment Wotan, he knew that all right.

Von Skalka pulled his sleeve. 'Over there,' he hissed. 'The road that leads round and out of the village towards the he –' The words died on his lips.

Immediately to their front, the door of what looked like a fisherman's hut had suddenly opened. For an instant a knife of yellow light stabbed the gloom and in it they could see a tall soldier muffled up in his greatcoat, with a bayoneted rifle slung over his right shoulder. There was no mistaking that piss-pot of a helmet that the Tommies wore. 'Sentry,' von Dodenburg hushed urgently. 'Schulze.'

Schulze needed no urging. For such a big man he moved remarkably silently. He darted forward body bent double, making hardly a sound. Von Dodenburg tensed as he crouched watching Schulze's progress towards the dark outline of the sentry standing on the little road, collar about his ears.

Suddenly he seemed to stiffen. Von Dodenburg could feel

his abrupt alertness. *He had spotted something!* Slowly he began to turn. Abruptly he saw the dark shadow creeping towards him. Madly he flung up his hands and fumbled with the strap of his rifle. Too late! Schulze dived forward. His brutally muscled shoulder smashed into the sentry's midriff. There was a stifled gasp of shock. The two of them went down in a tangled heap. For a few moments the two of them rolled back and forth on the wet road, each of the big men searching for an advantage, hugging each other like lovers. Then the sentry let his guard drop. Schulze didn't give him a second chance. The Hamburg Equalizer flashed, and the cruel brass knuckles smashed, with all Schulze's strength behind them, directly into the other man's upturned, contorted face.

Something snapped. Hot blood flooded Schulze's fist. The sentry heaved convulsively. Schulze needed all his tremendous strength to keep him trapped. Suddenly, with a dreadful bubbling sound, as if he might well be choking in his own blood, the Englishman went limp. His head flopped to one side, unconscious or dead, Schulze didn't know.

'Nobbled, sir,' he gasped a moment later. 'Well and truly nobbled.'

'Good. Let's move on. Look!' To the west the sky was suddenly rent by a violet, jagged fork of lightning, followed an instant later by a huge hollow boom like a fist being slammed down on a sheet of metal. 'We're in for a storm.' He blinked hard in the ugly bright-white light. 'God in heaven, it's as light as day. *Los!*'

Like fugitives fleeing for their lives, they slipped across the road, leaving the sentry stiffening in the first drops of the new rain, what looked like red vomit oozing from his slack mouth. At the double, panting with the effort and laden like mules with their equipment, they ran across the sodden fields, heading for the heights. Quickly the rain gained in intensity, lashing at their tortured young faces.

But von Dodenburg and his NCOs showed no mercy. They were here, there, and everywhere, haranguing, threatening, cajoling, promising, forcing the men to keep up and not lag behind. But these were the elite. All their young lives, ever since they had first joined the Hitler Youth, had been dedicated to peak physical fitness and a passionate devotion to the national socialist cause. They would not flag, for it had been instilled in their very bones that a German youth was as hard as Krupp steel. There was no place for weakness in the New Order that now ruled Europe.

As the ground started to rise the rain fell even harder, driving at their sodden uniforms like spikes, erupting from their packs in little spurts. It seemed as if the very earth was melting in this terrible downpour. It was the weather the world would undoubtedly end in.

And then they were on the heights, limbs trembling with the effort of that tremendous race, the young giants gasping for air like ancient asthmatics in the throes of a final attack. Still von Dodenburg had no mercy on them. Every minute counted. 'Over here the mortar crews,' he commanded, trying to control his own breath, hearing the words snatched out of his mouth by the terrific downpour. 'Hurry up . . . One mortar over here . . . The other on the other side of the road . . . Ensure you have the smoke ready . . . You'll need smoke when you retire to the beach . . . One never knows . . . Now then, where are those anti-personnel mines . . . Fuse and start planting them just along this line here at irregular intervals . . . '

Von Skalka was impressed by the efficiency of the young SS troopers. ' "The country rings around with loud alarms, and raw in fields the rude militia swarms," ' he quoted Dryden and then grinned, the raindrops streaming down his face as he remembered the last line of the poem, ' "then hasten to be drunk, the business of the day." '

Well, there would be no hastening off to get drunk for these harassed, panting giants in their soaked camouflaged uniforms. This night they would either die or live, as Fate decreed. The sombre thought reminded him of his own mission. Drying his hands on his camouflaged tunic the best he could, he took the clumsy wooden pistol butt from his belt, removed the pistol and began screwing the butt on to the pistol to make a small but highly effective rifle.

It was thus that von Dodenburg found him after organizing the defensive position and detailing a protesting Sergeant Schulze to take command of the heights. 'What's that for?' he asked, as von Skalka completed the screwing on of the telescopic sight to the strange little rifle.

Von Skalka shrugged easily, in spite of the pelting rain. 'Even a guide can fight, if necessary, *Hauptsturm*,' he answered.

Von Dodenburg grunted something and then forgot von Skalka. 'All right, the rest of you close up. We're going back to the village down there. And remember, if any one of you makes an unnecessary noise, I'll have the eggs off the offender – *with a blunt razor blade*!' With that terrible threat ringing in their ears, they set off once more, leaving the heights silent save for the steady hiss of the rain, and apparently unoccupied. The deadly little devices, with their three prongs peeping above the soaked soil, waited to bring mutilation and death to the unwary. Far off, down on the plain, there came the faint muted voices of many men.

CHAPTER 4

'The man is absolutely stark staring raving mad!' C cried over the telephone with quite unusual passion for him. 'Prime Minister, I don't think it will work.'

Churchill chuckled and, jerking the big cigar to the other side of his toothless mouth (he had his false teeth in the water glass next to him), he said without sympathy, 'You're just tired, Stewart, that's all.'

'Ten damned hours it took us from York to King's Cross – alerts and raids all over the damned place,' C said testily, 'and locked up with that maniac. In the end the doctors had to give him something to knock him out. I sat there half the time in fear of my life. Now I'm exhausted. I shall sleep the clock round when I hang up.'

Churchill, who needed little sleep said 'Yes, you must sleep, Stewart. But tell me this. Does he at least *look* like our fellow?'

'Yes, yes, the resemblance is quite striking. Same height, German of course, the nose'll have to be changed of course, and absolutely fanatically Nazi. Amazing, with his racial background.' Exhausted as he was, C's wonderment came through strongly. 'Really quite amazing. Do you think Hess might have Jewish blood in him?'

Churchill roared, his plump pink toothless face turning red, the tears streaming down his face for a moment. 'Jewish blood? My dear Stewart,' he stuttered and gasped, 'I say that *is* rare. Well, one thing is for certain, *now*, if anything happens, he certainly will have, won't he?' He wiped the tears from his cheeks with his pudgy knuckles and took a quick drink from his whisky.

'Yes, yes, I suppose he will, Prime Minister,' C admitted, as usual failing to see the irony of the proposed switch.

'Right, Stewart. Now that the gentleman in question is

safely lodged under guard at the Tower, I think you deserve a good night's rest. There will be time and enough to groom him for his, er, star role in years to come no doubt. Good night, Stewart.'

'Good night, Prime Minister.' There was a faint click at the other end and Churchill told himself that C had turned off the scrambler. He laid down the phone and did the same. He slumped back in the old armchair and puffed reflectively at his cigar, untroubled by the wail of the air-raid sirens far away to the east of the great city. The Air Ministry had already rung and Portal had informed that there was a series of raids taking place all over southern England. In the Air Ministry Chief's opinion most of them were feints – mere tip-and-run raids – and were not to be taken seriously. Why the Huns were sending them in, he didn't know.

Churchill forgot Portal, as all around him Number Ten slept, for it was already one in the morning. He had even sent the footman to bed; he would look after himself now until he retired. Some observers might have thought the fat old man was asleep, fallen into a doze that was a product of age and overindulgence, as he slumped in the old armchair, hand extended, the cigar ash growing longer and longer and threatening soon to fall onto the valuable eighteenth-century carpet.

But he wasn't. Churchill's brain was racing, as active as ever, mulling over the situation faster and more comprehensively than the brain of many a man a third of his age. Ever since Hess had landed in Scotland he had been depressed by that 'black dog' of his, though he had shown it to no one save his wife Clemmie. Now, however, things were beginning to fall into place again.

Since he had become the King's First Minister on 10 May 1940, just over a year before, he had led the country from defeat to defeat. Although discipline had been restored successfully, the British Army lacked spirit. They seemed unwilling to die for 'King and Country' as their fathers had done so eagerly in the Old War. He no longer believed that Britain and the British Empire could defeat Nazi Germany alone. Britain needed allies. Soon Russia would come in and he would make a pact with the Red Devil – anything that would help to fend off the Nazis and prevent the ruination of the British Empire. But most important of all was to ensure that Roosevelt brought the United States into the great global conflict. For the entry of America into the war would mean not just staving off defeat, but real victory!

The Hess Affair had threatened to destroy Roosevelt's trust in British intentions *vis-à-vis* Nazi Germany. Not that he was in any way blinded to what the American President's aims were for the British Empire. Those parlour pinks of his in Washington, all those left-wing troublemakers who had come in with Roosevelt's New Deal, wanted to dismember the Empire. They still saw Britain as an imperialist, colonial power suppressing the legitimate rights of the peoples under their control. Churchill smiled softly and wisely. How he wished the American President could spend a year – no, a mere month – trying to rule the Arabs and Jews fighting with each other in mandated Palestine, or the Hindus and Muslims in India. He'd change his tune about 'legitimate rights'.

He dismissed the thought and concentrated on Hess. It would take some time of course. He had already been examined by the army psychiatrist, a brigadier somebody or other, who had diagnosed Hitler's deputy as a psychopathic personality of the schizophrenic type. In his opinion, now that Hess's peace mission had been frustrated there was a danger of a marked depressive reaction. So there was already a body of opinion, small as yet, that felt that Hess was almost mad. That had to be worked upon – it might take years – until they could present the real madman.

Of course, they would have to be careful, very careful. The Swiss Red Cross envoy would have to be kept away from him until such time as it was thought suitable that *their* Hess could be interviewed. Nor would the prisoner ever be allowed into a hospital. Once in a hospital Hess might become a case for repatriation and that was simply not on.

The people presently guarding him – Grenadiers weren't they? – they'd have to be changed, as well. No one should be allowed to have too long a contact with Hess. He grinned. Let the Pioneer Corps take over next from the Grenadiers. They were used to mucking out messes! The situation down at Little Saxton would have to be kept in a state of constant flux all the time.

Slowly Churchill raised the hand bearing the cigar. The ash fell to the Chinese carpet unnoticed. Somewhere a clock ticked metallically. Now and again the storm lashed against the blacked-out windows. But the old man did not hear. His devious, cunning mind was too full of his schemes and plans for the future. Hess would die, he told himself, and then he would be resurrected, just when it suited the interests of the British people. 'A Second Coming,' he intoned with toothless gums. *The Second Coming of Rudolf Hess . . .'*

CHAPTER 5

It was 'Egg-and-Bacon Dicko' who first alerted the Home
Guard company that something strange was going on on the
height. Lance-Corporal Dickinson, fat and scarlet-faced, was
renowned throughout the whole battalion for his love of eggs-
and-bacon. Hence his nickname. 'Yer can have yer fancy
salmon and pheasants like what the gentry eat,' he was wont
to say, dragging out his vowels in the slow rustic Suffolk
manner. 'Ay, and yer fish and chips an' all. There's nowt to
beat a couple o' gammon rashers an' two nice fried eggs.' And
here he would rub his fat stomach in pleasurable anticipation. 'Brown eggs, mind yer.' As his favourite dish became
even scarcer, 'Egg-and-Bacon Dicko' had been known to
barter as much as twenty Woodbines for a couple of small
eggs, and he was once reputed to have been seen chasing a
piglet round with his bayonet during an exercise, crying, 'Just
a slice, that's all, just a slice, please!'

Fat and greedy though he was, he did have the country-
man's sense of smell and now he sniffed the damp air,
ignoring the rain beating down on his upturned face, like a
bloodhound trying to scent a fugitive. 'Yon smell's strange,'
he declared finally, after Colour-Sergeant Higgins had dug
him in the small of the back with the butt of his rifle and
commanded, 'Keep moving, Egg-and-Bacon! Keep moving
or you'll put the whole bloody line out – and yer know what
his nibs is like.' He indicated Major Pettinger advancing
through the rain-swept gloom to their front, revolver drawn.

'There a funny smell up yonder,' Egg-and-Bacon insisted,
'and I can smell it, so there, Sergeant.'

'What kind o' smell?' Higgins asked, pushing the fat man
forward with the rest, who were advancing across the sodden
field with their rifles across their chests at the high port.

'Baccy – baccy smell,' the other man answered, sniffing the

air again to make sure. 'But not like our baccy. Bit like them ruddy Pashas that they sell down in Ipswich.'

'You mean there's somebody up there?'

''Course. Cigarettes don't smoke themselves, do they, Sarge?'

'But this is a restricted area,' Colour-Sergeant Higgins said puzzled, 'and who in his right mind would be out on a night like this when it's raining cats and dogs?' He stopped short, and grabbed the corporal's arm, 'By God, you're right, Egg-and-Bacon! There is somebody up there, having a spit and a draw. I just saw the glow of a fag.'

'That's what I ruddy well said in the first place, Sarge,' Egg-and-Bacon Dicko said triumphantly, 'There's somebody up yonder.'

'What's all that chatter in the ranks?' Major Pettinger snapped irritably. 'What the devil is it?' He paused and the line of soldiers faltered to a halt in the pouring rain, bending their heads to it as if in submission.

'Old Egg –' Higgins corrected himself hastily. 'Lance-Corporal Dickinson here, sir, sez there's somebody on the height. And I just saw what looked like the end of a lit cigarette up there, sir.'

Pettinger reluctantly forgot the dreams of glory that had warmed him as they had stumbled through the rain-sodden fields in the dark. As a sixteen-year-old back in the Old War he had spent a summer holiday in Bournemouth in that beautiful summer when the Battle of the Somme had started on the other side of the Channel. As an impressionable patriotic boy he had spent hours listening to the guns, which could be quite easily heard in Bournemouth, of the tremendous opening barrage on that brilliant first day of July 1916. For a long time thereafter, his appetite fed by the jerky flickering newsreels of the time, he had imagined himself as a slim, dashing young infantry officer waving his ashplant and leading his shouting 'chaps' 'over the top'. That old dream, which had come back to him after all those years had now been rudely shattered by the fat stupid Dickinson, a common country yokel. 'Did you say there is someone up there?' he snapped. 'But who could it be, man? The Guards at the Hotel wouldn't be up there, especially on a night like this.'

'Poachers?' someone suggested.

'Go on,' Egg-and-Bacon Dicko, who knew a little about poaching himself, sneered. 'On a night like this! Besides, them poachers nobbled all the rabbits and hares around here ages ago. Fetch a fair price on the black market a nice fat hare does – '

'Oh do be quiet, Dickinson,' Pettinger snapped testily, 'Can't hear myself think.' He frowned, ignoring the rain-drops dripping off the rim of his helmet. The local population had been cleared out or had gone voluntarily back in June 1940 when an area of up to twenty miles inland from the Wash to the Rye had been declared a Defence Area and virtually every seaside hamlet and village had been taken over by the military. From Aldeburgh to a depth of three miles there wasn't a single civilian left. Even the small tenant farmers had been cleared out. So who the devil was up there?

'What do you think, sir?' Higgins broke the silence, eager to move on as he felt the cold rain working its way down his rough serge collar and along his back.

'Well, there's only one way to find out, Colour-Sergeant, isn't there?' Pettinger barked. 'Let's go and have a look.' He waved his revolver in the air, once more that lean, debonair young infantry officer going over the top on the Somme. *'Follow me!'*

'I swear she had two pair of tits,' Schulze was saying as he and Matz crouched beneath the trees, which kept a little of the downpour off them. 'They were stacked one set on top of the other.' As always with soldiers the world over on lonely wet nights like this, with nothing else to do, the subject was sex. 'Theme number one,' the *Wehrmacht* called it. 'I mean proper tits, with nipples and all and big enough to get yer head in between 'em and give 'em a good shake.'

'But you wasn't gonna waste time putting yer big fat turnip in between 'em,' Matz prompted. 'Get on to the sexy bit. Anything to warm me up on a shitting awful night like this.'

'God, you ain't got no soul, Matzi,' Schulze sighed and wiped his face with his big paw of a hand. 'Anyhow, as I was saying, she had this great big milk factory under her blouse and when I asked her if she fancied a titty roll, she sez to me, "Sergeant Schulze –" '

The light crack from below the height burst into his story, followed an instant later by the soft hiss of the trip flare exploding. In a flash, night was turned into day by the harsh, glowing, silver light of the flare. Schulze gasped as he saw the line of men in uniform, carrying weapons, lit by that unreal glare. He didn't hesitate. *'Stand to!'* he yelled urgently above the drumbeat of the pouring rain. 'Put on yer party frocks, lads. Come on, you cardboard soldiers, we're going to the frigging dance!' He whipped the stick grenade out of his dice-beaker, ripped out the china pin, counted three and flung it with all his brutal strength at the line of startled men below, just as the light faded.

The grenade exploded in a burst of angry violent flame. Egg-and-Bacon Dicko threw up his hands crazily, his fat guts, which had dearly loved fried bacon and egg, shattered and torn by the cruel metal. Slowly the dull pink snake of his intestines, smoking in the sudden cold, began to ooze from his ripped-open stomach. He fell into the mud screaming, trying in his moment of death to stuff them back.

Abruptly all was chaos, a mêlée of yelling, screaming men as the first ragged volley from the position on the height erupted and slapped into the line of surprised Home Guardsmen. Men were spun round by the impact, blood jetting from half a dozen wounds, screaming hysterically with pain. Others simply dropped their rifles as if they were too heavy for them and sank to the ground without a sound, like men too weary to carry on. A few, carried away by the unreasoning blood-lust of battle, charged forward, screaming obscenities, pumping the triggers of their rifles, held in hot hands that were suddenly wet with sweat, firing blank.

Colour Sergeant Higgins and Corporal Maltster, the veterans of the trenches in the Old War, were a couple of those few. Major Pettinger, hesitating at the base of the slope, as the bullets cut the air all around him, caught a glimpse of their demented faces as they plunged forward, yelling crazily, eyes glittering wildly in the light of the tracer. 'It's only blank, you fools!' he screamed at them above the vicious snap and crackle of the fire-fight. *'Blank...* ' His voice trailed away. They were not listening.

Bravely the little bunch of old men laboured up the base of the height, gasping for breath, but still shouting lustily until the machine-gunners saw them. A thin stream of tracer raced towards them as the Spandau opened up with its high-pitched hysterical hiss. Higgins went down first, clutching his skinny chest, a line of blood-red buttonholes suddenly stitched across it, his yellow false teeth bulging from his gaping mouth. Maltster followed an instant later, clawing the air like a man mounting the rungs of an invisible ladder. And then they were all gone, swept away by a merciless hail of bullets, thrown on the ground, mutilated and bleeding like a pile of useless offal dumped outside the door of a butcher's.

Major Pettinger still hesitated, as the survivors went to ground, hugging the wet earth as if it were a lover. He froze, fearing the red-hot impact of the first bullet. Slugs sucked the air about his ears. Dirt from ricochets stung his face. It sounded as if hundreds of bullets were being aimed directly at him. Absurdly he covered his helmet with his clasped hands like a child attempting to blot out some feared sound. 'Stop that firing!' he called to those above him. 'You fools, you're shooting at – '

A tracer bullet zipped close to his face. The sizzling phosphorescent tip broke away from the lead and fried into his right cheek. He yelped with agony. It was as if someone had deliberately ground out a burning cigarette into his soft flesh. The pain stung him into reality. This was not a tragic mistake. Whoever was up there on the hill was really firing to kill. *On the height there were Germans, real Germans!*

Frantically Major Pettinger dropped to the ground.

CHAPTER 7

Major Carruthers stirred uneasily in his bed. He had drunk quite a lot of whisky in the mess the night before. He had done so deliberately in an attempt to forget that he was stuck out here in the middle of nowhere while they fought a real war in the Middle East. As a result he had fallen into a heavy sleep almost immediately. Now he began to stir, as the muted crackle of an infantry fight started to penetrate into the dark recesses of his being.

He licked his parched lips and reached out for the bottle of lemonade he always kept handy on the night table when he had been drinking heavily in the mess. 'Damn and blast,' he cursed thickly, 'who the hell's holding an exercise at this ungodly hour?' He drank greedily, without turning on the bedside lamp, drinking straight from the bottle. Suddenly he remembered the pompous Home Guard major, who looked like a bank clerk. Of course, the old buffers were holding an exercise on the heights outside the village tonight. He heard the wind rattle against the tall windows of his bedroom and the hiss of the rain savagely slashing at the glass. 'Poor old sods,' he whispered huskily, 'out on a night like this. Ought to have been in their beds hours – '

He stopped short. There was something strange about that machine-gun now firing a long burst. A Bren couldn't fire that long without the magazine being reloaded or changed and the local Home Guards didn't have the Vickers, as some regional forces had. And it certainly wasn't one of those home-made weapons the press had ridiculed the year before – mortars made of stove-piping, hand-grenades fired from crossbows and the like.

He sat up, listening hard, the wind howling outside, lemonade bottle still in hand. Where the hell had he heard a gun like that before? Abruptly the weapon stopped the long burst and there was silence, save for the odd dry crack of a rifle. Still he didn't settle down in his bed again. *He couldn't!* That Home Guard machine-gun intrigued him too much.

Suddenly he had it! He and Douglas had been bringing up the rear of what was left of the company on the dead-straight road that led down the coast to Dunkirk, both sides lined with abandoned British Army vehicles and what looked like wet bundles of rags, which were dead Guardsmen, when a flare had sizzled into the sky. It was a red flare, which had hung there like an angel of impending doom, spluttering and sinister. They had been too groggy, knocked out by the days of endless marching, fighting, and retreating to react swiftly. Too late they caught sight of the coal-scuttle helmets bobbing up among the tall, stripped trees that lined the side of the road. Next moment there had been a tremendous burst of machine-gun fire (back in England he read the damned thing was capable of firing a thousand rounds per minute), and he and Douglas had gone down in a pitiful moaning heap, literally swept off their feet, bodies riddled with slugs. If the boys hadn't somehow pulled off a bayonet charge – God knows they had done it in their pitiful, exhausted state – he and Douglas would have been left there to bleed to death or would be in the German cage now.

'*Christ Almighty!*' Carruthers yelled out loud at the walls of the blacked-out room, '*that's a fucking Hun machine-gun!*'

CHAPTER 8

In that very same moment von Dodenburg knew, too, that they had been discovered. Even the thickest Tommy would surely know that something strange was happening in this remote arsehole of the world – and the men guarding Hess were the Tommies' elite, their own SS, the Grenadier Guards. He threw all caution to the wind. 'Drop the pick-axe handles!' he commanded, the wind from the sea tearing the words from his mouth, as they paused at the entrance to the village. 'There's trouble on the height.'

'"The sands of the desert are sodden red. Red with the blood of a square that has been broken."' Von Skalka quoted Kipling, almost as if to himself. '"The Gatling's jammed and the Colonel's dead. Play up and play the game."'

'Oh fucking shut up!' von Dodenburg cried in angry exasperation. Suddenly everything was beginning to go wrong. 'The bloody balloon – '

A helmeted head poked itself round the nearest corner. It was a piss-pot. Von Dodenburg caught a glimpse of the rifle being raised. He fired instinctively though his vision was spotty with the pouring rain. The tracer zipped in a lethal morse towards the Guardsman. He screamed shrilly. His head jerked back like that of a poorly controlled puppet. His rifle tumbled to the glistening wet cobbles. His legs crumbled beneath him last, not knowing that the upper half was already dead.

'Los!' von Dodenburg shrieked above the ragged fire beginning to erupt from all sides. *'Sturmangriff!'* He grinned with the cocky, savage arrogance of the SS. 'Follow me, men. The captain's got an hole in his arse!'

'The captain's got an hole in his arse!' they yelled lustily, and doubled behind him.

'God, what a battle cry!' von Skalka commented and then

he was running, too, zig-zagging wildly from side to side, as the slugs struck up vicious little sparks and spurts of flame on the cobbles around his flying heels.

Up front at the head of his running men, von Dodenburg felt the adrenalin spurting through his system. His hands holding the machine-pistol shook. He was gasping like a choking dog. The initial fear of even hardened combat veterans had been replaced by the thrill of the ultimate life-and-death situation of battle: kill or be killed! He ducked instinctively, as a burst of tommy-gun fire blasted down the centre of the street. Just behind him a trooper gasped, crumpled as if he had just been kicked in the balls, tried to keep going, bent double like a very old man, before sprawling face-first into the overflowing gutter. Unfeelingly, animated by the harsh demands of self-preservation, his comrades of a moment before trampled over his inert body with their heavy boots.

They swung round a corner, crowded together in the narrow village street. A stream of white tracer from the upper storey of the hotel where they held Hess scythed into them mercilessly, galvanizing the front rank into crazy grotesque movement like puppets worked by a puppet-master who had suddenly gone mad. Men fell everywhere, screaming, yelling for their mothers, cursing obscenely. In an instant the first rank had become a heap of writhing, twitching bodies.

Von Skalka skidded to a halt. Slugs ran the length of the wall nearby showering him with sharp little slivers of brick. He cursed and wiped the blood from his face. He was excited, perhaps a little fearful, yet completely in charge of himself. He glanced at his hand in the unreal white glare of the tracer bullets, as the machine-gun in the second floor continued to hammer away relentlessly and the SS went to earth. They were perfectly steady. He nodded his approval.

He pressed himself closer to the wall, as two cursing, excited young Wotan troopers, each holding an ankle, dragged the corpse of one of their comrades by, its brains spilling out of the huge scarlet hole in its head like grey pudding from a cracked bowl. 'Yer can see his shitting teeth through the back of his head,' the one kept repeating. 'Shitting teeth!'

Von Skalka made a quick assessment of the situation. Most of the defenders' fire was coming from the front of the house. Naturally so, because it was from that direction that the SS had first attacked. What would the defence be like at the side that faced the sea? If he remembered correctly from that weekend back in 1936, there was a collection of ramshackle fishermen's huts just across the narrow road there, and they were only a matter of a few yards from the hotel. If he could get that far, it might well be possible to rush the place. One shot was all he needed. By God, if Hess would only do him the favour of coming to a window, that would be that. He'd carry out his assignment and be off back to the dinghies. Here the situation was definitely bogging down into a real slogging match, and the SS were beginning to take heavy casualties.

Suddenly the bitter, half-crazed Sassoon verse came to mind. '"How many dead? As many as ever you wish. Don't count 'em; they're too many. Who'll buy my nice fresh corpses, two a penny?"' He shook his head as if to drive the awful words from his mind and then he was gone, disappearing into the glowing shadows.

CHAPTER 9

His dark un-German face contorted with both pain and absolute, ecstatic joy, Hess hopped on his good leg to the chair where lay his uniform. Ever since his imprisonment he had kept it there ready for this moment. Now it had come. *'Der Führer hat mich doch nicht in Stich gelassen,'** he cried fervently, tears of joy now beginning to stream down his face. 'He has sent his brave soldiers to rescue me.' He yelped with pain as his broken leg, now in a plaster cast, banged against a cupboard. He bit his teeth together to stifle the noise. He did not want the guard, who was still outside the locked door of his room to become suspicious.

There was another tremendous burst of machine-gun fire from the room above him and the plaster came raining down, as the windows shook and rattled furiously. 'Good,' he said aloud, speaking English, 'good.' The noise would cover any that he might make. But he had to get into that proud *Luftwaffe* uniform before it was too late.

With a gasp of relief, he slumped to the floor next to the chair, as somewhere nearby an angry voice began shouting, 'Stretcher-bearer, where the hell is the stretcher-bearer? I've got a wounded Guardsman here. Stretcher-bearer, I – ' The words ended in a sharp intake of breath, followed a moment later by a heavy falling sound, as if the speaker himself had just been hit.

Hess was deaf to all this. His mind was concentrated solely on now putting on the tunic over his pyjama top, trying to ignore the burning sensation in his leg every time he moved. 'Our meeting had hardly begun,' the Führer had once written in his *Mein Kampf*, 'when my Storm Troopers – for so they had become from that day forth – attacked. Like wolves

* 'The Führer hasn't let me down after all.'

they flung themselves in packs of eight and ten. How many of those men I never really knew until that day – at their head was gallant Rudolf, my present secretary!' How proud he had been when the Führer had dictated that to him in their prison cell in Landsberg so many years ago. Now he had sent his Storm Troopers all the way to this remote place to rescue his gallant Rudolf!

He paused and wiped away the tears that were beginning to flow yet once again at the thought and then fumbled again with the buttons of the tunic with fingers that were shaking with excitement. They would need to be able to identify him immediately. He could tell that the English were putting up a stiff resistance; he didn't want any more of those brave Storm Troopers sent to rescue him to die. He had to stop the killing as soon as possible!

He finished buttoning up the tunic. With his leg, it would be impossible to put on his breeches, but he must have his uniform cap. That would make him instantly recognizable. Using the chair as a kind of crutch, he hobbled over to where it lay on the table. He put it on, wincing with pain. But he had no time to worry about his leg. That damned machine-gun upstairs was hammering away again and outside the voices crying in German had faded away, as if the Storm Trooper attack might well have bogged down. 'But the Führer's brave boys won't give up,' a little voice inside his head whispered encouragingly. He had been hearing that voice – and others – a lot lately. They had tormented him. Now for the first time one was encouraging him. 'They'll hack you out,' it said.

Now he was almost ready. He started to hobble towards the tall, blacked-out window that faced the sea. Suddenly he halted in his painful progress, realizing that he had over-looked something. If his captors spotted him carrying out the plan, they would immediately unlock the door and seize him. Naturally they would. Hess's dark, mad face grew cunning. He had to make it impossible for them to do so. But how?

The chair, that was it. Of course. Painfully he retraced his steps, dragging the chair with him. His leg was on fire. An agonizing pain was beginning to burn right up it to the very thigh. Of course the English had not set it properly. They were a cunning, devious bunch. He knew they had been trying to poison him secretly, ever since he had failed to kill himself. That's why he had insisted that one of them should taste every meal and every drink before he partook of it. Now perhaps they were hoping he would die of blood-poisoning or some similar infection in his unattended wounded leg. But he'd escape them yet. Once back in the Reich he would order the most famous surgeons in the land to re-do his leg, perhaps even Professor Sauerbruch himself from the Berlin *la Charite*.* Yes, Sauerbruch it would be.

Mumbling crazily to himself, he dragged the chair to the locked door. Carefully, very carefully, he started to wedge it underneath the knob.

* A famous hospital.

CHAPTER 10

Pettinger knew he had to do something. Although the height had gone strangely silent – though the Hun devils were still up there, he knew that – there was one hell of a din coming from the Little Saxton direction. That meant the Guards were engaging the rest of them and that probably a general alert would have already been called. For all he knew, the regulars might well be on their way at this moment from the barracks at Ipswich. Obviously this wasn't a full-scale Hun invasion, simply some sort of commando-style raid that would be beaten back into the sea before first light.

He wiped the rain from his spectacles, listening to the soft murmurs of his men crouched in the dripping darkness all around, and considered. They could simply stay put until the regulars arrived, of course. The company had suffered grievously and no one, he supposed, would hold it against him for not having done anything more. After all, the chaps had blank ammo in their rifles.

But was that what they had trained for for so long and suffered so much ridicule? How those cheeky street urchins down in Ipswich had taunted them right at the beginning. *'Look, duck – and vanish!'* they had jeered, punning their 'LDV'* brassards! What would those same kids say now if they went to ground and did nothing? Besides, he knew that in other battalions in Essex and Kent that had come under fire last year there had been officers who had won medals for gallantry – the British Empire Medal and the like. There had been one who had even won the George Cross.

For a moment the fat, bespectacled bank manager, crouching there in the sodden darkness, warmed to the thought of *Major A. Pettinger, BEM (Military Division)*. Gosh,

* Local Defence Volunteers.

that would really raise his status in the community! They might even give him the battalion when old Smythe retired, which was soon. Pettinger swallowed hard, banishing the daydream, knowing that he couldn't wait for the regulars. He had to be seen to be doing something. But what?

It came to him in a flash, a ready-made solution, and he could have kicked himself for not having thought of it before. It might well have saved the lives of some good men. *The dead ground!* It had been his original intention to make his mock attack on the height from that direction anyway. That had been the tactical part of the exercise he had planned so carefully, crouching in the sitting room in front of the miserable flickering fire that was all that his wife Dora allowed him before five in the afternoon.

He cleared his throat carefully and called softly to the next man, some six feet away, 'Pass this on, will you.'

'Sir?'

'Keep your voice down, man!' he snapped urgently.

'Sorry, sir.'

'When I give the word, I want you chaps to follow me in single file. I shall head over there. Can you see those three oaks at ten o'clock? Look, there they are in that flash!'

'Yessir, I can see them,' the other man replied dutifully.

'I don't want anyone staying behind. There'll be trouble if anyone does. And stay close to me.'

'But what we gonna do, sir?' someone objected in a strange slurred lisp.

Pettinger recognized the sound. It was that idle man the others called 'Dirty' Jones. He had taken out his damned false teeth again. 'You're going to do as I order, Private Jones,' Pettinger said severely. 'Our boys are under attack at Little Saxton. I'm sure the regulars are already on their way from Ipswich, but we simply cannot just sit on our thumbs and let the Grenadiers be slaughtered by the Hun. We've got to do something to help them. And that is what we are going to do.'

'But, sir,' Dirty Jones began plaintively.

Major Pettinger cut him off with a harsh, 'Now no more

talk, Private Jones. Remember you are on active service. Under King's Regulations I can have you shot without trial for refusing to obey my orders, and also,' he added threateningly, 'for dropping out in the darkness. They call that desertion in the face of the enemy. Now get on passing the message.'

The talk of shooting reminded Pettinger of something. Clumsily, with hands that were wet and muddy, he undid his blouse pocket and took out the six bullets. Hastily he ejected the worthless blanks from his revolver and inserted the ball ammunition. He swung the chamber closed and cocked the trigger, feeling a great deal better. Now he told himself, it wasn't going to be all so damned one-sided. If the Hun shot at him, well then, he'd damn well shoot back – and shoot to kill!

He rose to his feet confidently, revolver in hand. 'All right, you men, are you ready?'

There was a hesitant, frightened murmur that they were. Pettinger overheard the fear in the voices of his middle-aged civilian soldiers. Proudly he brandished his revolver above his head and snapped, 'All right, then *follow me!*'

Reluctantly, heads bent like dumb animals being led to slaughter they followed . . .

Von Dodenburg raged. His attack on Hess's prison was stalled on all sides. The machine-gunner on that damned second floor held up all progress and his men were pinned down in the narrow street – it was little more than a lane – that led to the hotel. Now just when he could have used von Skalka's knowledge of the place, he had gone and damn well disappeared. One minute he had been there, carrying that strange rifle-pistol of his; the next he had vanished, and von Dodenburg was sure he was not one of the dead sprawled out in the street in wild, abandoned postures.

He dismissed von Skalka. Let the Viennese look after himself. Now he had less than an hour to rescue Hess and get back to the waiting boats. Time was running out on him rapidly. But what in three devils' name was he going to do? If only he had some heavy weapons. Even a small mortar might have done the trick; anything that could open a hole in the damned wall!

One of those ineffectual little round bombs the English used hissed spluttering redly through the downpour, struck the wall opposite and rolled into the gutter. It exploded and for an instant von Dodenburg caught a glimpse of the severed head of one of his troopers and it looked to him like an abandoned stuffed trophy; then he closed his eyes automatically and opened his mouth to prevent the blast bursting his eardrums. Brick splinters pattered down on his bent helmet and then it was over. No more casualties. Only a smoking hole in the tarmac. The little English grenades had more power than he had suspected.

Then he had it. *An improvised satchel charge!* Of course, three or four of the normal stick grenades tied together with a short fuse and hurled at a wall would blow a hole in it broad enough for a man to get through. But where? He craned his neck round the corner, trying not to see his poor dead soldiers and peered at the hotel.

Just to the right of the place there was a narrow passage, which was not covered from the windows or the big main door. A hole in the wall and they'd be into the bottom floor, where he knew Hess was held, in a flash. It was their only chance; for he was sure that the nearby garrisons would be alerted, in spite of the fact that they had cut the overhead telephone wires as they advanced on the village. The noise of the small-arms battle must have been heard for kilometres around.

'Here, you troopers,' he called to the grim-faced young soldiers grouped around him in the cover of the wall waiting for orders, 'Let me have four grenades.'

Swiftly the grenades were bundled together, lashed in place with a leather belt taken from one of the dead. Hastily, by the light of the flashes and explosions, he placed in the fuse. He knew SOP* was for him to order one of his men to carry out the task because an officer commanding troops should not risk his own life unnecessarily. But von Dodenburg had always led from the front and he was not going to change now. 'Listen,' he commanded, 'I'm going to breach that wall over there. I want covering fire. Don't take chances in aiming. Just bang away, but when I've mouseholed my way in I want you to come – and come crapping fast!'

In the sombre light, the men grinned. The Old Man was a real soldier, not one of those arrogant swine who cried, 'Do you want to live for ever, you dogs' and then let *them* do the dying.

Von Dodenburg took a deep breath and then willed himself to move. He went round the corner running all out, head tucked in between his shoulder, arms moving like pistons. Almost immediately the machine-gunner in the second storey spotted him. Tracer hissed towards him like a myriad angry red hornets. Wildly he zigzagged, vicious

* Standard Operating Procedure.

spurts of violet erupting at his flying heels, whining off the walls and thwacking solidly into the bodies of the dead.

Behind him a hellish volley of fire started up, deafening him in the tight confines of the little street. A crazy wild kaleidoscope of death and destruction flew by him – a man with no head, a boot with a foot in it, a cart of what looked like hay burning furiously, a Guardsman pressed against a wall, dead with shock, but somehow standing bolt upright as if on guard at Buckingham Palace – as he raced closer and closer to the building, hardly daring to believe that his luck was holding out so long.

Then there was a roaring, a hot hard slap of wind, a red-hot needle pricked him in the right thigh, something clubbed him at the back of his helmet. He couldn't help himself, he simply couldn't stay on his feet. He sprawled forward helplessly, the bundle of grenades tumbling from his suddenly nerveless fingers. Dimly aware of the vicious snap and crackle of slugs all around him, he just lay there absolutely, totally winded.

High above him in the second-floor bedroom, the floor covered in broken glass, the spent cartridge cases from the Vickers lying everywhere, Major Carruthers slapped the sweating gunner on the back and cried above the racket, 'Well done, Smith 192. You really got the bugger! That was a satchel charge he was going to try and shove up our arses!'

Behind them, his unwaxed moustaches drooping so that he looked like a stage Chinaman, CSM Douglas frowned. Even in the heat of battle he didn't like any of this familiarity between the officers and the rank-and-file. It wasn't good for discipline. He made a mental note to mention it to the CO in due course, when they had seen off these Jerries who had so surprisingly appeared from nowhere.

Carruthers, bare-headed and minus his tunic, a soldier's rifle clutched in his right hand (he had learned early enough in France that Hun snipers always took a man with a revolver to be an officer and singled him out as their first target), grinned at the sour look on the old NCO's face. He cried above the noise of the battle, 'Now don't put me on a fizzer for language unbecoming for an officer and a gentleman, Douglas!' Then he was serious. 'What are our casualties like, Sar'nt-Major?'

Douglas clicked to attention. 'Twenty dead and wounded and another fifteen unaccounted for, sir,' he barked.

Carruthers nodded his understanding and frowned. 'Over ten per cent of the company, eh, Sar'nt-Major.'

'Yessir. But we've given the buggers – excuse my French – a real bloody nose, sir. There must be at least forty of the buggers who've copped it out there in the street.'

'Communications, Sar'nt-Major?'

'Still cut, sir, and the Eighteen Set's bought it. Bullet right through the transmitter.'

'Well, we're holding our own here,' Carruthers said slowly. 'Can't think it can be long now before Command reacts – and I'm sure there'll be Hun ships off the coast which must have brought – '

'*Sir!*' a bare-headed young Guardsman, with blood trickling down the side of his head, stood swaying in the door. 'Permission to – '

'Get on with it,' Carruthers cut in brutally.

'Sir, I was guarding his nibs – Hess, I mean. Bullet came out of nowhere and knocked me fair dizzy for half a mo.'

'*Yes?*' Carruthers urged, leaning forward tensely.

'He's locked the door from the inside. I think I could hear him trying to get the blackout curtains – '

'Come on, Sar'nt-Major!' Carruthers sprang into action. 'He's going to signal to them, showing himself to his own people. Let's get that bloody door down!' He dashed from the room, followed by CSM Douglas.

Instinctively the machine-gunner, distracted by the interruption, took his eyes off the road below, still lit by the dying crimson flares.

It was a chance that a winded von Dodenburg had been waiting for. He seized it with both hands. He was up in an instant, pelting towards the shadows thrown by the wall, the rain beating fiercely down on his strained ashen face.

'Fuck that for a bloody tale!' the enraged gunner cried. He swung the Vickers round, thumbs poised over the firing trigger, jaw clenched angrily, and loosed off a vicious burst. Plaster and brickwork showered down on the running man as the slugs ripped the length of the wall above von Dodenburg's head. For an instant he faltered, shocked by the closeness of that angry salvo, then he was pelting on all out and into the dead ground afforded by the shadows and was gone out of sight.

'Oh, my Christ,' the Vickers gunner said weakly. 'Now I've ruddy well gorn and done it. Now they'll stick it right up our arse.'

CHAPTER 12

By now Major Pettinger's resolve and courage had vanished once more. They were getting ever closer to the German positions, he knew that. One false move and those terrible machine-guns that had already decimated his company would open up again, tearing his poor survivors apart. He prayed that the steady drumbeat of the pouring rain would hide any noise his weary old men might make, as they sloshed through the mud and sodden grass. Why, for heaven's sake, had he ever suggested trying to outflank the Huns? He should have left the battle to the regulars. Behind him someone slipped in the mud and fell to his knees with a muffled curse, his rifle rattling to the ground, and Major Pettinger jumped with surprise. Oh what a damn fool he was. Soldiering was not the job for a middle-aged bank manager who was too fat and out of shape. God, how he wished he was back home in front of the fire with his slippers on. Even Dora, his shrewish wife, with her constant nagging and iron curlers seemed attractive just now.

But in spite of his depressed, fearful mood, Major Pettinger carried on, plodding up the muddy slope, his body tense with fear and apprehension. Despite everything, he belonged to an older school of Englishmen who would never admit cowardice publicly. For the men of Pettinger's generation, all emotion, even fear, had to be suppressed. This suppression did not make them happier men, but it did give them backbone of a kind and a means of carrying on. It was a type of small town stoicism, completely unheroic, that enabled them to die – almost willingly – for causes they could hardly comprehend. They reduced it to that simple, naïvely patriotic formula, 'For King and Country'.

Thus Major Pettinger and his old men, men who should have been long abed, soaked to the skin and infinitely weary, went to their deaths. They had not realized, of course, that they were up against professionals, the supreme professionals of the SS. Von Dodenburg had spotted the 'dead ground' immediately and had ordered precautions to be taken in case the handful of defenders on the height might be outflanked. Now the Home Guardsmen ran straight into the hastily improvised minefield.

'Dirty' Jones was the first to catch his boot against the deadly little prongs. 'What the hell,' he cried as he stumbled. The earth below him erupted in an angry burst of cherry-red flame, and the thick lethal crump came an instant later. His face shattered and disintegrated like a soft-boiled egg shell struck by a heavy spoon. Blood, bone, flesh flew everywhere in a crimson flurry.

'*Mines!*' one of the veterans of the Old War shrieked in absolute terror. '*We're in a minefield!*' Then, he, too, was struck, the cruel steel pellets exploding at waist height, ripping his lower stomach apart, turning his thighs into a mess of bright-red fleshy goo.

Now mines were exploding on all sides, tearing the darkness apart with vivid, blinding flashes, flinging screaming, terrified men to all sides, bodies grotesquely mutilated, looking like the work of some crazy surgeon armed with a blunt tin-opener.

Screaming hysterically, Major Pettinger, out of control, stumbled forward, pistol on its lanyard bouncing up and down on his fat stomach, hands held in front of him like a blind man trying to grope his way through obstacles. He dodged a sudden smoking crater, lined with two of his old men, heads hanging limp, guts and feet blown off. Another mine exploded close to his right. The blast almost knocked him off his feet. A man screamed shrilly, '*Oh, my leg, my poor leg!*' As if in a slow motion film, he saw the man begin to fall, desperately trying to balance on his remaining leg, while the other one, still in its boot, lay on the torn ground, blood jetting out of the ragged, red-pulped stump as if out of a hose. He dodged the man's outstretched hands, gasping with horror.

Then the machine-guns were firing again from the height. Gleaming white tracer converged on the trapped men from both sides, seeming to converge on *him!* Something slammed into his left shoulder like a kick from a horse. He saved himself from falling just in time, hardly able to comprehend the sudden warm, wet feeling inside his shirt. Another stab to his side, as if a red-hot poker had been abruptly plunged into his lungs. He gasped with shock, his mouth suddenly full of the hot copper taste of fresh blood. But still he ran on. And then suddenly he was through, staggering and faltering, but still upright and moving, while behind him the screams and moans of his poor dying men were drowned by the steady chatter of the German machine-guns.

CHAPTER 13

Slowly face contorted with pain, teeth gritted together, the pearled sweat standing out on his furrowed brow, Hess started to pull the heavy curtains apart, balancing the best he could on one leg. Outside they were hammering on the door with fists and rifle butts. The chair was still holding, but it was beginning to give. With fingers that felt like clumsy sausages, he fumbled with the stiff rusty catches of the shutters he could grasp in the split between the curtains.

'Open this door, damn you!' someone was crying loudly above the snap and crackle of rifle fire. 'I demand you open this door – *immediately!*'

Hess took no notice. His attention was concentrated exclusively on opening the shutters and finally revealing himself to the Führer's Storm Troopers, who had come so far to rescue him. Now he knew in his crazed mind that Hitler had ordered him rescued not only because of their old friendship, but because the Führer needed him. Soon the Third Reich would march against the arch enemy, Soviet Russia, the same enemy they had fought against, indirectly, back in the 1920s, right at the start of national socialism's meteoric march to power. Now Adolf would need his advice and support, just as he had in those early days when they had fought side by side in those bloody battles in the Munich beer halls. His dark face lit up at the thought in spite of the terrible pain in his leg. '*Mein Führer,*' he cried, the sweat dripping from his brow, '*ich komme . . . ich komme . . .*' With one last desperate tug, he forced the shutter open.

Proudly he stood there, clad in his *Luftwaffe* tunic and cap, outlined clearly in the light streaming out of the room into the night, staring intently into the sodden darkness, trying to make out his rescuers. Suddenly, balancing the best he could, he flung out his right arm in the salute with which he had always welcomed the Führer at the annual party rallies at Nuremburg before the hysterically cheering massed ranks of Storm Troopers, Work Service, Hitler Youth, and all the rest of those enthusiastic selfless young people who had made Germany great again. *'Mein Führer,'* he cried, his dark eyes gleaming with fanatical madness, *'Sieg Heil!'*

Down below, hidden behind the tar-paper beach hut that smelled of tar, rope and stale fish, *Rittmeister* von Skalka whispered, unable to believe the evidence of his own eyes, *'Sakrament noch mal*... It's *him!'*

There was no mistaking the face at the window, clearly visible in the yellow light streaming out into the blackness. It was Rudolf Hess all right. He licked suddenly dry lips and raised his little rifle, ordering himself to breathe normally. For he knew he would get only one shot. One shot alone. If he failed the first time, Hess would duck, thinking it was the Tommy guards shooting at him.

His breathing normal now, the butt tucked deep into his shoulder, ignoring the heavy rain beating down on his hunched shoulders, he placed his finger carefully around the trigger, curling it there almost pleasurably, like a lover might around the breast of his girlfriend, feeling for the nipple.

A week from now, he told himself pleasurably, as Hess still postured at the window opposite, he'd be in Zurich with those mealy-mouthed, toadying Swiss bankers. God, how he disliked those Swiss-Germans, who only thought of money! From there, he'd cross into Unoccupied France and go on to Spain. He already had the necessary papers – he hadn't worked for the Gestapo so long for nothing. From Madrid he'd travel to Lisbon, where there'd be a second change of papers. Perhaps a month from now he'd be on a neutral freighter heading for South America and a new life, away from a war-torn, crazy Europe. *'Guten Tag, Herr Professor,'* he tried the title he desired so much with a grin and took first pressure. Hess still stood at the window, his right arm flung out in the 'German greeting'. The *Rittmeister*'s knuckle clasped around the trigger began to whiten...

Von Dodenburg slammed, winded and gasping, against the wall. He had done it! He had made the cover of the dead ground and the wall of the Hess prison was only metres away. He swallowed hard and tried hastily to control his breathing. Already he could hear the groan of heavy truck engines, interspersed with the thick, throaty bark of the mortars. Schulze's men were firing smoke. They were preparing for the retreat to the pick-up beach as the enemy arrived in force. There was no more time to be lost.

He spat dryly and raised his arm with the satchel charge, noting the stab of pain as he did so; he must have been hit somewhere or other. With his other hand he pulled the china pin that activated the four grenades. *'One, two, three...'*

From within the house there was what sounded like a shot, followed by the tinkle of broken glass and a cry of pain. He ignored the sounds. *'FOUR!'*

He flung the charge and ducked his head at the same instant. There was a tremendous, ear-splitting roar as the four grenades exploded. The hot blast slapped against his bent back, ripping and tugging at his uniform. Masonry and bricks tumbled down. Something slammed against his helmet, hard, very hard. For an instant he saw stars exploding in red and silver in front of his eyes. Then he blinked hard and they went away, and everything swung into focus.

Opposite him, the yellow light streaming out through it into the night, there was a great jagged smoking hole in the brickwork. He had done it. He had blasted a big enough hole in the wall for mouseholing.

As above him the machine-gun began hammering away once more, his men were already clambering into the dead ground from down the street and dropping gasping next to von Dodenburg, ready for his orders.

They were simple. As the big Guardsmen scampered through the smoking corridors, ready to meet the new challenge, he roared above the racket, *'After me, men!'*

They surged forward in a crazy, cheering bunch.

CHAPTER 14

Stumbling, falling, half-running, half-walking, his eyes behind his cracked glasses like those of a hurt, dumb child who has been beaten severely and does not know why, Major Pettinger, all alone now, crossed the little coastal road and tumbled to a stop. Out at sea, signal lamps were flashing urgently. Green flares hushed into the night sky and, punctuating the steady throb of ship's engines, there came the steady soft swish of paddles.

Dying on his feet as he was, absorbing the information with infinite slowness as if through a sea of cotton-wool, Major Pettinger realized that this was where they were going to re-embark. 'Hun coming back here,' he mumbled and sat down abruptly on the wet tarmac. 'Back here.'

He knew now that he was going to die, but the thought no longer frightened him. In a way he was glad. It was all going to end at last, and in a way heroically, like it had in the fervent dreams of his youth. No more pettifogging bank business; no more silly figures; no more balances; no more Dora with her headaches, moods, and tempers; and no more pleading with her to let him try in bed, 'Just one more time, *please*, my dear.'

Of course, he knew that his actions would not alter the outcome of the war one iota, just as his life and death would go completely unnoticed. Whether he lived or not would be of absolutely no significance to the world at large. Yet for him – and known only to him – the manner of his passing now was of vital importance. For once in his miserable, failed, petit bourgeois life, he would do something heroic. He would sacrifice himself for the 'cause'.

Pettinger wished he could get his flask out and have a final drink, but he knew the gesture might well spell the end. He could not afford to move much now. His shirt and tunic were full of blood. He was bleeding to death rapidly. He forgot the whisky and tried to take a firmer hold on the revolver with a hand that was becoming increasingly weaker. Out to sea some sort of quick-firing gun began to fire. White tracer shells streamed towards some target to his rear like glowing golf balls, curving over his head gracefully.

He was too weak to look at their target, but he guessed it might well be the regulars' convoy as it sped towards the embattled village.

He sat in the pouring rain, nursing his revolver, a fat, bedraggled, slightly absurd figure, waiting to die for 'King and Country'. From the village to his right there came a loud booming roar. Idly he wondered what it was; then he forgot about it and concentrated on not dying before they came back . . .

CHAPTER 15

'Look out!' von Dodenburg shrieked frantically, as he stumbled through the smoking rubble, 'At the head of the stairs.'

Behind him one of his troopers reacted more swiftly than the half-clad Guardsman. Before the big Tommy could fire, his Schmeisser, clasped tightly to his hip, burst into life. A stream of slugs ripped the length of the Englishman's vest. He screamed shrilly, let his rifle fall to the hall below and slumped over the banister, dead.

Another of the big Englishmen sprang from what might well have been the place's kitchen. (As the door opened, von Dodenburg could smell food.) He raised his hand to lob the grenade, but he didn't get a chance. A dozen weapons barked. He went down, the front of his collarless shirt flushing scarlet, the grenade still clutched in his hand. An instant later it exploded. The small of his back heaved – he was actually lifted off the floor for an instant by the explosion – then his spine blew out, the broken bone glistening like polished ivory in a welter of scarlet flesh and blood.

The opposition on the ground floor was almost broken. Wildly, as his men came to a bewildered halt in the debris-littered main hall, wondering what they should do next, von Dodenburg looked for the room in which the English were keeping Hess. Nothing seemed barred, the way one might expect from a place where the enemy was keeping an important prisoner. Then he spotted it. A stout oaken door, marred by what looked like blows from brass-shod rifle butts, with a chair overturned next to it, plus a chipped mug of tea and an ashtray. Of course, that was it! That was where the sentry guarding him sat.

'In there!' von Dodenburg commanded excitedly, knowing now that they had finally come to the end of their mission, as the sound of wild firing outside came ever clearer. 'They've got him in there, lads. . . . And for God's sake, don't bunch!' He jerked up his own Schmeisser and indicated with a brisk nod that his men should take up their positions at both sides of the closed door. 'And don't forget, no indiscriminate firing. The Deputy is in there.' He nodded to the trooper nearest him. 'You – the door.'

'*Jawohl, Hauptsturm!*' the young trooper, who was minus his helmet for some reason, slammed his cruelly shod dice-beaker against the door. With the lock already broken, it swung open more easily than the soldier had anticipated. He over-balanced, carried forward with the impetus of his kick.

Suddenly, startlingly, a single rifle shot rang out, magnified tenfold by the tight confines of the room. The helmetless trooper was blasted right back into the hall, as if propelled by a giant fist. For a moment he swayed, smiling stupidly, almost apologetically at von Dodenburg. Then he coughed, blood running down his hairless chin. Lumps of ghastly pink lung tissue dropped with a revolting squelching sound to the floor at his feet. Still smiling, his legs giving way beneath him like those of a new-born foal, he went down in the same instant that von Dodenburg, crazed by this last unnecessary death, which was as much his fault as that of the Englishman who had shot the boy, sprang through the door into the smoke-filled room.

A man as tall and as lean as he himself faced him, a livid scar down the side of his face. In spite of the ordinary infantryman's rifle he clutched in his hands, von Dodenburg knew instinctively he was an officer, one of breeding and culture and one, too, who had seen hard combat. He didn't hesitate. Even before Carruthers could jerk back the bolt to eject the spent cartridge, von Dodenburg, his face set wolfishly, pressed his own trigger. The Schmeisser chattered frenetically at his hip.

At that range the impact was so great that it spun the major round, as if he were performing some grotesque dance, the rifle falling from nerveless fingers, a cry welling up from deep within to be stifled the next moment as the blood flooded his shattered lungs. An instant later he slammed against the nearest wall and slowly, very slowly, as if he were fighting Death itself to remain on his feet and live, began to slide down to the floor, leaving a ghastly trail of bright, cherry-red blood on the wallpaper.

Suddenly the English officer sat down, head slumping to one side, already dead. Behind him an immensely tall man with the look of an old soldier about him cried something and made as if to dart forward, but thought better of it. Reluctantly, his nut-brown face, with its drooping, waxed moustache contorted with impotent rage, he began to raise his hands in surrender, his bitter, angry eyes flashing from the body of the dead officer slumped in the corner to von Dodenburg's face as he stood, mouth now gaping open with absolute, total surprise.

Behind the abruptly mesmerized officer, the others crowded in, gasping with shock, young faces registering their surprise, too, as they recognized the body, half-clad in uniform, lying in the centre of the room, hands crossed neatly over the chest, two coins weighing down the closed eyes, as if it had already been laid out by professional undertakers.

'Did you do this?' von Dodenburg asked, finally breaking the heavy, tense spell that hung over that scene of death. He pointed with a hand that shook a little at the neat, puckered scarlet bullet hole dead in the centre of the corpse's forehead. 'Was it your orders to shoot him,' he demanded in his slow careful English, 'if we try to – to get him?'

CSM Douglas remained cold and unafraid, even though he recognized the feared silver runes of the SS on the collar of the officer who was addressing him, and noted just how trigger-happy some of the young giants in their camouflaged tunics were. 'No, sir,' he answered with calm deliberation, staring the young officer straight in the eye. 'Your men killed him – one of you.'

'What?' von Dodenburg exploded, face full of disbelief. 'What did you say?'

'Look.' Calmly, without lowering his hands, CSM Douglas half turned, ignoring the rifles that were suddenly jerked up threateningly at him. He nodded at the window. 'There's where the bullet came in that killed him. *From outside!*'

Von Dodenburg strode quickly across the room and stared at the window with its cracked star of broken glass. Beyond, flares and star shells were sailing into the dark sky above the sea and he could hear the rapid, harsh thump-thump of 20 mm cannon. The E-boats were in trouble. Time was running out ever more rapidly. He turned to face the prisoner once more. 'But none of my soldiers were outside the house.' He stopped short, as the realization hit him. He gasped, as if struck suddenly in the solar plexus. 'Of course!' he said out loud, while his men stared at him in bewilderment for not shooting their prisoner out of hand for what he had obviously just done.

It had to be von Skalka, von Dodenburg told himself. He was the only one unaccounted for. Someone – God knows who? – had ordered him to kill Hess. Right from the outset that had been his intention. That explained the Luger. But who had given him that order? Why had Hess to die when they had come so damned close to rescuing him? Was there some traitor right at the top, because obviously *Rittmeister* von Skalka (if that was really the Austrian's name) had been infiltrated into their mission at the highest level? A lot of questions, he told himself, wondering desperately what he should do next, without any easy answers.

'Shall we take the corpse, *Hauptsturm*?' someone asked anxiously, as the sound of the firing got closer. 'I mean the Deputy, back to the boats?'

'What?' The corporal's question jerked von Dodenburg out of his spell. He realized that he would have to make a decision and make it fast. They might have only minutes left.

'Yes,' he snapped, suddenly decisive again, 'We take the Deputy's body with us. The Führer must know what happened here.'

A long burst of machine-gun fire ripped into his words and

the window shattered dramatically, showering the dead Deputy with broken glass.

'The buck-teethed buggers are right on our heels, sir!' a familiar Hamburg voice bellowed from outside. 'We've got to hoof it, sir, while we've got – ' There was a sudden burst of Schmeisser fire and Schulze outside cried, 'Try that one on for size, you frigging thin-shitters!'

It was Schulze with the rear-guard. There was no time to lose. The English were almost upon them.

Hastily he rapped out his orders. Four of the men slung their weapons and grasped the Deputy's dead body. 'What about the old Tommy?' someone cried excitedly. 'Do we shoot him, *Hauptsturm*–'

For an instant von Dodenburg looked at CSM Douglas's hard, impassive old sweat's face as if he were seriously considering the matter; then he shook his head. 'No,' he announced, 'let the old man live. There has been enough killing tonight as it is. Now move out.... Careful with that body, you men. *Los, los*!'

They clattered down the stairs in their heavy boots and out into the rain-swept gloom that was punctuated by the vicious stabs and flashes of enemy fire, leaving the old CSM to lower his hands slowly, two lone tears trickling down his wrinkled cheeks. A look of infinite sadness crossed his face as he bent down to close the dead officer's eyelids. Then he straightened up to his full height, every inch a Guardsman, and raised his hand to his peaked cap in salute, 'Permission' – just for an instant, but only for an instant, his voice threatened to break – 'permission to fall out, sir?'

CHAPTER 16

There was no mistaking the harsh crunch of the boots over the wet shingle. There was something arrogant and brutal about the sound so that it stood out from the rest of the noise of battle all around. Major Pettinger blinked and tried to penetrate the glowing gloom. Only a Hun could make a sound like that. A weak rage suddenly welled up within his dying body.

Did they really think that they could descend on England like this, kill and maim and destroy and get away with it? What kind of people did they take the English for? Truly his old men had been cooks and clerks, fitters, and that sort of thing, a part-time army. But they had risen above themselves, overcome their civilian fears and shown a kind of greatness in their manner of dying. Did the Huns really think they could come and push a people like that around and get away with it? Hadn't the great Old Man thundered defiantly when the country's fortunes had been at its lowest ebb that we would fight them on the beaches. Even in his dying state, he remembered those bold words, delivered in that bulldog growl, with a shiver of pleasure.

The steps came nearer. Pettinger summoned up the last of his strength. His hands seemed incredibly weak and he was panting as if he had run a race by the time he had cocked the hammer. Now slowly, very slowly, using both hands to lift the revolver, he began to raise the .38 and point it at the dark outline that now appeared in the line of his wavering, trembling, dying vision.

'"No! I am not Prince Hamlet, nor was meant to be."' Von Skalka quoted the Eliot poem happily to himself as he strode towards the dinghies. '"Am an attendant lord, one that will do to swell a progress, start a scene or two. I grow old. I grow old. I shall wear the bottoms of my trousers rolled.

Shall I part my hair behind? Do I dare eat a peach? I shall wear white trousers and walk upon the beach."' He stopped short, his mood of carefree happiness now that he had finally accomplished his mission vanishing in a flash. Something had moved on the little road to his front. He was sure of it. He dropped his right hand to the big clumsy wooden holster. Yes, definitely there was someone there between him and the dinghies. He tugged at the holster catch. Nothing! It refused to open. The damned thing had stuck. He stopped, body tensed at a half crouch.

Now he could see the dark object in the sitting man's hands, clearly outlined by the flares hissing up above the beach. He swallowed hard. It was a pistol, there was no mistaking that. And it was pointed directly at him! What was he going to do? For one wild moment he thought of flight back the way he had come. But already he could hear the commands coming from the embattled village – and they were in English. There was no escape that way.

Frantically he tugged yet again at the pistol holster, his body abruptly lathered in sweat. He could feel it trickling unpleasantly down the small of his back and his hair at the nape of his neck was standing on end. For the first time in his life, he was really afraid. He was going to die here, if he didn't do something quickly. But what?

'It's all right,' he croaked, trying but failing to make his voice light and confident. 'I'm English . . . I'm one of you.'

'No you're not,' Pettinger said through gritted teeth, trying to fight off the red mist that threatened to engulf him. 'You are a Hun, one of those blackguards who have invaded our shores – '

'Please no!' the *Rittmeister* choked, knowing that it was going to happen soon, frantically trying to free his pistol and failing, 'Please, don't – *DON'T!*'

Major Pettinger fired. The gun kicked, blasting itself free of his hands. Without another word he fell face forward onto the wet tarmac, crushing his glasses into his sightless eyes, and lay still.

But his aim had been true. *Rittmeister* von Skalka screamed high and shrill as his chest exploded and blew apart. Suddenly he found himself lying on his face in the wet shingle. His chest burned like no burn he'd ever experienced before. It ached as if someone had hit him with a mighty blow from a sledgehammer.

He tried to raise his head from the shingle. But he couldn't. Then he knew he was dying. For a moment he thought it ironic. He tried to laugh at the whole overwhelming irony of what was happening to him. All his great plans had gone totally wrong. But he couldn't. Instead his mouth was flooded with hot blood. He gasped and choked for breath.

'*"We have lingered in the chambers of the sea"*' – Absurdly and for no reason that he could fathom the last lines of *The Love Song of J. Alfred Prufrock* came singing into his mind – '*by sea-girls wreathed in seaweed red and brown . . .*'

Now he was fading fast, he knew it. The life force was running out of his body swiftly, as if someone had opened an invisible tap. There would be no South America now . . . no comfortable, obscure niche in some provincial university, teaching eighteenth-century English literature . . . no *Herr Professor. Ordnung ist das ganze Leben*, his dear old stuffy father had once pontificated in another world. But there was no order to life, no reason to it, no logic, no justice . . . His eyes were closing rapidly now. There was a great roar in his ears, louder than that of the sea. He was going . . . '*Till human voices wake us . . . and we drown . . .*'

Then he was dead.

DAY EIGHT

Saturday, 17 May 1941

CHAPTER 1

Bormann eyed the survivors with evident distaste. Their officer, a lean, typically arrogant SS swine had lined them up in the gleaming outer hall, just as they were, straight off the plane that had hurried them from France to the *Berghof*. They were dressed as they had been for the mission, tunics ripped and blood-stained, smeared with mud, their faces hollow, exhausted, and unshaven. It really was *not* the way the Führer liked to see the cannon-fodder. He preferred them immaculate, bursting with energy, bright eyes popping out of their silly young fanatical faces at the thought of being presented to the man who ruled the destiny of the Third Reich.

He shrugged his heavy shoulders slightly. But there was no alternative. The Führer wanted to see the survivors of the Hess Assault immediately, just as they were. He would be in for a surprise.

Bormann crooked a finger like a thick hairy sausage at von Dodenburg and beckoned to him to step forward.

Von Dodenburg, the pain of the bullet that had grazed his ribs still nagging (for he had refused a morphia injection) strode to where the Party Leader stood and clicked his heels. '*Hauptsturmbannführer* von Dodenburg and sixty men, SS Assault Regiment Wotan,' he barked, gaze fixed on Bormann's evil face, '*all present and correct, Reichsleiter!*'

Bormann appeared to wince as if the noise, echoing around the tall room, was too much for him. Casually he touched his hand to his forehead. 'Thank you, *Hauptsturm*,' he said easily, telling himself that this von Dodenburg, or whatever his damned name was, was another of these damned, toffee-nosed aristocrats trying to get on the national socialist bandwagon, 'You may stand your men at ease. I want to brief them.'

As von Dodenburg spun round, ribs hurting like hell, but back ramrod straight all the same, *he* told himself that Bormann was another one of those 'golden pheasants' with whom the Führer unfortunately surrounded himself. Fat-bellied former clerks and cooks, who preened themselves now in their chocolate-coloured uniforms, heavy with gold braid and party medals. He had taken an instinctive dislike to the fat, run-down secretary to the Führer the moment he had seen him. 'Parade,' he bellowed and noted as he did so that a heavily bearded Sergeant Schulze had a bottle of English whisky sticking out of his back pocket. *He*, for one, had not wasted his time in 'perfidious Albion', ' parade will stand at ease. *STAND AT EASE!*'

As one the survivors shot out their right boots and sagged a little on their left hip, the position of rest, while Bormann winced again at the stamp of all those steel-shod boots. Von Dodenburg told himself that perhaps he feared the roof of his precious *Berghof* (for he had been behind the building of the mountain retreat) might fall in.

'Soldiers, comrades!' Bormann began in his harsh clipped Mecklenburg accent, 'you have been summoned here so that the Führer personally can address you.' He paused, as if he half expected them to show some outward emotion at this great favour.

He was disappointed. Most of the survivors were Wotan's old hares. They were no longer impressionable. Indeed Sergeant Schulze was so unimpressed that he took the liberty of letting rip one of his long drawn-out and not unmusical farts, celebrated throughout the regiment for its staying power.

Bormann flushed a little and Schulze gave him a friendly smile. Silently he mouthed the word 'sorry'.

Von Dodenburg shook his head slightly. One of these days, Schulze would go too far and then... He dismissed the thought. In what was soon to come, Germany would have need of all the Sergeant Schulzes it could find, however irreverent they might be.

'Soon you will be ushered into the presence of our dear, beloved Führer,' Bormann continued. 'Most probably he will address you individually, asking about your person, families, how the battle went in England, things of that nature. Now remember this,' he raised a finger as if in warning, 'our Führer bears a terrible weight of responsibility on his shoulders. A lesser man would break under the awesome strain. So I must request you to spare our leader, who has done so much for Germany.' He paused, voice faltering and dabbed the corner of his right eye, as if the emotion was a little too much for him.

Von Dodenburg stared at the party official in disgust. The man was a mountebank, he told himself scornfully, a cheap, third-rate actor! Was this the kind of party official that his poor brave green-beaks had just sacrificed their lives for?

'So,' Bormann went on, 'I do not want any of you adding to the Führer's heavy burdens by saying anything that will depress him. Give him only good news. Tell him that what happened in England was all part of the day's work and you'd be glad to go over and do it again, sort of thing.' He smiled encouragingly. 'In short, be alert and cheerful, as a good German soldier always should be. Well, that's about it. I shall be calling you soon.' He nodded to von Dodenburg and reluctantly the latter went over to where Bormann waited, back now turned to the men. *'Hauptsturmbannführer,'* he said in a low voice, 'what of Party Comrade Hess?' He hesitated a fraction of a second and von Dodenburg could see the thin line of sweat glittering just above his upper lip, as if the Party Secretary was in some kind of emotional state, 'Is – is he really dead?'

'Jawohl,' von Dodenburg snapped, wishing Bormann would go away. He could barely be polite to the official.

'Are you sure?'

'Yes, I saw his body with my own eyes, as did a good dozen of my men, though' – von Dodenburg frowned – 'most of those men are, unfortunately, dead or missing now.'

'I see,' Bormann said, and it was easy to see the look of

sadness on his broad face was as fake as the tears had been a few minutes before. 'And of course, the filthy English shot him during the rescue attempt?' he ventured, eyeing von Dodenburg's unshaven face from the side, as if for some reason he did not wish to look at him directly.

'No, they did not!' von Dodenburg said sternly. 'An officer, a *Rittmeister* von Skalka, if that was his real name and title, of our force shot *Herr* Hess.'

'An accident?' Bormann said hastily, 'a tragic accident?'

'I doubt it most strongly.'

'How do you mean?'

'Herr Hess was dressed in his *Luftwaffe* uniform and was clearly visible in a lighted room. Any one of *my* men' – von Dodenburg emphasized the word harshly and significantly – 'would have recognized him easily. Yet he had been shot at a range of some twenty metres, cleanly through the centre of the forehead. A very professional assassination job, in my opinion.' He looked down sternly at the *Reichsleiter* who was sweating profusely now.

Bormann stared at him aghast. 'But why – who would – ' he stuttered aghast. 'How can you make such a dastardly statement, Captain? How can you prove it? *Where is the body of Party Comrade Hess?*'

CHAPTER 2

It had been no longer an orderly fighting retreat, but a panic-stricken flight. Suddenly the whole coast was ablaze, with Tommies everywhere. On the height where Major Pettinger's old men had died so purposely, a squadron of English tanks had taken up position and were machine-gunning the beach mercilessly.

Out at sea, too, the E-boats waiting to take them off were under attack. Running along the shingle beach at the head of the panting squad carrying Hess's body, von Dodenburg could see the stab and flash of cannon fire, with tracer zipping back and forth between the embattled ships in lethal fury. Anxiously he told himself that Hansen wouldn't be able to wait for them much longer; and the men knew it as well. They were no longer making any attempt to hold off their pursuers from Little Saxton. Instead they were pelting all out for where the dinghies were beginning to beach, clearly outlined in the cold, unfeeling, silver light of the star shells the Tommies were firing all the time. Only minutes were left now for them to make their escape and they would be abandoned if they didn't make it.

A gasping Sergeant Schulze, minus his helmet, appeared out of the garishly glowing gloom. 'There's a bunch of buggers... up front, sir,' he choked. 'Me and Matzi'll tackle him... That's him now.' He indicated further up the beach where someone, presumably Corporal Matz, was firing short, controlled bursts from a Schmeisser. 'Come back... to tell... you...' He looked at the four frightened green-beaks carrying Hess's body. 'What about him, sir?'

A frantic von Dodenburg knew what he meant. His whole force ran the risk of being wiped out if they didn't make the dinghies in a few more minutes. 'We've got to take him back!' he yelled, ducking as a burst of tracer from the height swept the beach, thwacking solidly into the dead body of one of his men, who had been killed previously. 'There's been a murder – a plot. We've got to have the proof that – '

'I'm off, sir!' Schulze cried, knowing that there was no time to waste on arguing. He doubled off into the darkness to join Matz, who was obviously being hard-pressed.

The English redoubled their efforts to prevent them escaping. They came pressing in boldly from all sides. A big man loomed out of the darkness to von Dodenburg's front, hand raised with a grenade in it. Von Dodenburg fired without aiming. The Englishman's hands fanned the air with the sheer unbearable agony of his wound. The grenade exploded at his feet, ripping them both off. For a moment he tottered on the two bloody stumps, the next he fell face downwards in the sand, sobbing like a broken-hearted child. They pushed on, the men gasping with the strain as they lugged the corpse through the sand on a door.

Out at sea, the sound of an airplane's engines began to drown the snarl and whine of the fast craft jockeying for the advantage at top speed. Von Dodenburg could have groaned out loud as the first flares began to descend like fallen angels. The Tommies had sent up a spotter plane. Once it had located the target, the fighter-bombers would soon follow. He had to get to the boats soon!

Fifty metres or so ahead of the party carrying Hess on the door, Matz and Schulze advanced side by side. Crouched like western gunslingers in a movie shoot-out, they fired from the hip, systematically scything the gloom with bursts of tracer, ignoring the fire coming their way, the cries for help, the yells of rage, the wild orders in a tongue they couldn't understand. 'We've got to carve a way through for the CO,' Schulze kept repeating through gritted teeth, as he kept up the fire, 'We've got to carve a way through!'

'But the buck-teethed buggers are everywhere, Schulzi!' Matz objected more than once.

Schulze did not seem to hear. Instead he kept repeating the words as if they were part of some prayer of hope.

Now up ahead, the ratings who had formed a kind of defensive perimeter around the boats and were blazing away wildly at anything that moved, English or German, were crying desperately into the glowing darkness, 'Over here, shipmates! Look lively, lads.'

'*Los . . . los!*' Von Dodenburg urged his own party desperately, as the noise of their pursuers from Little Saxton grew louder and louder, the bullets now digging up little spurts of sand at their heels. He spun round and as his men doubled by him, crouched and loosed off a burst at the shadowy figures to their rear. A Tommy came at him from the right, teeth bared in a wolfish grin of triumph. He lunged at von Dodenburg with his bayonet. Just in time, the SS officer parried the blow with his Schmeisser. Metal grated on metal. With a grunt, von Dodenburg forced up the other man's bayonet and then slammed the butt of the machine-pistol into his opponent's face. He went reeling back, spitting out smashed teeth.

Another came charging in. Frantically von Dodenburg brought down his machine-pistol. In a panic, he pressed the trigger. Nothing! He had a stoppage. The Tommy yelled. His eyes were red-rimmed and there was a trace of foam at his lips. He lunged vigorously, bayonet outstretched as if he were back at the depot charging the stuffed dummies. Von Dodenburg was quicker. He sprang to one side. The Tommy went reeling past him as von Dodenburg kicked him neatly between the buttocks sending him down, weapon falling from suddenly nerveless fingers, writhing and choking in his own vomit as he grabbed for his ruined testicles.

It was then, as he doubled after the others, that von Dodenburg stumbled and fell to his knees for an instant next to a corpse lying in the shingle and sand. He did not need to lift up that ghastly face, with the features still dripping off it like molten red wax. He knew who it was merely by the discreet, expensive smell that overpowered the stench of his own sweat. It was the French toilet water he had used during the few days he had known him. It was von Skalka, and he was very dead. *He* would never answer that great, over-whelming question that even at this moment of fear and pursuit, von Dodenburg would have dearly loved to have put to him. For an instant he stared down at the dead officer, wondering who had employed him to kill Hess, and then he was off again, wading into the icy water after the others who were trying to load Hess's body onto one of the bobbing, unruly dinghies, as the fire-fight grew and grew in bitter intensity . . .

Twenty minutes later, as Hansen steered the E-boat through the English motor torpedo boats closing in on them from both sides at a tremendous speed, its prow completely out of the water, trailing a thick white smokescreen behind her, the enemy torpedo had struck them amidships like a knell of doom. Almost at once the E-boat had broken up. The stern, the twin screws still churning furiously, had gone under at once, carrying with her the trapped sailors and soldiers. For its part the bow had reared upwards like a metal steeple, flinging the few panic-stricken survivors into the water, where they threshed madly to keep above the waves and cried frantically for help as the second E-boat hove to to pick them up.

For an age the bow reared upwards, the waves leaping up to devour it, only to retreat with an angry sullen hiss. Then, with a great rending, sucking sound, it was gone, sliding smoothly beneath the waves, taking the body of Rudolf Hess with it to the bottom of the North Sea...

CHAPTER 3

'Meine Herren, der Fuhrer des deutschen Reichs lässt bitten!' The gigantic, black uniformed SS aide, who was a head taller than even Schulze, bellowed at the top of his voice as if he were on a parade ground. Behind him the big doors were flung open by another giant in black.

Von Dodenburg barked an order and his weary soldiers snapped to attention. He gave the command to march forward and hoped the Führer would not see the looted bottle of English whisky in Sergeant Schulze's back pocket.

They marched into the big room to be stared at by the Führer's 'court'. They were all there, the officials, senior officers, the courtiers, the toadies. Keitel, ram-rod straight and wooden-faced; Jodl, pale and cunning; Speer, intelligent and looking bored; Goering, his fat cheeks rouged and playing with his uncut stones; Bormann, of course, humble and fawning, keeping in the background. There was even a prettyish woman in her early thirties, nibbling chocolates from a large gift box, whom everyone addressed as 'gracious miss'.

Von Dodenburg frowned as he stood stiffly at attention, waiting for the Führer to notice their presence. He was uneasy in this room, crowded with the elegant *Prominenz* and their scores of hangers-on and SS flunkies in breeches and riding boots, but wearing white coats over their tunics. Soon Germany might well be fighting for its life in the East, yet these fine young men were playing waiter to a crowd of middle-aged parasites. He could sense his men's unease, too. They felt out of place among all this power and elegance in their soiled, ripped, camouflaged uniforms, stinking of powder and sweat.

Then Hitler became aware of them. He broke off the conversation he was having with Speer, the architect. 'Linz, my dear Speer, will rival Paris one day, mark my words.' Von Dodenburg caught the tail end of the conversation as the Führer advanced upon him, both hands extended as if he were a long-lost friend. 'Why my dear Captain von Dodenburg,' he exclaimed in delight, his eyes sparkling with apparent pleasure, as he gazed up at the stern-faced young officer. To von Dodenburg's embarrassment he took his right hand in both of his and held it there. 'Now you must tell me what happened over there in England.' He beamed at a red-faced von Dodenburg. 'Loud and clear so that everyone can hear how you brave fellows tried and' – his face darkened for a moment and the exuberant note went from his voice, as if he were suddenly sad – 'failed to save dear Party Comrade Hess.'

Inwardly von Dodenburg felt a sense of doubt. The Führer's apparent sadness at Hess's death seemed somehow as feigned as had had Bormann's. It was almost as if he, too, were glad that his Deputy was out of the way now. It was all very puzzling. Why had so many good men had to die in an attempt to save a politician who had apparently been mad and who no one seemed to regret?

But obediently von Dodenburg stated at the top of his voice what had happened in England, feeling somewhat of a fool, while in the armchair near the big, open fire, the woman they had addressed as 'gracious miss' curled herself up and continued to munch chocolates.

There was a sudden heavy silence as he finished, the toadies all waiting for Hitler to make a comment before they made their own. Von Dodenburg, who would have given the earth at that moment for a drink, caught sight of Bormann lurking on the edge of the elegant throng, biting his thumbnail anxiously.

Hitler broke the uneasy silence. 'Then you are sure poor dear Party Comrade Hess is dead, Captain? I ask because there has been absolutely no mention of the fact on the English radio, that lying BBC of theirs. Not of the assault, nor even of the sinking of the E-boat. With so little to crow about these days, the English tend to claim the smallest success as a great victory. Why haven't they mentioned the victory, eh?'

'I do not know, *mein Führer*,' von Dodenburg stuttered, as if he were at fault. 'All I know is that I saw the Deputy dead – with a bullet through the centre of his forehead.' He stopped, feeling that this was not the occasion to mention the manner of Hess's murder, for that was how he saw it now.

'My poor dear Rudolf, shot in the head . . . ' The emotion in Hitler's voice was genuine now. Suddenly the toadies were all making sympathetic sounds and Keitel took out a handkerchief and blew his nose loudly, as if he were overcome by grief.

It was about then that the gigantic SS aide slid into the room, worked his way carefully through the *Prominenz* until he came to Bormann. He bent stiffly, as if he might well be wearing a corset beneath his black tunic, and whispered something in the Party Secretary's ear.

From where he stood next to the Führer, von Dodenburg could see over the latter's hunched shoulder how the expression on Bormann's face changed. From feigned sadness, the look was transformed to bewilderment and plain shock. He wondered what news the aide had just brought.

'I wonder if the English will bury him with due ceremony?' Hitler said sadly. 'I hope they do – '

'Mein Führer,' Bormann broke in, voice shaken and urgent.

Slowly Hitler turned round. 'What is it, Bormann?'

Before he answered, the Party Secretary nodded swiftly to the SS aide. He strode smartly to where von Dodenburg and his men stood, abruptly forgotten as the 'court' turned to Bormann, who had disturbed the Führer's sad reverie so startlingly. 'Out,' he hissed. 'Out at once! Move it, now!'

'But, *Obersturmbannführer*,' von Dodenburg objected, 'what in three devils' name is going on?'

'Out, for God's sake, get out!' He spread out his arms like a teacher ushering out a group of naughty children and forced them to the door, while Bormann hurried towards a puzzled, waiting Führer. The great doors closed behind them and for a few moments they simply stood there bewildered, while

Schulze carefully took a swig of his looted whisky before passing the bottle furtively to Matz, with a whispered, 'Knock that behind yer collar stud, but not too much, arse-with-ears. I've got my glassy orbits on you... '

Von Dodenburg ripped at his collar angrily and thought 'damn the protocol'. 'Now then, Colonel, I think I deserve an explanation, don't you?' He deliberately used the familiar form common to the officer caste of the SS, *comrade*.*

The aide looked carefully to right and left, as if he feared he might be overheard, and then led von Dodenburg to one side. 'We've just got the London papers from Lisbon. Our embassy people fly them in every day.'

'So, what have the London rags got to do with us?' von Dodenburg demanded, his anger growing by the instant.

'This. You said that you saw Hess dead, shot between the eyes or something, didn't you?'

'Yes, I did,' von Dodenburg answered hotly. 'Why?'

'Then how do you explain this, Captain von Dodenburg,' the other man countered coldly, proffering the newspaper he took from his excellent tunic. 'Take a look for yourself.' He handed the folded paper to von Dodenburg.

Completely bewildered by now, von Dodenburg opened it and read, *'Daily Mail. For King and Empire'*, and then, 'There's nothing. I don't understand.'

'Turn it over and look beneath where it says "Gordon Stands Supreme, sixteen shillings and sixpence per bottle",' the giant urged, his voice toneless, but his eyes suspicious, very suspicious now.

Von Dodenburg gasped. Next to the headline stating 'Nazi Leader Sees MO' there was that familiar face again, looking up at a jolly, tubby British Army doctor with a stethoscope round his neck, as if he were about to test the morose-looking party leader's lungs. Hastily he scanned the caption below, which meant nothing to him. 'Hitler's Number Two feels under the weather. "Nothing that a good dose of number

---

* 'Thou' instead of 'you'.

nine* won't cure," says Captain Heath of the Royal Army
Medical Corps.' Von Dodenburg looked at the stony-faced
SS aide. 'But I still don't understand,' he stuttered.

'Neither do we,' the other man rasped. 'That photograph
was taken yesterday.'

'But it couldn't have been,' von Dodenburg objected
angrily.

'Oh yes it was. There can be no doubt about that. Reuters
in Lisbon confirmed it immediately and we know they do not
lie. So how do you explain that *you* saw Hess dead yesterday?
Tell me that, *Hauptsturm*?'

Von Dodenburg licked his lips, looking around him wildly
as if seeking help. But none was forthcoming. 'I can't. But I *did*
see Hess – on my oath as an SS officer. Ask my men. They can
confirm it, one or two of them at least. Sergeant Schulze?'

The aide held up his white-gloved hand. Sergeant Schulze
stopped in his tracks, his unshaven face angry and menacing.
First they had been heroes, he told himself, now they were at
the bottom of the shit heap again. And the big, black-clad
flunkey was giving the CO trouble. He doubled a fist like a
steam-shovel. If only he could get him down a dark
alley . . .

'Whatever happened over there yesterday,' the aide said
icily, 'one thing is certain. You have failed in your mission.
Reichsleiter Bormann has ordered that you be returned to your
regiment in Poland immediately. A special convoy is being
prepared to take you there now. You will speak of this matter
no more. Nor will your men. From now onwards the Hess
Assault is to be regarded as *Geheime Reichssache*.'† He looked
hard at von Dodenburg. 'And you all know the penalty for
revealing a secret of that kind? It will be the axe.'††

For a moment it seemed that von Dodenburg might well
seize the taller officer. A vein ticked nervously at his temple

---

* A feared war-time laxative used in the British Army.
† Literally 'secret imperial matter', roughly top secret.
†† In Nazi Germany criminals were executed by axe.

and an anxious Schulze could see how his lean jaw had hardened, as it always did when he was about to go into combat. Perhaps now for the first time, he thought, the CO was learning that these brown-clad masters to whom he had dedicated his life, his youthful enthusiasm and idealism, were not as perfect as he had imagined in his national socialist fervour. 'Sir,' he said softly, 'I think I can hear the trucks outside.'

'What?' Von Dodenburg shook his head like a man trying to wake up out of a deep sleep. Then he remembered where he was, and that whatever had happened, there was nothing now that he could do about it. He clicked his heels together, not really looking at the supercilious giant. 'Permission to march off, sir?' he barked, his face revealing nothing now.

The giant waved his white-gloved hand. 'Yes, you may march off now,' he said casually, taking a silver cigarette case out of his elegant tunic pocket. He lit a cigarette and took a grateful draw on it, as if he could relax now that this unpleasant chore had been taken care of. Carefully he edged his bulk on the little card table against the wall, puffing at his cigarette, swinging one gleaming booted leg back and forth lazily as the ragged weary soldiers, shoulders bent as if in defeat, left.

'Cannon-fodder, my dear Colonel,' Bormann had whispered to him a few minutes before when he had given him his orders. 'Undoubtedly the new Russian front will soon settle their hash for them. Cannon-fodder, mere cannon-fodder, that's all . . .' The giant colonel sniffed, stubbed out his cigarette and hastily swallowed a cachou pastille. He rose and tugged at his tunic. Outside the trucks were already beginning to draw away. He shrugged and turned to go inside again, the survivors already forgotten.

The Hess Assault had passed into the secret history of World War Two.

Envoi

Shortly before one o'clock on the morning of 16 October 1946, they started to hang the *Prominenz*. The first was the ex-Foreign Minister von Ribbentrop, who had once said he would tell the Italians that Hess was 'crazy, absolutely crazy'. He told the two white-helmeted MPs who were taking him to the place of execution, 'I trust in the blood of the lamb who bears the sins of the world.' The two Americans were not impressed by the Nazi's sudden conversion.

He blinked as they took him into the room where it would take place. There it was as bright as day, though the official witnesses, including four Allied generals remained in the shadows. Suddenly the ex-Foreign Minister gasped as his hands were seized from behind and expertly tied together with a black shoelace. A moment later a blindfold was slipped over his eyes. Guided by an MP on each side, von Ribbentrop was led up the thirteen wooden steps that led to the gallows where Master-Sergeant Woods, with his fat, cruel face, waited to hang the first of the 'Nuremburg criminals'.

There the little party paused. The interpreter barked, 'State your name, prisoner. Loud and clear!'

'Joachim von Ribbentrop,' he called and then, as the little priest began to mumble the Act of Contrition, he cried with sudden energy, *'God protect Germany!'*

A moment later Master-Sergeant Woods had opened the door of the trap and the ex-Minister was dead, dangling down below grotesquely, face contorted a livid red, tongue hanging out of the side of his gaping mouth, trousers wet where he had evacuated his bowels with shock.

Now they followed swiftly, for the execution of the former Nazi *Prominenz* had to be carried out and the mess removed long before dawn and the ruined German city outside awoke. The last resting place of the Nazi leaders was going to remain a secret for all time, that was for sure.

Some died bravely, defiant to the last, crying, 'Everything for Germany!' Some pleaded for mercy and eternal forgiveness, whining, 'I beg the Lord to accept me up there graciously.' One went to the gallows in his underpants, refusing to dress, screaming crazily as they took him up the thirteen steps, *'Heil Hitler. Heil Hitler!'* And there was one who didn't go at all. The fat ex-head of the *Luftwaffe*, whose bombers had tried to wipe London off the map that night when it had all started. Two hours before he had written in his last letter to his wife, 'Germany's Imperial Marshal cannot allow himself to be hanged.' Thereupon he had taken cyanide and thus cheated the gallows.

At four that October morning, forty-odd years ago now, two American trucks, escorted by a guard convoy under the command of an American and French general, drew up outside Nuremburg's *Justizpalast*. Eleven wooden cases were hurriedly loaded onto the trucks and with their sirens howling the heavily armed convoy raced off into the darkness, an officer warning the journalists present that if they attempted to follow they would be shot.

One day later, the representative of the US Military Government in Munich informed the local city crematorium that at six-fifteen that same evening, the bodies of *twelve** American servicemen who had died of infectious diseases would be brought to the place for cremation.

Duly, that Wednesday evening American trucks appeared at the place carrying the coffins containing the dead bodies of Corporal Adam K. Johnson, Pfc Abraham H. Goldstein, a macabre joke that, First Lieutenant Robert T. Meroz, etc., etc. Swiftly, coffin after coffin was dealt with, the contents being passed to the lone German civilian allowed to be present, who ground them up laboriously into ashes with a pestle.

One day later, just before midnight, American GIs cordoned off the *Marienklausen* Bridge that runs over the Isar

* To throw anyone off the scent.

Canal. Here, as the church bell at the nearby *Wallfahrtskirche Maria Thalkirchen* struck the last note of midnight, the ashes of the former Nazi *Prominenz* were tipped unceremoniously into the dark, swiftly running water of the canal below. The last remains of the men who had once boasted that their brutal, brown-shirted regime would last a thousand years had vanished for all time. All of them – Hitler, Goering, Goebbels, von Ribbentrop – had gone, save one, the Führer's ex-Deputy, Rudolf Hess.

Or so it seemed, for he alone of the *Prominenz* had escaped the death sentence passed on the others at Nuremburg, and was now serving life in the 600-cell Spandau Prison, far away in Occupied Berlin. As far back as 1944, he had written to his wife that, 'I may as well tell you: I have completely lost my memory. The whole of the past swims in front of my mind in a grey mist. I cannot recollect even the most ordinary things.'

A year later he had come to the conclusion that his mission in 1941 had failed because he had been a victim of a Jewish plot. He had claimed that the Jews had 'some power' to hypnotize people without their knowledge; and in February 1945 he had made a list of prominent people who had been hypnotized this way. It included Anthony Eden, Winston Churchill, and naturally he himself.

When they had taken him to Nuremburg for his trial, he looked little like the fine upstanding party leader who had parachuted into Scotland in 1941. He had weighed less than 140 pounds, his once-thick hair was thinning and his face had been cadaverous. His fellow defendants had had trouble identifying him and when he had been shown photographs of his old party comrades, he had exclaimed hollowly, 'I remember nothing. I cannot remember.' Even when confronted with Goering, he had muttered morosely that he did not recognize him and that he was being poisoned systematically by his guards.

For the whole of the trial he had shown a complete lack of interest, once even bringing in a novel to read during the proceedings. Nor had he shown even the slightest interest in receiving a visit from his wife and infant son. Indeed, in the forty-odd years he has now been in Spandau, he has never asked to see his wife Ilse, nor his son Wolf, whom he last saw as a toddler, once. Why? Why is he so afraid of meeting the only person left – Ilse Hess – who really knows him?

Since 1947 he has now been Prisoner Number Seven in Spandau Prison. Once he had companions, other 'war criminals'. But the last of these, Speer, who had seemed so bored by von Dodenburg's account of the Hess Assault, was released in 1973 and is dead, just like the others. Now Prisoner Number Seven lives alone in the rambling red-brick prison, alternately guarded each month by British, American, Russian and French soldiers. He is ninety-three, half-blind and senile, the only inmate of the 600-cell jail.

But who is he? Is he really Hitler's Deputy? What plot – with him as the central character – was dreamed up that night of the bombs in London by those two devious, upper-class old Englishmen so long ago? What happened in Little Saxton (which has long slipped beneath the North Sea, a victim of erosion and the great floods of 1952) that day after the bloody failure of the Hess Assault? 'The loneliest man in the world,' the press call him. But who is he really, that old man in Spandau? *Who is Prisoner Number Seven?*